WHITE MAN
FALLING

ALMA BOOKS LTD
London House
243–253 Lower Mortlake Road
Richmond
Surrey TW9 2LL
United Kingdom
www.almabooks.com

White Man Falling first published by Alma Books Limited in 2006
Copyright © Mike Stocks, 2006

Mike Stocks asserts his moral right to be identified as the author of this
work in accordance with the Copyright, Designs and Patents
Act 1988

Printed in Jordan by the National Press

ISBN-13 (HARDBACK): 978-1-84688-009-4
ISBN-10 (HARDBACK): 1-84688-009-2
ISBN-13 (SPECIAL LIMITED EDITION): 978-1-84688-025-4
ISBN-10 (SPECIAL LIMITED EDITION): 1-84688-025-4

WHITE MAN FALLING

MIKE STOCKS

ALMA BOOKS

Book One

1

In 1888, the British laid out a grid of three-room bungalows in the town of Mullaipuram, in the state now known as Tamil Nadu in southern India. The bungalows were built for married NCOs in Her Majesty's Armed Forces. After Independence, they were acquired by the Indian Police Service and designated as housing for lower- and middle-ranking officers. These buildings still stand today, reabsorbed by India, their slipshod extensions pressing this way and that in the search for more space to collapse in eventually. Number 14/B is the home of Sub-Inspector (retired) R.M. Swaminathan. He carries a morbid fame in these parts for having once attempted suicide using only a puncture-repair kit.

With his wife and six daughters, Swami has lived at Number 14/B for ten years. On the day they moved in, he ripped out the interior doors and broke them up for firewood. Why would an Appa and Amma put a door between themselves and their children? Better to sleep together, side by side on the floor, your wife snoring like a pond of croaking frogs, your youngest babbling unconscious nonsense as her knees twitch amiably against the backs of your thighs.

Swami, Amma and three of the girls are watching the youngest girl dancing Bharatanatyam-style to a raga playing tinnily on an antiquated Murphy two-in-one tape player. Her name is Leela. She has a skinny and imperious facility in the art. There is a language to speak by small modulations in gesture, a semantics to convey with the angle of the elbow. A semi-trained instinct tells her what is the best phrase her body should reveal at each moment, leaving her mind to do something else in a place she can never remember afterwards.

Amma performs the entire dance vicariously, using only one eyebrow. This is a talent that comes with middle age. Very good, she is thinking, very nice – thank God she's still so young. Particles of gram flour lie in the wrinkles of Amma's knuckles. "Six daughters and no son to lighten the load" – that's what people say of her.

There is something else that people say of this family: "Six dancing girls and a father who can't walk!" The taunt is almost true. Two years ago, Swami administered a mild custodial beating to a Very Guilty Suspect in the lock-up of Mullaipuram Police Station, but whereas the VGS suffered five minutes of terror and a single cracked rib – which was surely the least he could expect for being so guilty – Swami suffered an intercerebral haemorrhage in the left hemisphere. The stroke left him with speech and mobility problems. Perhaps he'd been a sitting duck for it, given his high blood pressure, his greediness with food and his lack of exercise – but he prefers to think that it was set off by the acute stress brought on by selflessly beating up a criminal in the line of duty. And for evermore, Amma has resented the VGS for causing this misfortune to befall her husband. Wasn't the fellow the cause of all her misery? Because of him, hadn't her husband lost his job and seen his salary replaced by a half-pay disability pension? And worse than any of these hardships, Swami has lost his pride.

"Appa, see!" one of his daughters shouts, entranced by Leela's haughty signature in resolving the dance.

Yes yes, I see. Seeing is something I can still do...

"Tea, Appa?"

The question is put a few seconds after the music dies, before Swami has adjusted to its absence. When a father watches his daughter dance like that, he needs a moment to die as well.

"Appa, tea?"

Tea, always tea. Do they think I enjoy passing water every three minutes, when it takes me so long to get there and take my thing out?

He grunts as he hauls himself to his feet.

"Wife," he says. "Tea," he says. "My books," he says.

He can risk short sentences. More than that and he hardly knows what oddities may come sidling out of his sloping mouth.

His wife carries a white plastic chair and a folding table to the noisy verandah – a fine vantage point for the day-long Mullaipuram rush hour – and sets them up. Jodhi, the eldest girl, drags out a plastic crate of books and papers. Swami follows her with his slow, sad limp. Outside, he tests the gradations of the day's hustle and blare with a cocked ear, and watches a former colleague walking past on his way to an evening shift. The man gives a lacklustre salutation. Swami returns the gesture gravely, with his good hand. *That man hasn't stopped to talk to me since my stroke.*

It's late afternoon on a January day that will not remain ordinary for much longer. The rainy season has passed, having done its worst. Mullaipuram at this hour is hot dirty air and 110 decibels of hysterical honking traffic. Swami collapses, in a controlled fashion, into the hard seat. The verandah looks out over a ruined British wall to the busy Madurai road; on the other side of the road are shops selling electrical and plumbing supplies. Buses, lorries, old Ambassador taxis and the slick new cars of the middle classes tailgate one another casually, parping without cease, scattering the black-and-yellow autorickshaws, the families on scooters and bicycles, and those unfortunates who are merely walking. A fetid ditch lies under the ruined wall, as though to catch the crumbling brickwork as it falls. Half the policemen in Mullaipuram piss in it every day.

"Which book, Appa?"

"*Eight*," he says. "*Songs*," he adds. He is tired, and defeated, and in such circumstances what in the world is there to do but read 2,000-year-old poems about love?

Jodhi fingers through the books, head down, frowning slightly. A petal from the jasmine flowers in her hair flutters down. There is a slight dampness visible at the junction of the sleeve and tunic of her *chudidhar*, an odour residing there, not unpleasant.

"*The Eight Songs*," she mutters dubiously, "*The Eight Songs*... What colour is it?"

A nasty whip of temper cracks within Swami – *doesn't she know anything about anything?* – and "Blue!" he shouts; then, curiously, "Four Hundred!"

This puzzling numerical rebuke doesn't seem to faze her.

"Yes Appa," she says. "So sorry. Getting tea."

She places *The Eight Songs* on the table, and his exercise book and pen, arranges them tenderly and withdraws.

Swami turns the pages, brooding about his daughters: there is Jodhi, the academic one and the eldest, with her calm unnerving acceptance, who is in the third year of her B.A. in English Literature at the Madurai University-affiliated local college, inexplicably studying the books of some foreign devils rather than those of the Sangam poets or the great Kalki; there is Kamala, the domestic one, now finished with school and studying, who fusses around them all like Amma at Pongal time, and is forever sewing lurid pencil cases to sell at the market for a few extra rupees; there is Pushpa, the witty one, who has a temper on her, and who is the cleverest girl in her school year; there are the twins, Suhanya and Anitha, who live in their own little world, and who were the obvious choices to send away to Swami's brother and childless wife in Coimbatore – to give away, almost – after Swami's stroke left him unable to support all his family; and there is Leela, the youngest, just eleven years old and everyone's spoilt and naughty favourite, who always has something mischievous to say, and who can dance like Nataraja until the other five weep in wonder.

Jodhi, Kamala, Pushpa, Suhanya, Anitha and Leela – Swami recites the mantra of their names while he opens his exercise book and places it to the top right of the table – *loving daughters, pretty daughters, talented daughters, dutiful daughters, lively daughters...*

Six daughters! What was Lord Vadivela thinking of, giving me six daughters and no sons? How could anyone find dowries for six daughters, let alone a cripple like me on a half-pay pension?

Jodhi's marriage has been at the forefront of Swami's and Amma's anxieties for a long time. "How will we marry this daughter of ours?" – this is what his wife is always saying, or thinking, or stopping herself from saying, or pretending not to be thinking. Most of their savings have gone on Swami's medical expenses. "These days you need a new Honda scooter with indicators and everything if you want a very good good-boy dowry," Amma worries. "Jodhi would have to be a computer programmer or an engineer to get a good boy without a very good good-boy dowry – how can an English Literature student get a good boy, when we can't even afford a new bicycle? What kind of good boy does a bicycle get? Do we want some low-down worthless boy wobbling around on a Gupta Hero Bicycle? But if we take out a loan for a scooter, then how will we get very good good-boy dowries for the other five girls? Where will they get their good boys?"

Swami does not have answers to any of these questions. He only knows that it's a matter of personal honour and inviolable religious duty to marry off his daughters at Bollywood-blockbuster expense, and the first instalment of this bankrupting epic could be coming soon. Trusting in Lord Ganesha, the remover of obstacles, some months ago Amma had set to work with one of Jodhi's numerous aunties in finding a potential match for Jodhi. Oh, these two formidable ladies, they have firm ideas as to what kind of boy he should be: a suitable boy from their own Vanniyar community, a dutiful boy, a kind boy with a first-rate education, a boy with prospects, a boy of varied accomplishments, a boy good-looking enough to merit their own lovely Jodhi, a boy whose skin colour isn't too dark, a boy without bad smoking or drinking habits, a boy with respect for the old traditions, a good Hindu super gem of a boy into whose A1 household Jodhi can be happily entrusted.

To put it more concisely, Amma has taken it into her head to bag the most expensive boy in India.

Jodhi's auntie claims to have found just such a boy. His name is Mohan. He is a distant acquaintance of the family, and possibly a relation, being a cousin of Amma's sister's cousin's friend's tea-stall owner's brother's people, who happen to be related to Swami's brother's wife's sister's father-in-law, via the father-in-law's mother, who is dead now, but who had close family links with the tea-stall owner, or the sister, or somebody else; and he lives with his parents and extended family in a brand-new apartment complex in the third-best district of the nearby town of Thenpalani. His father, whose name is so long and unpronounceable that he is universally known as Mr P, holds a respectable position on the railways, while his mother Mrs P is a housewife. There are two other brothers who unfortunately, for the purposes of Amma's six-daughtered matrimonial masterplan, score her idiosyncratic and very lowest rating of "useless". The younger brother Anand is very useless indeed because he is expert in sleeping and in being expelled from educational establishments for world-champion laziness – people say he is so lazy that he eats bananas with the skins on – and he is known to write poetry and also to stare for hours on end at mundane objects for reasons no one has succeeded in pinpointing. The much older brother Devan – thirty-two going on forty – is even more uselessly useless than the younger one, because he is unforgivably happily married. But the middle brother, Mohan... he is not useless in any department, he gets Amma's highest ranking in every aspect, his attributes make her mouth water. Take, for example, his educational accomplishments: they are exemplary. Not only does he have a first-class degree from Madurai University in Computer Programming, but he has also won a nationally prestigious and lucrative scholarship to study for an M.Sc. in Applied Computer Programming at the South Indian Institute of Integrated Information Technology in Bangalore. In a matter of months he will be heading off to that place with all the other very clever high-fliers. After another year, he'll be earning like a film star. Amma and Jodhi's auntie are in full agreement: the boy is a *very good* good boy.

On the verandah, flicking through *The Eight Songs*, Swami shakes his head uneasily at the thought of him, this Mohan, this supernatural being. *There is something wrong with this boy.* Of that he is convinced. Why would the parents of this young Krishna even consider his own poor Jodhi, dowryless as she is? But his wife won't listen, and who can control a mother when it comes to plotting the welfare of her children? Already the priests of both families have consulted their charts and scrolls, and those two learned gentlemen are as one in confirming that with Guru on the ascendant in the sixth house of

Mohan's horoscope, and with Sukran favourably placed in Jodhi's fifth house, everything augurs well for long-term marital bliss.

Never mind planetary movements and the stars, Swami complains – we don't have any money! But Amma won't listen to such matter-of-fact objections. She trusts in God. She trusts in lots of gods. She trusts in all of them, every last one, even the ones that nobody else can be bothered with any more, even the goddess Santoshi Mata, even Maangadu Amman, who is especially obscure. The priests have already been asked to decide on an auspicious date and time for the first pre-engagement visit, and that meeting is only a few days away.

The forefinger of Swami's good hand traces the path of a love poem written in the full glorious flowering of ancient Tamil culture. He nods in melancholy appreciation of the poem's beauty. As he reads, he can see his moustache lurking at the base of his field of vision. Just as a young woman is considered peculiar unless she is wearing jasmine flowers in her hair, "A man is not a man without a moustache" – so his mother had told him, nearly thirty years ago. *And is a man a man, who cannot walk or talk or sing? And is a man a man, who cannot make his daughters scream in mock terror by picking them up and trumpeting like an elephant? And is a man a man, who has no work to do and no way of purchasing a brand new Honda scooter – with indicators and European crash helmet and all the trimmings – for his daughters, who all deserve their very good good boys? No. There is nothing I am good for but reading and thinking. What kind of a man,* Swami would like to know, *is that?*

He turns back to the poem and digests the words sombrely. A few lines strike him, so his finger revisits them:

*"On the night of their marriage ceremony
the low will be the high and the low,
the high will be the low and the high."*

He copies out the lines in his notebook, thinking how they are true: not just in birth and death are the rich and the poor equal, but in sexual congress, when all become beasts, and gods. Then he writes a comment underneath: *Perhaps everyone who has ever lived is somehow one person only.* There is a comfort in such notions. And it is insights like these which offer a small hint as to the extraordinary fate that is going to overtake him.

He remembers how much his body had shaken with terror and desire on his own wedding night. His wife, sixteen years old then, had been so very beautiful. "Film star matrimonials" – some wit had come up with the phrase early on, during the morning of the ceremony; a perfect description for such a handsome couple, it was still doing the rounds eighteen hours later on platform five of Mullaipuram station, when a vast wedding party had waved them off on their three-day honeymoon. Later, his heartbeat drumming against hers, the train moaning past dark-drenched villages, he had entered her and had known she would conceive immediately. That was the beginning of Jodhi, right then at the beginning of the marriage.

Inside the bungalow, Amma is reaching for a large volume called the *Tirukkural* that is face up on a shelf, so that, some twenty-two years after creating her, she can chastise her eldest daughter.

"What is the number Appa is shouting at you?" she scolds.

"Four Hundred, Amma."

"Why are you so naughty, provoking him all the time?" she asks, pursing her lips as she searches the pages.

"But Amma, I don't know anything about all this

Classical Tamil that Appa reads." Jodhi prefers Graham Greene and Evelyn Waugh and E.M. Forster. Her dissertation is on English novelists of the 1930s.

The "Four Hundred" with which Swami had re-buked Jodhi refers to a couplet from the *Tirukkural*, otherwise known as *The Sacred Couplets*, by the ancient poet Tiruvalluvar. There are 1,330 sacred couplets in *The Sacred Couplets*. And although no one has fully comprehended the scale of Swami's achievement, nor its connotations, since losing his employment he has memorized all of them by heart, like some kind of divinely blessed holy man.

Jodhi, Kamala, Pushpa and Leela wait for Amma to find sacred couplet Four Hundred, suspended as always between sincere filial respect and dread hilarity. Amma mouths the page numbers with exaggerated respect – she can read, but she hasn't made a habit of it.

"Sacred couplet Four Hundred is in section forty of Part One of *The Sacred Couplets*," she begins. She always begins like that. And she always pauses before reciting the words of wisdom:

"The learning that you achieve in this birth
Will benefit you in all seven births."

Silence from the six girls.

"Let us reflect on this thought-provoking nugget of wisdom," she tries, gamely.

The girls try very hard not to giggle or to catch one another's eye. Quite recently Leela, forgetting the num-ber with which Appa had chastised her, had generated an entirely random Nine Hundred and Thirteen to Amma.

"Sacred couplet Nine Hundred and Thirteen is in section ninety-two of Part Three of *The Sacred Couplets*," Amma had said:

*"The false embrace of loose women is like
That of a cursed corpse in the dark."*

Her face! They had all collapsed with laughter. Pushpa and Leela had slumped to the ground helplessly and cried in pain from the general hysteria. Even Amma had joined in. It was the tension, which had to find release somewhere in that unhappy bungalow. But Appa had reacted very badly, and in the evening he had tried to drown himself in a bucket of water.

2

Mullaipuram is situated on the hot, flat plains of Tamil Nadu. An isolated goitre of rock protrudes from the face of the settlement. The rock is only seventy metres high, but it is visible for many miles. Rival South Indian dynasties – the Cholas, the Pandyas and the Pallavas – fought for control of it for centuries. Then Tipu Sultan, the British and the French fought over it for a further two hundred years, bequeathing ungraceful additions to the ancient and ruined fortifications. No one fights over it now. An employee of the Tamil Nadu Board of Tourism climbs up it every day and sits in the cool of a dungeon to wait for tourists who do not come, tourists who will never come, tourists who will go to Madurai and Chennai and Pondicherry but who will never come to Mullaipuram, not even with a pistol at their temple. This fellow has a pee, eats his tiffin, takes a nap, then climbs down some four hours early and goes back home to his wife.

The rock carries on regardless, like they do.

Swami often goes on small trips into town. For short distances he limps, although a round trip to the nearest shop might take him twenty minutes. For longer trips he uses an antiquated three-wheeled wheelchair purloined from an amputee beggar by police colleagues. Usually one of his daughters pushes him, but when none of the girls is available he employs a thirteen-year-old Christian boy called Alexander – the son of a poor widowed flower-seller who lives in a shack built against the crumbling compound wall of the Indian Police Service bungalows. For five rupees an hour the boy bounces him across the potholed streets. "What are you doing, squandering our daughters' dowries on that stupid beggar boy?" Amma is always complaining. She has a soft spot for that boy. She sneaks him snacks like *vadai* whenever Swami isn't looking.

Alexander earns ten rupees today, because none of the girls is available to push Swami into town. They are too busy being harangued, beautified and instructed by Amma, for this is a very important day. In only one hour, that mighty young god of the Information Technology Era, Mohan P, B.Sc. – holder of this year's illustrious *Sri Aandiappan Swamigal Tamil Nadu Information Superhighway Endowment Scholarship* – is due to descend on Swami's family with his direct relations and indirect relations and maternal confidantes and household neighbours and every Raman and Krishnan from Thenpalani who has a nosy nature and an hour to spare.

Swami has promised Amma that he will be back in plenty of time to wash his face, comb his hair, change his shirt and look distinguished. Alexander is pushing him down Station Street, in the shadow of the rock. Swami is thinking about the shocking age of that great outcrop, which mocks the living matter swarming around it. And that, you know, is a consolation. They are returning from the police station, which Swami likes to visit once a week or so to listen to the latest goings-on. There is a long-running case gripping Mullaipuram. The dissolute son of a state politician long known for his extreme Eve-teasing and sexual harassment of young women has been charged with rape, and although the best and brightest brains of the Indian Police Service have been assigned to the case, it looks as though the accused might not get off scot-free.

"*Shaani*," Swami warns periodically, as the cow pats loom up; Alexander, absorbed in the hostile press of the crowded street and the sheer effort of wheeling a grown man down the rubbish-strewn road in the high heat of the day, has a habit of stepping into them in his bare feet.

Swami looks at his watch. "Hurry up," he grunts.

* * *

Amma, Jodhi, Kamala, Pushpa, Leela, Granddaddy, Auntie and Uncle on Appa's side, Auntie and Uncle and Auntie and Uncle and Auntie and Auntie and Auntie on Amma's side, two of Amma's close cousins (fellow gurus in the mysterious arts of matchmaking), and an unmanageable number of random well-wishers and gossip-ravenous neighbours are all crowding the little bungalow of Number 14/B. Jodhi has barely said a word from the moment she woke up this morning until now, patiently submitting to whatever Amma tells her to do, even when what Amma is telling her to do is incompatible with everything else that Amma is telling her to do. Granddaddy too does not speak. Ever since his wife, Amma's own mother, died ten years ago, he has preferred music to people, obsessively playing his flute all day long. It is a special flute, fashioned by his own hand from a storm-damaged sacred peepul tree in his ancestral village; it is a flute which he regards as god – god whom he can carry tenderly in his hands, god whom he can render his very breath to and worship with music; it is a flute that he resents being parted from for any longer than it takes to swallow the meagre amount of rice and pepper water that his family can persuade him to eat for the sustenance of his scrawny frame, because who in his right mind would voluntarily divide from god, even for a minute? As he plays, everyone else except Jodhi is talking non-stop. None of them can imagine the chaos that is shortly going to be unleashed.

"Why did you wear this when I told you to wear that?"

"What time will they come?"

"Give it to me Auntie, I'll do it."

"Where's Appa?"

"Respected Granddaddy, please stop playing your flute, my head is hurting."

"Father, now remember what I said, as soon as they arrive I'm taking the flute, just this once – the boy's family don't want to listen to you and your flute."

"Sister, what will you do if this boy is the ugliest boy in Tamil Nadu?"

"Leela! Don't bother your sister, you've seen his photo, you know he's a nice-looking boy."

"Truly truly ugly, so ugly that we all scream and run away?"

"Leela, enough! Leave your sister alone!"

"Yes Amma – but what if we all faint from an inability to withstand his skin-puckering ugliness?"

"LEELA!"

"Where's Appa?"

"Shall I eat this?"

"What time is it?"

And then the panic, because "Amma, Amma, Amma they're here!"

"What? Don't be silly, don't, you, I... Oh my God they're here, they're so early, where's Appa?! Jodhi go and sit, Sisters, Brother come with me, Kamala take Granddaddy's flute away – oh my God, why are they so early?! Oh my God – *where's Appa?!*"

While Amma and Pushpa and a dense crowd of

uncles and aunties and a surge of minor hangers-on
go out onto the verandah as an advance welcome party,
and while Kamala wrestles decorously with Granddaddy
over possession of the flute, and while other aunties
and uncles and sisters arrange Jodhi in the designated
chair, Leela and Pushpa rush to the window and ogle
in high excitement at what is taking place outside. A
small burgundy Maruthi van is disgorging a village
onto the roadside – boys, girls, women, men, middle-
aged relatives, antique patriarchs, shifty ne'er-do-wells,
chortling householders, bespectacled intimates, incapacitated crones, complaining extras and a range of
hungry freeloaders.

"Ayyo-yo-yo it's an army!"

"I never saw so many people in one Maruthi van."

"Which one is the hero?"

"Where is he?"

"Ayyo-yo-yo look at that fat lady! Who is that fat
lady?"

"Oh that is so fat!"

"That is very fat!"

"Did you ever see a lady so fat as that? Is that the
Mummy?"

"A lady as fat as that must sit in the middle of the van,
or it will fall over, isn't it?"

"There he is – here is our Mohan! Here is our Sita's
Rama! He is coming!"

"Don't be so stupid."

"Jodhi, I think your boy is the very tallest person there!
He is very handsome!"

"But goodness what a very fat lady!" Leela repeats. "I
can't stop looking at her!"

"Good afternoon," says a deep and unfamiliar voice.

Leela turns round to find that half her extended family,
and a fair portion of the immediate neighbourhood, is
staring at her, limp with dismay, while Mr P – a large,

dark, hairy and not entirely un-fat personage himself, who has slipped away from the throng outside and has just this moment entered the bungalow – is framed in the doorway of the room. He conducts a slow sweep of all the mortified faces looking up at him, and settles his gaze on Leela. She screams.

"Somebody give me my flute," says Granddaddy, into the void.

* * *

Swami is looking at his watch every few seconds by the time Alexander gets him to within half a mile of home. "Push!" and "Faster!" he is saying to poor little Alexander, who is doing his best, but whose skinny undernourished thirteen-year-old body is not best-suited to a task like this. Straining and sweating to keep a good pace going, Alexander gives a high-pitched grunt as he forces Swami's wheelchair over a hump of fetid rags. Swami lurches in his 'seat. "Watch it," a woman in front of them says angrily, feeling the chair's footrest bang into her Achilles tendon.

When it happens, it happens as these things ought to happen, in a manner appropriate to the clichés that witnesses will later attach to it – "suddenly", "in a flash", "out of nowhere".

Suddenly, in a flash, out of nowhere, a white man falls out of the sky. He bounces on the hard dirt road, directly in front of Swami – somehow he lands in a gap between the swarming pedestrians, although not without knocking a small boy off balance. The screams seem to begin instantly and from everywhere. Swami gazes down at his feet to where the man is lying in the kind of mangled position one would expect. He is looking at an ageing hippy with dirty blond-grey locks and a creased face almost orange from years of exposure to the sun.

Their gazes lock together, and Swami knows that the white man is moments from death. The expression on the man's face is turning from confusion and pain towards a strange new place, somewhere between peace and vacancy.

A riot is developing around the dying man and Swami, surrounded as they are by angry onlookers, but neither of them is aware of this. *I'm here*, Swami finds himself communicating to this man, *I'm here* – it is an instinctive offering, though what is being offered is unclear. And when he does this, he hears in his mind the *I'm going* of the white man's dying consciousness – he sees it, and feels it, and knows it; it is as clear and powerful as a panoramic view from a high peak on a cloudless day. The white man is already leaving this world.

"I didn't know..." the white man sighs. Who knows what he didn't know, and to whom he is speaking? His eyes turn inwards to greet the death waiting within him.

The whole thing is happening in seconds, but to Swami it feels like minutes. He tears his gaze away from the fresh dead face and looks up to where the man might have fallen from, a seven-storey building with a neon sign: "*Hotel Ambuli – full A/C – non-veg*".

"Saar," Alexander squeals, trying to hang on to the wheelchair as hundreds of individuals turn into a mob. Swami feels the chair rocking this way and that. A woman is now standing over the mangled white man and beating him ferociously with her husband's tiffin can. With her other hand she grips her howling infant, the boy who had lost his balance and fallen over.

"He nearly landed on my precious son!" she screeches, thwacking the metal container into a dead man's head. "My son could have been killed by this snow-faced sky demon!" The mob eggs her on. Spittle flies out of her mouth, then springs back on its own trail to hang from her chin.

"Saar!" Alexander yelps desperately. He is no longer holding the wheelchair, he has been wrenched away.

"My – little – son," the woman pants, cracking down the unlikely weapon. "My – tiny – son is – precious!" Now more people have joined in, using their bare hands, as men shout to each other, at each other, to God and at the world. Swami is still in his chair, the white man's bloody head inches from his feet. He isn't scared at all, he hasn't felt as peaceful for a long time. *Snow-faced sky demon*, he finds himself thinking, *that's good*. The chair tips back and he's over, lying there in the dirt with the dead man. People are scrambling over him and over each other, piling in to get at the white man and beat him: he's white, after all, which makes a change, and he's dead, so it doesn't really matter. Chances like these don't grow on trees.

Swami briefly sees Hotel Ambuli again through the flailing arms and legs – "*What a Refreshing Place to Stay, for your Busyness and your Holiday*" – then feels bare feet trampling him. He wonders if this is his death, and hears himself calling God, *Rama, Rama, Rama*, but not out of fear. It is more out of politeness, as one would call to friendly neighbours through the half-open door of their house – quietly, in case they were busy, or sleeping.

Whistles are ringing, batons are flashing, members of the mob are being grabbed by the collar, by the hair, by the seat of the pants, and sent spinning. The police are here and are weighing in. They lash out and force their way through, calling everyone sons of prostitutes in their time-honoured and reassuring fashion. The intent of the people goes this way and that way for a few seconds, then sensibly goes that way for good. The mob divides into individuals again, onlookers only.

"Well Brother, what are you doing down there?"

Swami is looking up at the prodigious moustache of his old friend and colleague from Mullaipuram Police

Station, Sub-Inspector K.P. Murugesan. He opens his mouth to say something.

"Dead, tiffin – didn't know!" he says. It isn't what he'd planned to say, but since the stroke he can't be too fussy.

"Are you hurt?" Murugesan asks, speaking to him but looking with dread at the corpse.

"No."

"Saar!" Alexander shouts, finally wriggling his way through and taking his position behind the toppled wheelchair.

"Don't worry boy, he's very fine." says Murugesan. "A bit shocked. We'll get him up. Hey! You and you! Come here!"

Two constables lever the wheelchair up, then get Swami to his feet. He collapses into his chair, half-dazed and abruptly exhausted, as Alexander brushes him down with the dirtiest rag in Tamil Nadu.

"Go home now Brother, have some tea, leave me to deal with this god-almighty disaster. My God, a dead white man," Murugesan laments, appalled, "there'll be hell to pay!"

"Dead before," Swami says, indicating the body with his eyes.

"Yes yes, never mind these details." Murugesan looks disappointed. "Dead before they beat him?"

"Mm."

"Alive when he landed or dead already?"

"Living."

"My God," Murugesan mutters, looking up at Hotel Ambuli, "what does it mean?"

* * *

A choice between Granddaddy playing his flute continuously and Granddaddy continuously asking for his flute back is not much of a choice. Granddaddy is playing his flute. The immediate family members of both clans are corralled together in the little lounge. The most significant elders and one unidentified baby have been allocated the shiny blue fraying sofa. Two or three dozen other people are thronging the remaining two rooms of the bungalow and the small back plot outside. Some of these people are hungry. They are stripping Number 14/B of edibles with the automatic efficiency of a swarm of locusts. Meanwhile, Leela is miles away, mortified and hiding – "Such a little monkey," Mr P keeps saying, ambiguously – and Swami is missing. A disinterested commentator might hazard the opinion that this is not the smoothest possible start to a pre-engagement meeting, but the principal players in both families are coping.

"Oh yes, I'm sure he'll be here any moment!" Mrs P says in the cosy crowded room. "We aren't worried, please don't concern yourselves."

Her husband is mm-hmming enthusiastically in kindly support of his wife's small talk, enjoying being at the centre of so much excitement and activity, so many interested well-wishers.

"Appa is maybe held up at the police station by some important problem," Pushpa suggests shyly, wanting to make her father seem very grand.

"A long career in the police, I heard," chips in an uncle of the boy.

"Oh yes, very long career," Amma answers, "more than twenty years."

"And still they are asking his advice!" Anand chips in, deadpan and mischievous, causing Amma's left eyebrow to scale her forehead independently of her right eyebrow. She is suspicious of this younger brother because he needs a haircut and because he says smart things and because she can feel a funny throbbing near her left elbow. If her right eyebrow scales her forehead independently of her left eyebrow, then he'll really be in trouble.

"Shut up," says the gloom-laden Devan, scolding his younger brother.

For a moment Amma thinks he is speaking to her, and her right eyebrow quivers; while she doesn't actively dislike this older brother, she doesn't wholly approve of him because he is already married.

"Government desk job is distinct possibility!" screeches Swami's brother's wife, from nowhere, and without a shred of evidence.

Government desk job? No one says anything for a moment, as though to mark the fact that Swami's brother's wife has over-egged the pudding. The unmarried young people on both sides examine each other discreetly, Mohan and Anand sizing up the sisters, the sisters sizing up Mohan and Anand. Amma takes a moment to range her unqualified admiration over the petrified features of that perfect middle brother, the saintly Mohan.

"How many melodies he knows!" says Mrs P at last, nodding admiringly at Granddaddy – everybody turns to look at Granddaddy – from whom a flourish has just emanated; his reedy tunes are yet to imprint themselves in everlasting tedium on Mrs P's neurons.

"But when you ask him about it, he says he can't remember anything, he just plays what comes out," says an unidentified voice from somewhere over by the door, where second-tier supporters of the pre-engagement meeting are craning their necks to watch the fun.

"That is the gods," Mrs P says approvingly. "Our elders are closest to the God. That is only one of many reasons why we are giving you our respect," she adds, addressing her remarks to the oblivious Granddaddy and to a head-waggling stump-toothed aged parent of her own.

Amma nods gratefully. Amma is in awe of authentically fat women. Not only are fat women rich enough to buy lots of expensive fattening foodstuffs, they have enough free time in which to eat it. Amma loves to see two fat wealthy ladies crammed nonchalantly into a creaking cycle rickshaw while some 45-kg fellow with pipe-cleaner legs strains to pedal them up a long, slow incline – especially in the hot season. Amma regrets that she will never have enough money or leisure to be grotesquely corpulent.

There is a quarter-minute of free-falling speechlessness in this small packed room.

"What about your studies and what-all?" says Mohan – that human super-entity of cutting-edge computational developments – to Jodhi. Such excitement! Rapt observers near and far try not to ease their buttocks into new positions expectantly, or to seem in any way as though this might be a significant incident deserving of the utmost attention. For these are the first ever words spoken between Jodhi and Mohan. Certainly some incoherent mumblings and shy glances of mutual terror were exchanged when Jodhi and Mohan were first introduced, but since then – nothing. Just vacant faces staring at whoever is speaking, and flat, clipped voices responding to anything that is being said to them. Who knows if these two youngsters are head over heels in love or half crazed with horror? Some say it's much the same thing. The couple are sitting side by side in white plastic chairs, like a King and Queen down on their luck; a court of parents and elders are seated near them; making up the loyal subjects are brothers and sisters and uncles and aunties and cousins and intimates, all perching on armrests and table corners and small protuberances of furniture, or sitting all over the floor.

What about your studies... Amma's eyes bulge out of her head as she gazes at Jodhi and wills her to reply. Jodhi swallows and shifts in her seat. *What about your studies,*

Amma thinks, *what about your studies, what about your studies... DAUGHTER, SPEAK!*

"Eng. Lit.," Jodhi says.

"I know that," says Mohan. "Eng. Lit.," he says. "Like him," he says, gesturing at his younger brother, "before he was—"

"Very very very very!" Mr P bellows, incomprehensibly. He doesn't want his younger son's latest expulsion from college broadcast willy-nilly at the pre-engagement meeting, though he knows that everyone knows.

Amma beams at Mohan. What a beautiful boy, she is thinking. Actually, what an incredible salary he'll soon be earning – that is a more accurate rendering of her thoughts – but his good looks are certainly a bonus.

Amma's sister picks up a plate of fried snacks and offers them around.

"No no no, no," Mrs P says, taking one, taking two, taking three *murukku* as everyone watches admiringly.

"You see," Mr P begins in a new and solemn voice, "now that we are having such a jolly time, the thing is, you see, dowry is the thing, we'd better think about dowry situation, that's the thing."

"Dowry situation," murmurs Amma with a head-wobble like a Thanjavur doll, as though there is nothing that can make her feel more soporifically at ease than this matter, as though there is scarcely a topic under the sun or even beyond the edges of the known universe that she would enjoy investigating further than this one, at this time, in this place, under the tongue-lolling, neck-craning, eye-bright scrutiny of her neighbours. "Husband better come first," she says.

"Who is your favourite English author and what-all?" Mohan blurts out at Jodhi. He is on a roll now. He is not so very interested in the dowry situation.

"I don't know," Jodhi answers, startled. "I like Graham Greene."

"I can make world-champion-beating anagram out of Graham Greene. Possibly several," her suitor confides.

Jodhi isn't sure what to do with this information, but she nods gratefully, and the two Ammas share their little smiles. And then there is some shouting and commotion outside, a turning of heads, something of a small-scale bungalow-constrained non-fatal stampede, an "Oh my God!" from a startled Kamala and a bum note from Granddaddy and a booming "The little monkey!" from Mr P as Leela fights her way into the room, panting "Amma Amma Amma!" She trips over an ankle and dives full-length into the throng, shouting:

"Amma, a flying white man fell on Appa!"

3

Swami – bare-chested, slack-breasted and yawning – is standing in the doorless doorway of the bedroom, still in his sheetlike lungi, looking out at Amma and Kamala. The mother and daughter rose half an hour ago, bathed themselves in the cool dark, and then went outside to pour water from a vessel and pray to Surya, the sun, who was rising too. Women of Amma's caste do not normally worship in this way. Maybe that is why she does it. Now she and Kamala are performing puja to the family gods who live in the little wall-mounted shrine. For every dawn of her married life, Amma has sought to see God and to be seen by God in this way. Later, the other three girls will get up reluctantly, and Kamala will draw a *kolam* design on their doorstep with rice-flour paste.

Swami loosens his lungi so that he can tighten it again around his waist – it is something he has learnt to do with one hand.

But how many times has the sun risen, Swami thinks. By how many people has the sun been worshipped? If you multiplied the one number by the other number, what kind of number would you get? Swami is always thinking thoughts like these, but what else has he been thinking about during this past week? Of how Jodhi has lost her chance of a very good good boy because of him?

Of course. Of how his wife is embarrassed by him? Yes, that too. Of how he'd like to lie down on his sleeping mat, and go to sleep, and never wake up, just like the white man, the dying white man who said "I didn't know..." as he left this world for some other place? Yes yes, all these thoughts and more have come to him often in his misery and his wonder, as well as strange ruminations and meditations concerning death gazes, the strange pink-white whites of a white man's eyes, and that moment when the balance of power between a new brief light and an old one is superseded by a dull glaze. *The fellow just – went away...* "I'm here," Swami had said to him, from some part of his mind he hadn't known was there. "I'm going," the man had responded. *It was neither speech nor thought, it was transparent communication, it existed outside any frameworks I understand, it was...* And the curious thing was, Swami had felt so calm as the white man was dying. Only later, under the indignity of everyone's fascination, had he felt even worse than before. For when Swami tries to convey the deeper resonances of his responses – to his wife, to his relatives, and to any of the neighbours and acquaintances who have been coming by to enquire after his welfare – they don't listen properly. They don't want to hear him mumbling about abstract topics, it's too difficult. They want to know what it is like to have a white man fall on top of you. No one takes a blind bit of notice when Swami grits his teeth in frustration and tries, for the hundredth time, to explain that the white man did not fall *on* him – "Not fall *me*," he fumes. They want to ask yes-no questions as to whether white men bounce, and if the fellow was bleeding, and whether he had blond hair; they want to know what she looked like, that spittle-flecked mother who beat the dead white man over the head with her husband's tiffin can, while the little boy in her frenzied grip was sent lurching this way and that. As for Amma, what she really wants to know is this: "How could this happen at such a time? How could he do such a thing?"

Who knows if it is the white man she is referring to, or Swami.

When there is no hunger or pain or fear, what is peace or its absence except a state of mind one chooses? Swami knows this, but *I can't endure any more* is the background mantra playing over and over in his mind at this moment as he watches his beautiful wife at prayer; he is at the mercy of fore-thoughts that ricochet between half a dozen extreme problems: the white man, Jodhi's prospects, his crippled future, ultimate meanings, his humiliation, his wife's anger – and partly, it is true, his breakfast.

When he was a newly married man nearly thirty years ago, and he used to watch Amma's morning puja, he would tease her afterwards, saying, "Yes yes, this early-morning high devotion is all very well in Tamil Nadu, where the sun gets up with us, but there are places on this earth where the sun gets up at 2.30 a.m., and then what would you do?" In reply, she would coyly hint at how hard it would be to leave her husband's arms at that time – but she would do it, because his welfare and the welfare of their family depended on the protection of the gods. But there have been few such teases and loving hints since Swami lost the ability to say four words together in the right order, and there have been even fewer since Jodhi's divinely handsome and accomplished mate was marched out of the pre-engagement meeting by his mortified family because of the rollicking embarrassment of a white man falling on the father of the prospective bride. Though the *Vedas* and the *Brahmanas* and the *Upanishads* make no reference to snow-faced sky demons plummeting from the heavens to expire on innocent Hindus, though the *Mahabharata* and the *Ramayana* and the *Puranas* contain no indication as to what such incidents may portend, though the 2,685 verses of the *Lawbook of Manu* are incontrovertibly silent on this topic, nevertheless the parents of Mohan have taken a broad view that such an event is not auspicious.

The small, roughly made cabinet of the family shrine is fixed halfway up the living-room wall. On the inside of the open doors are cheap prints of Ganesha and the eight Lakshmis. Within, on a shelf, amongst flower petals and brass plates showing scenes from the sacred texts, and next to a small stock of oil, wicks, clarified butter and lamps, are murtis of Murugan and Mariamman – little statuettes representing the Gods. Samayapuram Mariamman, the feminine power who conquers evil and heals disorder, went wooshing up the family worship rankings shortly after Swami's stroke, when Amma desired sight of a god who could really understand her family's plight. But as for Lord Murugan, the youthful warrior god, he can never be displaced in Amma's affection. The protection he affords is all-encompassing, and the boons he grants are legendary. And anyway he is so handsome and virile. Sometimes Swami is envious of Lord Murugan, particularly on special occasions when Amma bathes him in coconut milk and dresses him and feeds him devotedly.

Behind Swami, the other three girls are stirring on their mats, under their thin blankets.

"Get up," Swami says in a kindly way, once Amma and Kamala are done.

"Don't snap at them for nothing," Amma snaps, for nothing, brushing past him and into the kitchen to steam some idlis for breakfast. Since the catastrophe, she has barely spoken to him except like this. She is still in maternal despair about what happened. For the first time in her married life, she is ashamed of her husband. Swami doesn't blame her, he knows she only wants what is best for Jodhi... *But is it my fault that people think a white man fell on me? Or is it my fate?* That second thought is worse than the first. But maybe it is his fate.

Poor Swami, he is a laughing stock. On the day after the incident, he was the lead story in the local newspaper. FLYING FOREIGNER LANDS ON RETIRED WHEELCHAIR COP, was the headline. He is famous. When he goes into town, young men scream "Keep back!" and point at the sky theatrically, as though more foreigners might plummet down at any moment. Jokers follow his painful progress down the streets, arching their necks and looking up as they rap out their outlandish predictions:

"Mr George Bush!"

"Michael Jackson!"

"Bernard Matthews!"

Nobody knows who Bernard Matthews is, except the wit who first said it, a fellow who happens to know a thing or two about European turkey-farming, but everyone thinks Bernard Matthews is a wonderful name, one that can bear much repeating. And yesterday, as Pushpa was wheeling Swami to the second-hand booksellers who lay their wares out on cloths near the spice market, a plastic baby-doll came hurtling down from a second-storey window and bounced off his knee, to the helpless hilarity of a bunch of rowdies.

There is, Swami now knows, no worse feeling than being roundly ridiculed in front of your own daughter. *And is a man a man...* he had thought to himself at that time, stony-faced, almost crying.

Swami trails past Amma in the kitchen and out into the little yard behind the bungalow.

I've lost all my dignity outside this small compound, and most of it within.

He steps into the toilet, closes the makeshift door and squats down slowly and awkwardly over the hole, with his lungi hitched up over his knees. He winces

as burning sensations shoot up his left arm; acutely
painful, they nearly always occur when he squats down,
ever since the stroke dumped one half of his body
outside the control of his brain. There is nothing to be
done about this, the doctor says.

Since this is the only place in India where Swami can
weep, Swami weeps.

* * *

Of all the police personnel in the town of Mullaipuram,
surely it is K.P. Murugesan who has the best moustache.
Not that it is the biggest or the longest or the most
spectacularly sculpted, for any stupid fellow can break
a record, but K.P. Murugesan's moustache is generally
believed to be naturally fuller and bushier and stiffer and
better-shaped and altogether more impressive than any
other moustache one might encounter across the entire
Indian Police Service of Tamil Nadu. The moustache
of K.P. Murugesan has been photographed in IPS
journals, has featured in the nightmares of convicted
criminals, and has even been mentioned in passing by
an admiring member of the State Legislative Assembly.
This moustache: it really is a god of moustaches,
women look at it and wobble their heads in awe – and
who can wonder, when it juts from his face like wings
from an aeroplane, like a mighty load of timber in a bull
elephant's strong trunk?

Murugesan is Swami's oldest colleague in the Police.
The two of them attended the Police Training Academy
together, more than twenty-five years ago, but they
only got to know each other very well some twelve
years back, when Swami was posted to Mullaipuram.
Murugesan had shown Swami the ropes. It has to
be said that those ropes, in those days, were not the
cleanest ropes around, and since then they have only

got grubbier. The policemen of Mullaipuram are not consistently renowned for being entirely incorruptible in all circumstances. For example, whenever there is a crackdown on a vice den in Mullaipuram, the police and the gangsters negotiate in advance as to how many paid volunteers should be arrested during the raid, thus keeping the newspapers happy with photogenic crime-busting operations, whilst safeguarding the kickbacks that flow from the den, through several tiers of the IPS's finest, all the way up to the wife of the District Super, who has expensive tastes in European crockery. Even so, amongst this formidable legion of law-enforcers, Murugesan and Swami have always prided themselves on being slightly less corrupt than some of the others.

It is these superior ethical values that are informing Murugesan's expression today, as he walks through Mullaipuram's early-morning streets to visit Swami. The gaze above his hairy outcrop has a slightly harassed aspect; the violent demise of a white man in a small South Indian town was always going to spell trouble for those unfortunate personnel assigned to the case, and Murugesan is feeling anxious because he is one of the investigating officers.

Forces and pressures far above Murugesan's sphere of control are pushing and pulling at the case. Aware of the potential damage to tourism that could spread across the entire state of Tamil Nadu, various regional government agencies are overtly anxious to see the case concluded as quickly and as tidily as possible; it is known that the Chief Minister of Tamil Nadu is hopping mad and advocating a speedy low-profile resolution; and as for DDR – Doraisamy Devanamapettai Rajendran, the filthy-rich domineering Mr Mullaipuram of this town, who is also a State Legislature political hopeful and an influential member of Mullaipuram District Police Board of Governors and the owner of five hotels and a score of other businesses, including Hotel Ambuli from which the unfortunate white man is suspected to have fallen... well, he's got half the town in his pocket. He's already been telling Murugesan's superiors that nothing could be worse for the prosperity of Mullaipuram, nothing could be more detrimental to the operation of natural justice, nothing could be more contrary to the principles of effective police investigation, "than if that bouncing white man is found to have been killed in *my hotel!*" In brief, anyone with a sliver of common sense is agreed that this case is a clear instance of suicide by an unidentifiable foreign drifter of low worth and no importance.

But when did common sense hold unfettered sway over one second of time or one atom of matter? Several western consulates, anxious to know from where the victim hails, have been urging the Indian authorities to reveal the nationality and identity of the dead man; central government officials in Delhi, under pressure from a concerned American Embassy, are also dissatisfied with the response of the authorities in Tamil Nadu. So pressed this way and that way to do one thing or another thing, Murugesan's bosses are trying to find responses which seem proactive and useful while being the opposite. This is why it has been decided, at the highest levels of political futility, that Swami will be taken by Murugesan to a Madurai morgue, to confirm formally that the body currently lying there is the same one that fell on him a week earlier.

Murugesan turns into Swami's street, and starts thinking about Amma's breakfast idlis, which are famous.

* * *

Jodhi, Kamala and Pushpa are standing outside the toilet waiting for Appa to come out. Kamala has a bar of soap, Jodhi holds a jug of water, and Pushpa bears a small towel. They wait in a row, talking in very quiet voices against the background noise of traffic.

"Taking very long time," Kamala hisses.

"Taking longer every day," Jodhi whispers, sadly.

Everyone is feeling very sorry for Jodhi now that Appa has ruined her life. They marvel at her courage in the face of adversity.

At last Appa comes out and moves up and down this row of dutiful daughters. First he stares at the top of Jodhi's head as she pours water over his hand. Then he looks at the top of Kamala's head as she dispenses and receives the soap which he jiggles around in one hand. Then he looks at the top of Jodhi's head once more as she pours water again. Finally he looks at the top of Pushpa's head as she dries him with the towel. It is a solemn process.

The tops of my children's heads are beautiful... He would like to touch their cheeks lovingly, but daren't. It would make him weep again.

"Appa," says Leela, coming out from the kitchen in her school uniform as she hands Jodhi a stiffly ironed and starched shirt, "Mr Murugesan is come."

Swami nods.

Jodhi hands the shirt to her father, who puts it on awkwardly. She itches to do the buttons up, but Swami does it by himself. He is halfway through when he reminds himself that she has lost her happiness because of him; *let the girl put my shirt on me if she wants to.*

"You girls," Swami says, when she's finished. "What," he says, "what when," he tries, "when what."

"Appa?"

"College?"

"Yes Appa, going to college today."

"Attending practicals," Pushpa confides.

"Good girl," says Swami.

"No college for me Appa," Kamala says. "Staying here with you only, Appa."

"Good girl. Hurry three," he tells Pushpa. "To, through – over," he tries. Hurry up is what he was aiming for.

Inside the bungalow, Amma is speaking on the phone. Something about the way she is saying "Okay" and "Very good" and "Very happy" and "I will do the needful" and "Most kindly of you" and "Yes yes we will fix it without delay most certainly" is entering their minds as significant, and drawing them inside.

"Rest assured," says Amma, smiling anxiously as she speaks, "we are most happy to hear this news, very happy."

Inside, Appa greets Murugesan with a nod as everyone gathers around Amma.

"I don't know how to thank you," Amma trills, on the point of tears. "Such a good boy! Yes very soon. Goodboy! – I mean, Goodbye!" she says, laughing girlishly.

She puts the receiver down, then picks it up again to polish it on the edge of her sari, trying not to cry as all the girls except Jodhi beg her to tell them the news. She replaces the receiver back in its cradle, and gently drapes a little cloth over it.

"God is doing this for you, Jodhi," she says at last. "Boy's family want to visit again, even after everything that happened, even though a white man fell on Appa."

"*Didn't*—" Appa blurts wearily, but no one takes the slightest bit of notice. Jodhi's hand is clamped over her mouth in shock, and her three sisters are exclaiming "Ayyo-yo-yoooooooooooo!" over and over again.

"Boy is wanting this most particularly," Amma says, "he is insistent, so Mother and Father have finally agreed, despite the descent of the snow-faced sky demon."

"Very happy news," Murugesan says, as Swami burns in shame to be the obstacle that has occasioned such a concession.

"God is all-powerful," Amma says huskily, knowing that this development is an example of the all-encompassing protection, the legendary boons, for which Lord Murugan is famous. "Go!" she barks at Leela, fiddling on a shelf for twenty rupees, "run to the market before school and buy three coconuts!" Later she will go to the temple and make an offering of them.

4

That is all I am these days, a passenger escorted from this place to that place by people who have no interest in what I say or think... From his passenger window, Swami watches the fields giving way to fetid plots of wasteland, to hideous corporate company headquarters, to fields again, to a row of tottering roadside stalls, then more benighted plots. The car is approaching the outskirts of Madurai, where the morgue is located, and Murugesan, driving, has not made a tactful job of explaining why Swami is being asked to confirm that the body being held there is the white man's corpse. It is clear to Swami that he is being used by Mullaipuram Police as a diversionary pawn in a game of political pressures. *Only because no one is interested in what I do or say am I being asked to do something and say something.*

"Good news about this boy," Murugesan offers in a conciliatory tone, after some hesitation, wobbling the steering wheel fractionally so that a small stray puppy in the road ahead might – with a bit of luck – pass under the speeding car without being squashed. It's the first thing either of them has said for ten minutes.

The car jolts slightly.

"What is he like, this boy?"

"Gnngow," Swami answers.

"Oh-oh," Murugesan says, nodding.

I don't know, is what Swami had tried to say. *Don't pretend to understand me, Murugesan...*

As a driver, Murugesan is in a realm of his own. He is so superior to the slapdash norm as to be an impressive menace on an almost moment-by-moment basis, routinely forcing other road users to give way or join him in death. This is the only aspect of the journey Swami takes any pleasure in. Each time a near-miss situation arises, he hankers after his life's conclusion, where he imagines sanctuary might lie. But no, when Murugesan overtakes a lorry on a blind side, then the oncoming drivers lurch to their side of the road in horror, and when Murugesan hurls the car here and there to avoid being squeezed between two buses, he somehow always makes the gap.

Murugesan is feeling anxious about Swami's silence. He doesn't realize that Swami is feeling disempowered and offended. He thinks that his old friend is suspicious about something. But why, he wonders? After all, Swami's been around, he knows the score, he understands that in the application of law and order – especially as interpreted through the eyes of the Mullaipuram police – justice can sometimes take a circuitous path... What is he up to, this old friend of mine, Murugesan asks himself – what's going on in that old head of his?

"So then," he says emphatically, screeching the car into the hospital car park. He jumps out of the car and walks round to Swami's side to help him out.

It is a while since Swami has been to the Johansson Memorial Post-Mortem Centre attached to a private hospital in Madurai – not since he was a serving police officer, clogged up in an interminable case involving two vicious and vengeful family clans in an ever-simmering, fifty-year land dispute.

Inside, once they have passed from the 35°C heat

of the corridor to the constant 4°C cold of Mortuary Two, Murugesan walks patiently beside the shuffling, shivering Swami, leading him past shrouded bodies on slabs; here and there a foot or a hand pokes out from under the shrouds. A pair of mortuary attendants are playing cards on the floor; they leap up sharply and run to assist – Dalits, wrapped up in their ragged mufflers and their mended woollen balaclavas. Murugesan waves them away, and they stand together, watching the police officer and his disabled companion. No one has a kind word for these fellows, even though their responsibilities can be onerous. Sometimes they have to conduct post-mortems themselves, cutting the bodies open crudely, yanking the organs out, and shouting what they discover to a doctor twenty metres away. That doctor, disdainful of some low fellow's dirty old toddy-sozzled kicked-to-death carcass, will be hunched over the post-mortem paperwork, filling it in briskly, not even looking up from his forms. It is the kind of thing that happens nearly every week, but only to the bodies of poor men and women. There is no chance of the white fellow's body being subjected to this system. Even after death, his whiteness grants him some privileges.

They pass through the door at the end of Mortuary Two, and wait in a shabby little antechamber outside the deep-freeze room until the technician inside is ready for them. Swami sits blank-faced on the single chair. Murugesan stalks his own shadow under the harsh strip lights.

"You're lucky you're not a police officer these days," Murugesan says. "D.D. Rajendran has gone completely crazy, he's breathing fire on the backside of every officer in Mullaipuram about the reputation of his damn hotel."

Swami doesn't answer.

"Every year it gets worse with that fellow, he's got too

many people in his pocket, he's virtually running the police service in our town." Murugesan looks across at Swami, who is sulking. "So you see," Murugesan continues, made uneasy by the silence – what is wrong with Swami today? – "so you see, about this case, they just want me to take a deposition from you, that this is the same fellow and all."

"Who him? Who is?" Swami asks, looking up – it's the same question he'd asked in the car.

"Just some dumb hippy," Murugesan answers, deflecting it again. "Who knows, he could be any western dopehead."

"Papers?"

"Papers I'm not knowing about," says Murugesan. "Maybe papers, maybe not papers. All I'm knowing is this, I'm not knowing anything about papers."

"Oh," Swami says. "Slike that," he says, offended that he is not trusted enough to be in the loop.

"It's like that," Murugesan repeats; there is an unavoidable little cover-up going on that Swami, with all his experience, ought to sense and understand; but Swami just doesn't get it. For Swami, all this cloak-and-dagger stuff is just another indication that he is no longer regarded as a worthwhile human being.

A door opens and a technician jumps out.

"Okay, come." Behind him is a brief flash of grey-white leg on a metal trolley.

* * *

Amma is determined that the second pre-engagement meeting will be considerably more successful than the first. For starters, to guarantee Swami's presence at the great event and to ensure that nothing spectacular happens to him, it has been decided that he will not be allowed out of the house beforehand. Granddaddy, on the contrary, is to be respectfully banished – which will not be difficult, since his attendance last time had been so against his will as to necessitate abduction. As for the general tone of the affair, Amma is being much more rigorous about the number and quality of participants; after all, a house bursting at the seams, a disastrously behaved youngest daughter, a husband turning up not merely late but half-brained by a white man... such indignities cannot be risked again. So there are to be fewer relatives from both sides and no hangers-on, there are to be better-drilled daughters, there is to be a new sari for Jodhi, there are to be extra special titbits for Mrs P, there is to be a stately, dignified Swami sitting underneath the photo of himself in full ceremonial uniform and nodding sagely at every word which the mighty sire of Mohan might utter... With such techniques is Amma hoping to convince her guests that Jodhi is a good girl from a good family, a girl more than deserving of Mohan.

* * *

"A drug-addled Indian who fell out of a hotel window would be ashes in the river by now," Murugesan says. "Why should this fellow get different treatment? What is so important about him, the dirty rapist?"

"Heh?"

"Ah well," Murugesan says, apparently annoyed with himself as he waves an arm ineffectually, "you might as well know, there are rumours about this fellow."

Rapist? Swami feels shock. He looks at his friend reproachfully, assuming the admission is accidental, as Murugesan prowls around the aluminium trolley. He can see he will get no further explanation. And here is the corpse. Shivering, Swami looks down at the frozen matter that had once enfolded a human life. Poor fellow, Swami tut-tuts to himself automatically, taking in the details. The eyes are closed and will never open again, unless some boffin peels the lids back. Wherever the body has escaped the dark hues of injury and trauma, death has given the deeply tanned skin a grisly lustre, as though a faint grey matt varnish has been applied. But much of the skin surface is obscured by livid contusions and abrasions, and the face itself is very badly beaten. Swami can hardly recognize him, which goes to show that tiffin cans, when full of rice and sambar, and when wielded by mothers protecting their tiny precious sons, make effective weapons. Swami tries to see beyond the purple swellings and the dried black blood, through to the face of the man he had seen alive, when life was animating him for a few final seconds. *Poor fellow,* he repeats, automatically, but his sympathy is shallow and merely going through the motions, because it is difficult to link this frozen slab of beaten body to the living-dying man with whom Swami had connected. *Yes,* Swami realizes, *it's not his humanity I was granted access to, not the rapist of this world, but the spirit beyond it – and what does his spirit have to do with this bag of cutlets?* He stands over the corpse. Murugesan, looking on a little nervously, thinks he is scrutinizing it closely, but Swami is somewhere else, reliving the strange communication between his spirit and the white man's spirit, more vividly now than any time since it happened, and an inscrutable expression descends on his face as he stares unseeing at the corpse. *What did he want from me?*

"Don't worry about all that business," Murugesan says uneasily, after a few moments, "it's nothing important."

Swami jolts out of his reverie: "What?"

"Not our business," Murugesan says, pointing vaguely to the chest. Swami peers intently and sees three cigarette burns, two on the left side of the left nipple, and one almost fully on the nipple itself, half-obscured by the bruised and bloody condition of the corpse. He hadn't noticed them before, but now that Murugesan has pointed them out, there they are.

Why did he have to speak just then? Swami asks himself, scowling, resentful at having his attention diverted to these small strange circles; *for a moment, just for a moment, I was close...*

"Fashion thing," Murugesan says, improbably, of the burns. "Who knows why these hippies do this kind of thing?" He is shaking his head rather too theatrically. "You know, once in Goa I saw a hippy who had piercings *on the back of his neck!* These westerners, they roam around pretending to be as natural as trees, but all they do is drink beer and take drugs for three months, then go home on a jumbo jet when it gets too hot."

Swami can't help smiling at the caricature.

"Anyway you'd better sign the form," says Murugesan, sighing. "I know this is the fellow, you know this is the fellow, everyone knows this is the fellow, there has never been any doubt that this is the fellow, nor are there any other dead white fellows within one hundred miles of here, but you'd better sign the form all the same to say that this is the fellow."

Yes give me the form and I'll sign it. That is my role.

On the drive back to Mullaipuram little is said. Murugesan is sure that Swami is wondering about the cigarette burns, while Swami is thinking about the dowries of his six daughters, and vaguely hoping for an immediate fatal collision. He has life insurance. They would be better off without him.

5

What a contrast, what a relief, what a godsend! – so Amma is thinking, a couple of weeks later, as she plays host to the boy's family for a second time. She radiates smiles around the stalwarts of the boy's immediate party, as Mr P regales them all with one of his most fascinating railway anecdotes.

"That was in the days when one could thrash the porters," he is saying, by way of explanation.

"Those were the days," Anand murmurs, looking at all Amma's daughters with an expressionless face, hoping he'll force an involuntary smile out of one of them. Jodhi and Leela come close.

"Five billion passenger journeys every year! 1.6 million employees! 39,000 miles of track! Our state-owned Indian Railways is still the glory of India!" Mr P affirms.

"Ah yes," says Swami gravely, in a deep and reassuring voice, with a slowly nodding head, his greying temples freshly clippered, his shirt collar starched and ironed into a flawless graceful plane, his moustache trimmed and shaped and – yes – subtly enhanced with black dye, at Amma's request.

Who could have foreseen this, Amma is asking herself. One week her husband ruins everything by offering himself as a landing strip for a death-wish foreigner, while the next he is this dignified presence who seems to be impressing the formidable P family. She looks around the room in a state of nervous satisfaction. Kamala is taking an empty dish into the kitchen for replenishing, while Leela and Pushpa are paragons of daughterly obedience, with not even a hint of any whispering or joking or fidgeting. Amma has finally made the girls understand how desperate their situation is. We are poverty-stricken, she had pleaded, we can only just afford to eat, we pay for your education in debts, we are going to the wall, and if Jodhi bags a boy then that is one daughter who won't end up on the street, so you MUST behave... The two girls had ended up whimpering in self-pity and shame.

Amma nods and smiles at Mrs P, who is reciting impressive biodata not just for Mohan – surely that prodigy will be earning in excess of 300,000 rupees per annum in no time at all? – but for Anand as well. But although Amma's "most wonderful"s and "very excellent"s sound animated, it is difficult for her to simulate interest in that haircut-shy college drop-out. Her true focus is on Mohan. She catches him glancing repeatedly at her Jodhi. From the way his hungry, tongue-like glances flick all over her daughter, she can see he is besotted. Is this our future son-in-law? Amma wonders dreamily. She looks over to Swami, as if he might know. Seated like this in his best clothes, quiet and serious and smiling, he looks almost as impressive as the fine figure of a man he'd been before the stroke. Amma watches in amazement as everyone directs conversation to him respectfully. Everyone except Mohan. He has been mugging up on the web for titbits about English Literature, for Jodhi's benefit, and now, excited, he lets rip:

"How many plays did William Shakespeare write?"

A roomful of synchronized eyeballs swivel around to

him and then swivel back to Jodhi. Jodhi flushes. The
burden of being engaging and interesting lies heavily
upon her, but what is to be done with such a question,
one that kills conversation stone-dead and diverts everyone's attention to her slightly quivering chin?

"I think it was thirty-seven..."

The eyeballs rotate back to Mohan, as everyone an-
ticipates a fascinating rejoinder to Jodhi's remark.

"Correct," says Mohan.

There is a long and uncomfortable pause. Just as
Amma and Mrs P are on the cusp of ending it with
some chat, he sputters into action again.

"Which are your favourites, the Tragedies, the
Comedies, or the Histories?" he blurts. He's doing his
best. Yesterday he even got hold of a western self-help
book called *How to Attract Women*.

"The Tragedies," Jodhi half speaks and half whispers,
almost incapacitated by the fathomless depths of her
embarrassment.

"What is," says Mohan, screwing his eyes up in fierce
concentration as he strains for something interesting to
say, "what is," he repeats, now roaming the outermost
boundaries of conversational desolation, "what is... what
is the best play that Shakespeare ever wrote..."

Anand stifles a snort of laughter.

"...*and*," Mohan adds, suddenly inspired, "what are
three main reasons why it—"

"But – what are you *doing*?!" Mr P interrupts.

"Mohan is crazy about Shakespeare!" Anand an-
nounces, grinning.

"Shut up you little idiot," Devan says.

"Now now," trills Mrs P to all her menfolk in a brittle
tone, while a few aunties and uncles from both sides
make a hearty chortling show of pretending not to be
embarrassed.

Swami looks across at Mr P approvingly: *if this was*

my boy, that's exactly what I'd say to the little idiot, if I could speak. Then he directs a forbidding stare at Pushpa and Leela; despite everything that has been bellowed at them, they look to be on the point of a giggling fit. It's the boy Anand's fault – he has charm, and a naughty streak.

"The youngsters are a little nervous, it's only to be expected," Amma offers.

"They should have a few moments alone," suggests Mrs P, "get to know each other..."

"No no, not necessary," Jodhi yelps.

"Yes yes," Amma says, "that is very wonderful idea, and anyway I was just about to send Jodhi out for milk – Jodhi, Jodhi, please go and buy milk for more tea for our honoured guests."

"Oh no, no no no," says Mrs P, "please don't worry about tea for us, not necessary." She rather fancies a glass. She stands up and pulls Mohan to his feet. "We don't want any tea, but you go with her, my son, accompany her as she goes to the shop and carry the milk back for her."

"Yes, why not get to know each other a little," says Mr P, also standing up, slightly angry with himself for his outburst, "but please," he adds, "please, no need for any more tea for us."

"No tea," Mrs P confirms politely. She's gasping for it.

"Eighty-two," Swami says, while Amma is saying, "You must have tea, you must have tea!"

"What what?" asks Mr P, puzzled.

"Eighty-two," Kamala repeats. "Appa knows *The Sacred Couplets* – off by heart," she admits, with a dash of pride.

The visitors gaze at the head of the household with supplementary respect; anyone who memorizes *The Sacred Couplets* is definitely special.

"Eighty-two!" Mr P breathes, "eighty-two is it? Well let

us see it, let us see couplet eighty-two! Off by heart, you say..."

"No no no," Amma is fretting, "there is no need to have a look, it's just his little game—" but it's too late. Kamala already has *The Sacred Couplets* down from the shelf and is passing it to her. Amma takes the book in her hands and tries to glare at Swami in such a way as will be interpreted as a gaze of loving admiration to everyone but him – a skill one acquires little by little, after about fifteen years of marriage. "Well then," she says, thumbing the pages, "now then, eighty-two..."

Mr P is highly excited by this turn of events. He loves a bit of tension. He once lost 30,000 rupees on a bet. "Off by heart, is it?" he keeps saying, "off by heart!"

Silence steals over the little living area as Amma finds the page. Jodhi, Kamala, Pushpa and Leela watch in apprehension; what if it's another Nine Hundred and Thirteen, Pushpa is thinking in horror? Who knows what Appa is capable of at the moment?

"Sacred couplet Eighty-Two is in section nine of Part One of *The Sacred Couplets*," Amma recites in a quiet voice – is that the *pada-pada-pada* of her heart that everyone can hear? She scans the lines slowly. Her face relaxes:

"It is wrong to drink even the nectar of immortality
If your honoured guests stay thirsty."

How should this triumph be described? The guests are enraptured by their host's erudite display of grace and hospitality. Mr P can't stop braying like a drunken donkey, and he's *still* saying "Off by heart! Off by heart, is it?"; Anand, who is in love with literature even though he is one of the worse poets ever to scrape nib across paper, is saying "respect, man" in English; Devan is nodding profoundly; Mrs Devan is muttering "couplet eighty-two", as though meaning to lodge it in her memory; and Mrs P looks to be close to tears that someone has said something so beautiful to her family.

Amma wobbles her head, as though to confirm "Yes, this is my husband – pre-eminent scholarly genius in Mullaipuram and all South India". Even Swami, chronically depressed as he is, has to work hard not to beam with satisfaction.

"What is the nectar of immortality?" Mohan asks.

"Go!" his father tells him, "get the milk, and then we will find out!" He pushes him out of the room, and Amma trails Jodhi behind him, and away they go together, the two young people, loping awkwardly down the street.

* * *

It is 9 p.m. on a Friday evening – the family priests had been particular on the timing of this unorthodox second pre-engagement meeting, which has to be so overtly auspicious as to counter the debacle of the first – and Mullaipuram is throbbing with people who are shopping and promenading in the cool night. The traffic is nose-to-tail on every road, at every junction, with pedestrians cramming into the space between the cars and the shops: whole families, old friends, husbands and wives, mothers and daughters and sons, girls walking in pairs with elbows linked, boys walking in threes with their forearms across one another's shoulders, all of them milling around and weaving in and out of the mass. There are strings of lights over every stall, music blaring from shops, resting cows, altercations, some drunks, a street drama taken from the *Mahabharata*, large insects butting into lamps, bats tumbling overhead in the night air. Jodhi, burning with embarrassment, in mortal fear of stumbling into a friend, leads Mohan off the main street and down a side road, where the Tamil Nadu Milk Board has an outlet.

Mohan takes a sly sideways glance at Jodhi's figure, and gulps involuntarily from an excess of admiration. Jodhi takes a quick peak at Mohan, and has to admit to herself that he is certainly a handsome boy. She waits for him to speak, but he does not speak. She realizes that she must speak, but speech has deserted her. Walking side by side, both of them building up to saying something, they pass a tethered goat chewing on a plastic bag, and at last Mohan is inspired to break the silence. It's true that he is the holder of the *Sri Aandiappan Swamigal Tamil Nadu Information Superhighway Endowment Scholarship*, and it's true that he can write computer programs in C++ of dazzling elegance and utility, but...

"Goat," he says.

Though mining remote nooks and crannies of their brains, they arrive at their destination without excavating any further conversational jewels. In silence Jodhi buys a floppy plastic sachet of milk from the sullen boy sitting in the open hatch of the Milk Board outlet. As soon as it is in her hands Mohan snatches at it, blurting "Let me carry it!" as though her life will be at risk if he doesn't – but his reaction is so abrupt that Jodhi instinctively steps backwards. In the confused tussle, Mohan's grab at the milk sends the sachet flying down the street.

"So sorry!" Jodhi cries, mortified.

"It didn't explode!" he exclaims in relief, and scampers off to recover it; then he takes it back to the boy selling milk, and barks, "Wash this dirty thing!"

Following this little adventure, they set off for home, still incapable of finding anything sensible to say. Just as they get back, he whispers, much too late, "What is your email address?"

"Ah, here are the young wanderers!" says Mr P, slightly annoyed – he had been on the verge of raising the subject of the dowry – "Here they are, talking talking talking, talking away!"

Jodhi takes the milk into the kitchen, and Amma rushes in after her. She clatters around in a frenzy for a few moments, then "Yes?" she whispers, "yes?"

"Amma?"

"Yes?"

"Amma, yes what Amma?"

Amma rolls her eyes as she opens the valve on the gas canister under the bench and lights the one-ring hob.

"What do you mean with your 'Amma yes what Amma?'" she hisses, "what did he say!?"

"Nothing." Jodhi cuts a corner from the sachet, then pours the milk into a vessel as her mother looks on ominously.

"What do you mean, 'Nothing'? You tell me now everything he said!"

"But Amma—"

"No but-butting, speak Daughter!"

Jodhi leans back against the wall and wraps her arms around her ribs, shrugging.

"He said 'Goat', 'Let me carry it', 'It didn't explode' and 'Wash this dirty thing'."

Amma's eyes goggle in her head.

"What are you talking about, you stupid girl!"

"Amma, this is what he said."

"Nothing else?"

"He asked for my email address."

Amma stirs the tea over the gas ring with triumphant vigour: "There," she crows, "I knew it, he's mad about you!" But on a whim she stops stirring and points a finger at Jodhi accusingly: "You don't have an email address do you?"

"No Amma, of course not."

Amma nods and goes back to her stirring, then stops mid-stir and jabs another finger at Jodhi: "Why not? What is the matter with you, how can you expect to impress a boy like that if you don't even have an email address? The boy can build computer-supers before breakfast!"

"But Amma, it was you and Appa who wouldn't let me have an email address because of all the dirty doings in the internet cafés."

"How can you expect to bag a boy like Mohan if you don't have an email address, you silly girl?" Amma accuses her, wide-eyed. "You get hold of an email address immediately! How much do they cost? Where do they sell them?"

In the living area Mr P, after a significant glance from his wife, is about to come to an important matter. He clears his throat tactfully and gives his moustache a tweak or two:

"So you see," he says, "so you see, we have come to the time when certain issues must be talked about."

Oh no, Swami thinks, as he nods sagely.

"What I mean to get at is that, as you know, the normal thing to do, in these circumstances, at this stage, before any firm ideas occur as to whether the two young people will, will, will..."

Everyone hangs on his words, two gaggles of family members open-mouthed with interest at this meeting point of marriage and money.

"...come to an arrangement," Mr P continues, "as I'm sure you understand, is this business of the dowry situation. Dowry situation must be under discussion."

Oh God, Appa thinks.

Amma, who has come back in to make some space for the tea, wobbles her head.

There is the noise of car doors being slammed outside, directly in front of the bungalow.

"So we were wondering if you are wanting to give us best indication," Mr P suggests, "about your, ah, ah, ah-hm, your, hm-hm, your, that is... position."

Dear God...

There is a knock at the front door; Kamala gets up from the floor and answers it. Everyone gets a brief glimpse of two very large gentlemen on the doorstep before Kamala steps out, easing the door closed behind her. Swami looks across at Mr P, rather miserably.

"Dowry," he says, "dowry," as everyone waits for more, "Thousand—"

"What what?"

"—Fifty-nine!" he manages to blurt out in a rush.

Mr P is calling for *The Sacred Couplets* with some enthusiasm once again, but here is Kamala, stepping back inside, tugging at Swami's arm and whispering that he should go outside.

"Who is it?" Amma asks.

"Two gentlemen," Kamala says, "very urgent business."

"Most sorry," Swami says, struggling to his feet.

"He will go and then come," Amma says.

"Yes, please go and then come," Mr P agrees.

Everyone watches Swami limp across to the front door, and sees him greeting the visitors in the moment before he closes the door behind him.

"So sorry, he will return as soon as possible," Amma says.

"Damn police business," says Swami's brother reassuringly.

"They're still asking his advice?" asks Mr P.

"Relentlessly," says the brother. "Only the other day he travelled to Madurai to offer important pointers in a tricky case."

"Investigation was in complete deadlock," Amma confirms.

"He is certainly a very clever fellow," Mr P says. "But what about this couplet, please be reciting," he implores Amma.

As soon as Swami goes outside, he knows something is wrong. The expressions on the faces of the two gentlemen are only arbitrarily polite, and the car waiting for them on the side of the road – back door open, engine still running – is a Mercedes.

"Sorry for the disturbance," one of the goons says. "Mr Rajendran wants to talk with you."

DDR? Owner of Hotel Ambuli? Wants to talk with me?
"Yes?"

"Please come," says the other goon. "Mr Rajendran will explain."

"But—"

"No buts. Mr Rajendran is very busy."

"Daughter!" Swami pleads, pointing back inside, eyes bulging in panic. "Wedding! Hour," he says, "then you," he tries, "you then," he says, "then then," he finishes.

"Let's go," says one of the men, and he grabs Swami's arm.

"Then," says Swami, spluttering.

"Let's go," says the other fellow, grabbing him firmly.

"No!" Swami shouts.

Inside the bungalow, they all look up.

"Some disturbance," Amma says. She slips to the front door and peers out. As she opens the door, Swami is sitting down in the dusty road and pleading "No!", while the two men are trying to pick him up and bundle him into the car. Amma screeches, and everyone rushes outside or to the window.

"Appa!" Swami's daughters are screaming and wailing, "Appa!"

"Oh God oh God oh God, what are you doing, where are you taking my husband?" Amma moans, wringing her hands.

"We'll bring him back soon," one of the men says, getting in next to Swami as the other one takes the driver's seat.

"HUSBAND!" Amma wails, hurling herself at the Mercedes just as it lurches off. She drops to her knees in the street in a cloud of dust, where her daughters join her, sobbing and pleading, "Appa, Appa, Appa!"

6

DDR – Mr Mullaipuram himself – enjoys his wealth. His extensive business interests have secured a life of luxury and influence for him and his family, and he has built himself a very large house with generous lands on the outskirts of town. It is called Mullaipuram Mansions. Standing by the electric gates of the compound are two uniformed security guards who spring to attention whenever a Mercedes goes in or out, as one does now, with a very anxious Swami inside it. Roaming the grounds behind the gates are peculiar breeds of dog of complicated European lineage, which snap and scrap nervily in the shade of a vast old banyan tree. And as Swami is escorted gravely through the many chambers of the house, he sees dozens of household staff, all bowing and scraping about their business as they serve their master and his clan: men in suits whispering into mobile phones, old retainers in dhotis and lungis, servants cleaning and polishing, right down to a small boy who is improbably propelling a wheelbarrow down a long hallway, in which wheelbarrow slumps a dog. This is Bobby, DDR's favourite pet, an obese and ill-mannered paraplegic dachshund; the boy's role in life is to cart Bobby backwards and forwards between various family members for tickles, and to give Bobby hourly massages and limb stretches.

How DDR, with all his quirks and oddities and his very modest natural abilities, became and remains rich is a question for which logic is of limited use; he is as irrational, inconsistent, bad-tempered, emotive, vain, far-fetched, sentimental and credulous as many other inexplicably rich people in this world. At the helm of his business ventures he deals, bullies, bribes, invests, sells, employs, rewards, intrigues, patronizes and punishes according to his own anarchic impulses – and who knows how it works?

Why this formidable figure has abducted Swami is easy to speculate upon, although Swami himself, waiting in a little office where he's been deposited, has no idea as yet. The truth is, although DDR is rich, he is not happy, and the anxiety this causes him can make him suspicious about everything to the point of paranoia. A white man falling out of his hotel has not exactly helped things. So when he came to know, via sources unfamiliar with the real context of the incident, that Swami went to Madurai to view the body of the white man, he got it into his head that Swami is conducting an independent freelance investigation into murder.

When it comes to white men, DDR is indifferent, he takes little interest, he is neither for them nor against them; but in this instance there are one or two small details behind the fatal descent of the snow-faced sky demon that might be best left unexplored, especially since he is manoeuvring to be a candidate for one of two linked yet competing political factions in the forthcoming State Legislature elections, and so cannot allow a whiff of scandal to develop – at least, not a new whiff that is appreciably worse than the background whiff attending him generally. He has spent a small fortune on his democratic ideal of being elected no matter what, and he is not about to see this commitment to the worthy voters of Mullaipuram – proven, after all, in hard cash

– be jeopardized by the misguided bumblings of some loose-cannon law-enforcer of yesteryear.

Swami was served a glass of tea by a kindly looking servant long ago, and has finished it. He has been waiting for nearly an hour. His need to go to the toilet is becoming acute. There are pains shooting down his left side. As for his emotional condition, it is not bearing up – *so humiliating, so humiliating, so humiliating,* he moans to himself, a memory loop playing back in his mind time after time, one in which he is bundled into the Mercedes while the appalled family of the Mohan boy look on – *and they were all admiring me so much!* But what can he do right now but wait, and try (but fail) not to think about his humiliation, his bladder, Jodhi, Mohan, Amma, *The Sacred Couplets*, a Mercedes with the engine running and the back door open, and whatever unknown ordeal may lie ahead of him... *Afterwards*, he tries to tell himself sternly, *afterwards I can break down, but right now I must endure.*

There is a photograph of DDR's spiritual guide and guru on the wall, and from time to time he tries to distract himself with it. It is a framed, black-and-white photograph of a man in a loincloth standing under a peepul tree; there is a simple tattooed line spiralling upwards from under his feet, up and around each of his legs, into the loincloth, then out of the loincloth, up and around his chest in five or six long slow loops, around his neck and head and up to the top of his shaven crown, all the way up his outstretched arms to the very tips of his longest fingers, which point at the heavens: "His Holiness Sri Sri Dravidananda Gurkkal attaining enlightenment in Malayamaruthapuram village, 1993", reads the caption.

Enlighten me, mighty godhead, Swami begs.

As Swami implores the aid of the gods, DDR arrives at last, so presumably they aren't listening. The arrival is heralded by distant thuds and shouts from diverse sources, as though people are fleeing an imminent catastrophe; next there is a growing indistinct commotion as a shouting man approaches down a long corridor, which turns into brief snatches of words – little poems of abuse – as the great man gets nearer and nearer ("May earth fall into their mouths! I'll light a fire beneath their haunches if they're lucky!"), until finally the door is thrown open violently.

Here he is. In form he seems similar to any other middle-aged, middle-height, middle-brow, overfed shady character who loves his children and cheats on his wife with loose women and prostitutes, with his jolly little paunch bulging above his jolly little genitals, wearing his home-spun linen Nehru suit – a humble and severe attire as favoured by a certain class of élite politicians and hefty goondas across the length and breadth of India... but in function he is a mightier beast, and Swami stands up respectfully.

"Who are you? Can't remember why you're here," DDR admits, wiping his sweaty brow with a handkerchief and slumping wearily into a chair, while two flunkeys rush to stand by his side. "What's your name?"

"Swam ah-Swam," Swami answers. "Swimmy," he adds.

"What?"

"Ah-swim ah-sw-w-w-w ah Swami."

"*What?*"

R.M. Swaminathan, sir – that's all Swami wants to say. *R.M. Swaminathan! Is it really so difficult to say my own name? Is that so much to ask?* Yes, it is too much to ask, and Swami doesn't bother trying again.

"Who is this clown?" DDR says to his flunkeys, after a few moments, palms out in disbelief.

"This is R.M. Swaminathan, sir, the retired Sub-Inspector who—"

"Oh-ho!" DDR cries, leaping to his feet, energized by this new understanding, "now I remember! So this is you, so here you are, is it, Sub-Inspector, *retired*, R.M. Swaminathan?" And he stands over Swami, enraged, as though Swami should explain himself. But what can Swami explain?

"Sir?" Swami says, feebly.

"Yes here you are, our *retired* Sub-Inspector, taking it into his head to go to Madurai and see the stinking corpse of that damn *Vellaikaaran*, that *white man* falling from my hotel window, the selfish *Vellaikaaran* pig! This is you, is it?! You're the man?!"

"Sir—"

DDR likes to talk. He is also fond of shouting. As for ranting, it is a particular speciality, it really warms the cockles of his heart. Flailing his arms around in fury, jerking his head this way and that, he unleashes some preliminary rants on poor old Swami, who is trying but failing to figure out whether this encounter is very dangerous indeed or merely very upsetting.

"Poking about in secret," DDR charges him, "conducting private investigations, going above the heads of the authorities, jeopardizing the official investigation – so that's the way you want it, is it, that's your game, this is how you reward the esteemed Indian Police Service who employed you for twenty years, who pay your pension! This is what you do, setting yourself up as some crazy Inspector Eagle, sniffing around foreign dead bodies, following your own crazy agenda—"

"No—"

"Spying!"

"Sir—"

"Cheating!"

"I—"

"Snooping!"

"But—"

"Don't interrupt me!" DDR abruptly screams. So far he's been warming up, but now he seems to be getting into his stride, grabbing theatrically at a handful of his lush coconut-oiled hair and pulling at it in fury.

"What do you think you're playing at?!" he bellows. "What right do you have to start your own investigations into crimes, what do you think the IPS is there for?"

Swami isn't sure if he is allowed to speak yet. *What crimes? What is wrong with this fellow, why does he think I'm poking around, why does he think I'm investigating crimes?*

"Ninety-five," he tries, in desperation, but his persecutor doesn't seem to notice.

"Oh this is serious," DDR is muttering now, shaking his head sadly in the manner of a man who isn't relishing the unfortunate choices ahead; "you should have thought about what you were doing, you don't realize the consequences of your bumbling – the day you chose to go over the heads of the police, the day you decided there was dirty business to investigate, the day you poked around needlessly, that will come to be seen as the worst day of your life if you're not very careful, retired Sub-Inspector..."

DDR sits down at last, breathing heavily, mopping his brow. One of his flunkeys is nodding, in solemn admiration of the performance, while the other flunkey pours his boss a glass of chilled Miranda fizzy drink.

Not a clue what he's talking about, Swami thinks, very frightened now, and as miserable as it is possible to be. *If DDR takes it into his head to destroy me, there is no defence...*

"Very sorry," Swami mumbles.

"What?"

"Very." Swami repeats. "Blame all," he says indicating himself. He wipes his eyes with his sleeve – *this kind of fellow, he will only understand submission.*

DDR taps on the desk.

"What did you find out?" he asks suspiciously.

"Nothing."

"What do you think happened?"

"Nothing."

"Who do you suspect killed him?"

"No," Swami starts, and "one," he finishes.

"Why shouldn't I get your pension stopped?!" DDR abruptly screeches, voice catching with rage, jumping up once again and bouncing around the room. "Don't you realize who I am? Don't you know what-and-all committees I sit on? Why shouldn't I get you evicted from your accommodation? Don't you know there is a shortage of accommodation for serving police officers? What will you do, you and your herd of women, on the street?!"

Swami is suffering too much humiliation and anxiety in his life. He has been enduring the onslaughts for two years, and this is the moment that he can no longer endure it. He folds – *not this, not this, not this as well as everything* – and every meagre shred of pride and dignity and hope comes oozing out of him in an instant; he slumps forwards, his head banging on the edge of the desk and staying there. In abrupt, heaving gasps he starts to sob.

"Ayyo-yo!" DDR blurts, surprised – he's gone too far, he detests the sight of a weeping man. "Hey, stop it! Hey, stop it, I say!"

"Hey get up you," the flunkeys are joining in, "no blubbing on the desktop, get up!" and they are pulling him up roughly, but it makes no difference, his body might be under their control but his weeping is something else, he is getting it from somewhere deeper and more desolate than they have known or imagined.

"Sir, urinating," one of the flunkeys says apologetically to DDR, as he struggles to master Swami's floppy arms.

DDR stares aghast at the lake of urine expanding over the marble slabs from its source at the end of Swami's left trouser leg. At that moment the boy comes into the room with his wheelbarrow, so that Bobby can have one of his many daily fondles. The boy stands in the doorway hesitantly, staring at the sobbing Swami, the wheelbarrow sticking into the room. Bobby – lolling and obese and also, it should be said, incontinent – lies there like an undersized bloated water-buffalo.

"Get out!" DDR snaps at the boy, but at the same time he moves over to give Bobby a tickle behind the ears, so that the boy, not knowing what to do, stands on one leg and looks frightened. "For God's sake will you stop crying!" DDR pleads with Swami, still tickling the dog in a mechanical frenzy, "What are you doing sobbing on my desk and pissing on my floor, don't you understand the way things work, weren't you in the police for twenty years?" He stares down at Swami, who is still weeping inconsolably. "It's really just basic elementary business practice," DDR explains to one of his flunkeys in an aside, "to apply a little pressure. Oh, forget it, take him home," he orders in disgust, but then as soon as the flunkeys are trying to haul Swami up again he contra-dicts himself, "No no, leave him there, get out now."

So the flunkeys leave, and the gardener's boy is sent away too, leaving behind them a weeping Swami, a bemused boss, and a wheelbarrow of pedigree paraplegic dachshund.

Nothing much is said for a time while DDR stands over Swami and watches him weep. "Come come," he tries, feebly, "let us not be unduly pessimistic," but he gets no response. He looks at his watch, nearly gives Swami a pat on the shoulder, nearly opens the door to bellow, "Get this blubbing fool out of here!" At last he sits down in exasperation and says, "All right all right, I wasn't going to stop your pension, it was just my little threat, I just don't want you sniffing around this white man. The reputation of my hotels is a valuable commodity, don't you understand? What's the matter with you, haven't you ever leant on anyone to get what you want?" Still no response from Swami, and just as DDR is wondering if Swami is ever going to move or lift his head up, just as a bizarre thought comes to him about Swami having his own wheelbarrow and being carted around, like Bobby, from place to place, he hears something.

"What?"

"Six!" Swami repeats in a whisper, raising his tear-stained face. "Six!"

"More numbers? Six? Six what?"

"Daughters! No money!" His head goes down once more and then comes up again. "Job – no! No – dowry!"

"Yes yes but—"

"No... talking, no..."

"All right."

"...respect—"

"But—"

"No," Swami groans, in desolation, "elefates."

"What?"

"Elefa. Ele... phants," Swami snivels, thinking of those long-lost times when he would pick his screaming daughters up and trumpet majestically.

"No elephants..." DDR echoes helplessly, "yes yes that is very bad," he agrees. He scratches his head. "But – I was just giving you small instructive fright, you didn't let me get to the end. It's a question of correct procedure," he adds, pained, as if Swami is guilty of a breach of etiquette. "I was going to frighten the daylights out of you and then offer to get your disability pension moved up to full pay as long as you keep your nose out of this business – after all, you got your disability in the line of duty. I am definitely super-supporter of the police!" This is true, he supports them in all kinds of ways. They are no slouches in supporting him, either.

After he has made this generous offer – which has come to him spontaneously – he strokes Bobby's nape with long, slow sweeps of his hand, and wonders to himself whether he'll fulfil the promise or not.

Swami lifts his head cautiously. He looks at the slobbering hound in the wheelbarrow, which is ecstatic under his master's attentions, then up to DDR. When he tries to speak, nothing comes out at first. He tries again and there is not much difference. At last he gives up and just says, "No talking," then holds his head in his hands once more.

"The Mahatma himself observed a vow of silence on Mondays," DDR observes. There is a long pause before he continues. "My guru hasn't spoken in over fifteen years," he says at last, and he gestures towards the photograph of Sri Sri Dravidananda Gurkkal, a man whose mysterious encircling tattoo is said by his devotees to have been present at birth; a man who stands in front of a tree for twelve hours a day, every day, doing nothing, saying nothing, not moving, while thousands and thousands and thousands of pilgrims watch enraptured; a man around whom has grown up a vast ashram complex, a minor town, and an ever-expanding programme of charitable endeavours, all founded and funded and managed by his inspired devotees; a godhead, whose silence is said to have penetrated to the starting point of the centre of the spiral of all knowledge.

7

Swami is sitting on a white plastic chair on the verandah of Number 14/B, gazing unseeing into the belching traffic, occasionally glancing at his books in a faraway fashion; he has done little else since being returned to his family from D.D. Rajendran's house some four or five days ago. But what about Amma? Why is she coming out onto the verandah every few minutes, peering down the road anxiously, and clicking her tongue in frustration before going back inside?

Swami takes no notice of her comings and goings, and Amma takes no notice of Swami. Amma has stopped speaking to Swami. If this seems rather harsh of Amma, given Swami's lamentable psychological condition at present, and the extensive indignities to which he has been subjected, it should perhaps be pointed out in her defence that Swami has decided to stop speaking at all.

Amma comes out onto the verandah again and at last sees what she's been waiting for – Jodhi and Pushpa returning from college, threading their way up the obstacle course of the senses that is this street.

"Hurry up!" Amma mouths, watching her two pretty daughters walking back home – rather reluctantly, it seems – arm in arm in their dark-green *chudidhars*. "Well?" she demands as Jodhi gets within hearing range. "Did you send it?"

"Oh no Amma, not again, I can't stand it, please let me get into the house and—"

"Never mind all this and all that and all those other things too, I am wanting to know, did you send it?"

"Yes Amma."

"And?"

"Yes Amma?"

"And did the boy reply?!" Amma splutters in frustration.

"Yes Amma."

"I knew it!" Amma crows.

The parents of Mohan might have given up on the union of Jodhi and their boy, on the grounds that such a match would be straightforward utter lunacy, but Amma is not convinced that straightforward utter lunacy is an insurmountable bar to marriage. What she is convinced of is that Mohan is smitten with Jodhi, smitten beyond the furthest creaking strains of logic and reason. She knows a thing or two, does Amma. Her husband might have been flattened by a flying white man and held to ridicule by the entire town and then subsequently abducted in the back of a Mercedes by two enormous goondas under the unobstructed gaze of the parents of Jodhi's boy during the pre-engagement meeting – but it will take worse than that to force Amma into giving up.

"You come with me," she instructs Jodhi, ominously.

"Hello Appa," Jodhi says, with something like longing.

"Hello Appa," Pushpa tries too.

Swami looks up from his book, gazes at both girls in turn and smiles for some seconds wistfully – but only with his mouth, a forced smile of apology and submission. Then he disappears back into himself like an alcoholic turning to the bottle.

"I want to sit with Appa," Jodhi complains, as Amma mutters in disbelief at what her husband has come to.

"Does a bird sing to a stone?" Amma says brutally, and pulls her inside the bungalow, into the bedroom, where they both sit down cross-legged on the floor.

There would be a kind of wisdom, Swami realizes, very, very slowly, *in being a stone*... and his mind strays far, far away, playing in the shadow of this little idea.

"Give me that, that, that thing, that *email* thing," Amma is demanding of Jodhi in the bedroom, as Leela and Pushpa and Kamala eavesdrop in the living area without a giggle, or a sound, or a smile – somehow, with Appa being silent as a stone and Amma being obsessed with Jodhi's boy, nothing in life is funny or fun at the moment.

Sighing, Jodhi takes a printout of an email from her bag and hands it to her mother.

Amma unfolds it and scans the English words. "Well? What does it say?" she asks with an anxious look.

"It's all nonsense," Jodhi says sullenly. "It's too embarrassing to read it Amma, please don't make me!"

"*Read!*" Amma orders, thrusting it at her.

"'Dear Jodhi, I am thousand times grateful to you that you are replying to my unworthy humble email,'" Jodhi translates in a sheepish monotone, as a look of beatific satisfaction settles on Amma's face, "'I am more than thousand times grateful to you, I am thousand times a thousand times a thousand times grateful to you. That is one billion times.'"

"He's besotted!" Amma declares.

"Amma, it's you who's telling me exactly how to reply to his emails," Jodhi responds with a certain slyness, "maybe he's besotted with you."

"Don't be so stupid my daughter!" Her hands fly up in irritation at Jodhi's insolence. "I am a tired mother with a stone for a husband and six ungrateful daughters, while you are a beautiful young girl who speaks English and goes to university and sends emails and – what do you understand about everything and anything?" Amma cries, placing her fingers on her temples, fingers that have prepared thousands of meals for her family, fingers that have pounded and kneaded and chopped and sliced and washed and stirred and mixed and whisked and beaten and blended and stuffed and shredded and minced... Her tear-touched eyes express every trial and tribulation and indignity of her life, each hardship, disadvantage, compromise, defeat and hard-won advance. "What you understand about everything and anything is exactly nothing and nothing, that's what you understand about everything and anything! Now read me some more!"

"No Amma," Jodhi begs, "I don't want to, I want to eat and forget about all this."

But Amma is thirsty for the unexpurgated wit and wisdom of Mohan. "Read!" she orders.

"Amma," Jodhi tries, in a cunning and desperate rearguard action, "isn't obedience to parents very important?"

"That is the most important thing there is," Amma agrees.

"And being truthful?"

"That is also the most important thing there is."

"And accepting fate?"

"That is another thing that is the most important thing there is."

"Amma, they can't all be the most important thing there is."

"Yes they can. That shows how very important they all are," says Amma.

Jodhi shakes her head.

"If obeying parents and being truthful and accepting fate are so important, why are we encouraging Mohan to go behind his parents' back, and why are we deceiving him, and why don't we just accept that he is not for me?"

"Questions, questions!" Amma splutters. "Haven't you heard what the elders say? 'A thousand lies may be uttered when a marriage needs to be solemnized!' – that is what the elders say! Just you obey me, and you be truthful to me, and you accept the fate I get for you! That is the most important thing there is! That is enough for us! How can I control what the boy does? He's half-mad with love for you, nothing can stop him, not even if there is a third pre-engagement meeting and Appa does something terrible like, like..." But Amma, her mouth open, her head shaking, her arms waving in the air helplessly, is not able to conjure up any hypothetical catastrophes worse than the real catastrophes that have already taken place, it is too tall an order, and so she is forced to settle for "...something very very very very bad! Nothing can stop this boy, his parents will realize that, one day! I know these things! Daughter, you will be the daughter-in-law of that family! Now read me some more!"

* * *

K.P. Murugesan may have a singularly impressive moustache, but it is also the case that in times of unusual stress he sometimes experiences a twitch on the left side of his upper lip. If it weren't for the moustache, you'd hardly notice this affliction, but when his anxiety levels are too high, then the effect of the tic is exaggerated by the magnificence of the moustache, so that the outermost edge of the hairy edifice quivers up and down a good inch. It is an arresting spectacle. Murugesan fervently wishes that he didn't have this tic; it is very inconvenient to have his most anxious states signalled so transparently. However, he wouldn't dream of solving the problem by shaving off the moustache. Let's be sensible about this – a man without a moustache would be a laughing stock in Mullaipuram.

Once more he is making his way to Swami's bungalow on a delicate mission. Though questions about the fate and identity of the dead white man have receded from Indian and foreign consciousness after a couple of weeks of official obfuscation and delay, yet the issue of what, exactly, retired Sub-Inspector R.M. Swaminathan is up to in connection with the case is coming to the fore. It is a matter of acute interest to some of Murugesan's fellow police officers, because one of them saw Swami being taken to the home of D.D. Rajendran – being chauffeur-driven in a Mercedes, no less – and other officers, the ones with more reason than most to worry about the ramifications of the white man's death, have the feeling that Swami's visit to DDR does not bode well for them. It is well-known that DDR himself had been complaining in vociferous terms about some halfwit retired crippled cop poking around in matters that didn't concern him – and yet now that same fellow has been observed travelling by Mercedes to DDR's house! Has Swami not only indulged in a freelance investigation, but stumbled across some incriminating evidence? Why else would DDR turn from treating such a lowly fellow with contempt to treating him with elaborate respect?

While such speculations about Swami were raging for a day or two between factions within the station, a new detail emerged about DDR's apparent fear of Swami, a detail so striking as to convince even Murugesan, Swami's closest colleague within the Mullaipuram police, that his old friend might be posing a danger to them all. As soon as this new information had come to light, a couple of hot-headed younger men had wanted to pay a visit to Swami, but wiser, older heads had prevailed; which is why Murugesan, upper lip poised on the edge of twitchability, is threading his way through Mullaipuram to Swami's house.

Murugesan puffs his chest out and brushes his khaki

shirt smooth as he strides past Hotel Ambuli – there it is, that's the place where all this trouble started. How typical of a westerner to eject himself from a window at the slightest provocation and cause all this trouble, Murugesan thinks. Murugesan has never been to Europe or to the United States, but he can't help feeling that in such strange places there must be countless people forever hurling themselves out of open windows in their despair at not having been born in the sacred *Punyabhoomi*, the beloved *Bharata Mata*, the incomparable Mother India. The streets must be knee-deep in corpses, he thinks, shaking his head sadly.

When he reaches Swami's house a while later, he sees Swami on the verandah, gazing into a book in what appears to be a condition of profound serenity. He feels more awkward than he had imagined he would, and tries to remind himself that this man is his old friend. He would never knowingly harm me, Murugesan reassures himself; there must be some innocent explanation behind all his trouble-making – unless his suffering has just made him go plain mad.

"Well Brother, reading the ancients as ever," is Murugesan's greeting as he mounts the battered steps to the verandah. "And what do the ancients teach us this evening about this complicated world of ours?"

Swami looks up; Swami gazes at Murugesan without surprise or expression; Swami looks at Murugesan for some time – Murugesan's smile fades from his face as he waits for a response but does not get one – and then Swami looks away from him, into the traffic.

Swami is in the lattermost stages of despair and breakdown; he is going to kill himself today.

Murugesan's moustache twitches at once. What is this, he is thinking. Swami isn't speaking to me? Swami won't acknowledge me? Swami is so appalled by this dirty business with the white man – dirty business in which I was barely involved at all, dirty business that he might have been part of too if the stroke hadn't got him first – that he despises me?

Murugesan sits down on one of the steps, in front and to the left of Swami, the better to conceal his moustache which is now twitching every few seconds. An instant tide of sweat is surging over him, the kind of sweat that can only be produced by a man who has experienced a shock of dismay in thirty-eight degrees centigrade at ninety per cent humidity.

"My old friend Swaminathan," he says at last, looking over his shoulder at the immobile, unresponsive Swami. "I know how it must seem to you, this business, I know you've looked into it, this white man's death, I know you watched him die…" Murugesan strokes his moustache sagely, in order to fetter its independence. "You looked into his eyes, he granted you his last look on this earth, I know that. He has made big impression on you. And I know that you wanted to know everything about it, but we wouldn't tell you much. Yes, that is our fault, my fault. I should have told you everything. I didn't want to trouble you." He takes his hand away and the moustache is off again. A small boy walking past slows down and takes a good long look. "What I want to tell you now, what I promise you, is this – there is no killer of this white man. The white man killed himself. That is the truth." Murugesan waits for a reaction, but gets none, not for any part of his admission; he has already said more than he intended, but there is something about Swami's silence that leads him on to say more, and more, and more; his hands grope the air as though trying to find the right way to shape his explanation. "What you should know is that the fellow was not only a drug addict but a 100% guilty VGS, a dirty rapist. A year ago he raped a chambermaid in a Chennai hotel. Okay?" Still no response from Swami. "An Indian would have ended up in prison, definitely, but being a westerner the evidence had to be absolutely pukka. So, you see? It was like that. This VGS of the very highest order walks free because he is white, and then one day he comes passing through Mullaipuram – what to do? A couple of the men paid him a small visit, he panicked, he jumped. That is the 100% truth of the matter. Brother, what is the point of looking into all this and stirring up trouble? Brother? Swami? Why won't you speak to me? Me, your friend and brother for more than twenty years?"

Swami hasn't heard a word. He knows he's going to kill himself, almost immediately – but how? On the outside he is without expression, as calm as the corpse he intends to become, but on the inside his thoughts are turning over the practicalities. How? How does a man who can't walk more than a quarter-mile from home kill himself? How does a man who has half a dozen daughters tracking his every move kill himself? *Even in killing myself I need help, but there is no help for this.*

"Swami? Brother?"

Murugesan looks at his old friend, bewildered, but his old friend isn't looking back. His old friend is studiously ignoring him. Murugesan puts a finger on his upper lip to stop the quivering once more; he has never felt so dismayed. He gets up, walks around Swami tentatively, as though not sure what to expect. Then he knocks on the door and slips into the bungalow.

Amma comes out of the kitchen wearily, saying, "Welcome, Brother, did you get through to him?"

"Get through to him?"

"My husband is talking to you?"

"He won't say a word to me," Murugesan admits, shamefaced, wondering what Swami has told his wife, wondering how much she knows about the death of the white man and the conduct of the police officers of Mullaipuram.

"For five days now he is silent like this," Amma tells him. "I don't know what it is. He is on strike or something, but on strike from what? He wasn't doing anything anyway!"

"Amma, Appa is too unhappy," Kamala says from the bedroom, where she and her sisters are disconsolately watching a film on the black-and-white TV.

"Amma, Appa is too depressed," Jodhi says.

"Amma, I want Appa back," Leela says, and abruptly starts crying.

"Amma is too unhappy too!" Amma raps. "Amma is too depressed too! But Amma still speaks and cooks and looks after her daughters!" She turns on her heel and stamps outside into the bungalow's little backyard, where she bursts into tears.

A miserable Murugesan glances in on Swami's miserable daughters, then follows a miserable Amma outside.

They stand there, trying to compose themselves, Amma murmuring "Ayyo-yo-yo" at the tribulations of her life, Murugesan wondering what to do about Swami.

"Why do you look so anxious?" Amma says, with a slightly bitter twang.

"Swami, that is why, Swami is worrying us at the station – I think he is playing some strange game with his old colleagues. He saw D.D. Rajendran, you know that?"

"Know it? How could I not know it?! They came for him in the middle of the second pre-engagement meeting!"

"Do you know why they met each other?"

"I know nothing about my husband any more."

"Sister, yesterday I heard something from a friend who's a traffic cop. He was making an inquiry to an administrator in the Office of Police Welfare, and he ended up being told that DDR is behind a submission to the Pensions Committee of the Police Board of Control for Swami's disability pension to be reviewed—"

"Ayyo-yo-yooooo!" Amma shrieks – how can things get even worse like this?!

"No no Sister, calm yourself, they are talking of increasing it from half pay to full pay – and he'll probably get it, you know how these things work with men like DDR."

Amma's new expression – how to describe it? She looks like a woman who has had so many hopes dashed in recent times that another hope looming up is as much a source of terror as anticipation.

"Full pension?"

"Full pension."

"*Full* pension?"

"Yes yes, very fullest whole pension."

"Why, Brother? – why would DDR try to get us a full pension? What does he care whether we live or starve?"

"Exactly, Sister. Swami's got something on DDR, is what I'm thinking, so DDR is buying his silence."

There is a long pause as Amma contemplates this information.

"Why is he buying so much of it?!" She sniffs. "Still..." She scratches at her head. "Somehow my husband is trying to help his daughters, even if he has switched off from life. If we get a full pension, that would be very wonderful," and she wonders if she should start being kinder to Swami again.

8

Leela is lying on the cool cement floor of the living area, on her side, with her head in Pushpa's lap. She has stopped crying. They watch TV listlessly, some 1970s film in which super VVIP film star M.G. Ramachandran – later to be Chief Minister of Tamil Nadu – is fighting dozens of assailants simultaneously, divesting them of their vicious array of machetes as though enjoying some harmless funfair game and sending each one of them flying through air – where they appear to linger rather higher and longer than is strictly natural – before they come crashing down on car roofs and conveniently placed stacks of cardboard boxes and handily heaped piles of rotting vegetables. Pushpa is stroking Leela's hair as she watches, and occasionally insulting her younger sister with an affectionate "You big baby!"

Jodhi sits cross-legged close by.

"What about Kamala?" She asks, during a lull in the action.

"Amma sent her shopping," Leela says.

Their sadness feels as though it is altering the nature of the moments they are passing through; each minute in front of that TV feels like an age. The film is lurching from scene to scene, and now MGR is temporarily befuddled by lust, his eyes rolling in his head as a group of plump beaming beauties dance a chastely suggestive routine around him.

"Easy for MGR," Pushpa says. "Gets rid of his enemies easy as anything, has girls dancing around him morning, noon and night, solves all problems, and later he'll be nearly kissing number-one sweetheart." No one answers. "Easy for him," Pushpa sighs once more, and then, for good measure, she finishes off by slapping Leela on the rump and declaring "You big baby!"

"Jodhi, will you ever kiss Mohan?" Leela asks. "He is very handsome."

"Don't talk to me about Mohan," Jodhi begs her. "Don't talk to me about kissing. Don't talk to me about Mohan and kissing."

"Okay okay."

"Or kissing and Mohan."

"Okay. Only asking. Why don't you like him anyway?"

"You wouldn't understand, you're too young."

"Understand what?"

"Real life," Jodhi sighs morosely.

"Anand also is very handsome," Leela declares, and Jodhi says nothing. "Devan is a fat pig," Leela observes, by way of conclusion.

Soon they will have to rouse themselves and help Amma to cook the evening meal. Amma will make the chapatti dough, and Pushpa will knead it while Leela grinds cloves and fenugreek and cumin seeds to the finest powder. Kamala and Jodhi will chop and slice and sizzle under Amma's directions. Instead of happy banter there will be shouting from Amma, until all of them stop talking for fear of irritating her, and this will make Amma feel guilty, so she will nag them to speak up for themselves, to not be like their silent father. Someone will probably burst into tears, and something will go wrong with the food because of all the upset. Appa will refuse to come in and eat with them, he will sit by himself on the verandah and stare at the metal tray of food that they will bring out to him. Perhaps he will eat some of it. Perhaps he won't touch it.

Each of the girls is dreading the evening ahead.

"What to do about Appa?" Pushpa asks, after a lull in their desultory chat, and she sniffles involuntarily.

"Just sitting there and never responding to anything," Jodhi replies.

"Can't go on like this," Pushpa says.

"Let's not upset Leela again," Jodhi tries, briskly.

Pushpa thinks about doling out another slap on Leela's rump, and another "You big baby!", but she hasn't the heart for it. She moves Leela's head round in her lap, closes her sister's eyes for her, and softly strokes her cheek.

"Very nice," Leela sighs.

"Shall we sit with Appa?" Pushpa asks; but nobody answers. They have sat and sat and sat again with Appa, they have sat cross-legged at his feet as the Mullaipuram evening has passed into night; they have sat on the verandah's edge and chatted in low voices while Appa has stared relentlessly into his books; they have sat with him while being berated by their mother for wasting their time; they have sat with him one at a time and they have sat with him all together, and Leela has even sat on his knee, where she remained for ten minutes, waiting for Appa to cuddle her or tell her to get off. Swami did neither.

"What to do?" Jodhi whispers under her breath, in relation to all the problems of this world, concrete and abstract, personal and universal. The simple hopelessness of her question sums up all their feelings so precisely that Pushpa instinctively repeats it, "Yes, what to do?" – and Leela too: "What to do?" she is saying, "What to do?..."

The front door swings open and Kamala bustles in with a bulging shopping bag in each hand, bunches of coriander and lady's finger sticking out of the top, brinjal, onions, mangoes and cabbage underneath. They hear her going into the kitchen, but they don't bother looking round. MGR is cruising around Chennai in an open-topped sports car, successfully evading the attention of not merely every gun-toting, lip-curling, villainous car-driving gangster in the criminal underworld, but also of all the forces available to an overly officious police inspector who has got hold of the wrong end of the stick and is trying to arrest him. Kamala comes and stands in the doorway to the bedroom for a moment, watching the action.

"Where's Appa?" she asks.

"Where do you think, Kamala? Just outside."

"No he's not."

Kamala turns round and goes out into the backyard, where Amma and Murugesan are still talking.

"Hello Uncle, excuse me, Amma, where's Appa? Did he go out?"

"He's at the front."

"No, Amma, he must have gone out, come and see."

Kamala leads Amma and Murugesan through the bungalow to the verandah, and the three other girls traipse out behind them. Swami is not there. Amma and the four girls look up and down the street, each of them ayyo-yo-yoing, trying to pick out his head, his shirt, his broken gait, among all those pedestrians.

"Hardly moves for five days," Amma complains, pulling at the rings on her fingers frantically, "then disappears without telling us where he's going and when he's coming back!"

"Calm yourself, my daughters," Murugesan says to the girls, "be calm, Sister," he tells Amma, "what are you worried about? Did you want him to sit here without moving for ever? Can't a man go for a walk before his evening meal?" He is not used to being surrounded by so many womenfolk without another man, he doesn't know how to react, and he even feels slightly annoyed that his words of comfort are not having the slightest effect.

"Ayyo-yooooooooo," Amma gasps. "What did we do in our previous life to deserve this? What black deeds did I commit?!"

"He'll be back for dinner," Murugesan says brusquely. "I have to go now."

He strides off down the street, leaving five anxious women behind him. None of them notices, here on the verandah of Number 14/B, the copy of *The Sacred Couplets* lying open (at section thirty-five of Part One) on the white plastic chair. At the bottom of the page is a ring of blue ink around sacred couplet Three Hundred and Fifty:

Cleave to that One who cleaves to nothing,
and so by cleaving cease to cleave.

* * *

You would imagine that the last minutes of a man's life feel different in kind to other minutes. Perhaps some surprising aspects of love crystallize as never before. Perhaps some unknown mental infrastructure, submerged in the consciousness, comes out into the open and is meaningful, or perhaps the mind carries on doing what it does, but with a sharp awareness that soon it won't. Perhaps rank terror comes howling and gurning down the narrowing chambers of earthly consciousness to render us appalled and knowing. Perhaps the end comes like a gift that one accepts, or perhaps – but none of these "perhaps" happens to be Swami's perhaps. He shuffles down the dusty roads of Mullaipuram in much the same frame of mind now as he has been in for days. He is empty. There is nothing left of him any more except a self-esteem so low as to be its own unavoidable deathtrap. He ignores the greeting of an acquaintance – doesn't hear it or see it – and ignores too some fellow playing to the gallery with his warning shout about falling foreigners. Only a week ago the residents of Mullaipuram were still delighting in such witticisms, but today no one heeds the call, and the man who makes the joke slinks away embarrassed. It's possible there is something so ominous in Swami's aura that people are unconsciously picking it up. But what do these speculations matter? Swami is limping towards his death, stepping over the dead dog outside Anbumani's Motor Car Fixings, heading for the cross-roads at Begum Street and Muthiahmudali Street, next to the bus station.

Swami has elected to be comprehensively and irre-versibly run over by a bus, on the grounds that being run over by a bus is something he is capable of doing. And anyway, people are always being run over by buses in Mullaipuram. Even people who have no intention of being run over by buses in Mullaipuram are often run over by buses in Mullaipuram – such a fate is one of the natural hazards of this place. How could it not be, given the location of the town as a hub between three big cities, the crowded streets, the multitude of buses, and the recklessness of the drivers who swing their dilapidated monsters out of the station with brutal disregard for the pedestrians packed against the corners of the junction?

Where, in Swami's thoughts, are Amma, Jodhi, Pushpa, Kamala, Suhanya, Anitha and Leela at this moment, as he sees ahead of him the place he has in mind, and as the buses lurch and swing round, one after the other? Everywhere and nowhere, that's where. He is so convinced of his superfluousness to this world that all the things that most link him to it have fallen away, and whereas once he tortured himself to the point of despair as to how he wasn't able to look after his family properly, now and for the past week he has submitted to a new dynamic: because he cannot, therefore he won't.

"Bidis, cigarettes, betel leaves!" the street vendors are calling, "watches, combs, batteries!" they shout, "satchels, sandals, pencils!" – but nothing is getting through to Swami apart from the sight that his eyes are fixed on ahead, the almost unbroken convoy of buses swinging round the corner of the junction, and now his distinct, dragging limp is carrying him across the last thirty steps of his life. But he is too close to the shops, so he begins to edge out towards the interface of traffic and pedestrians, smelling the buses going past and feeling the heat of their exhaust fumes in his face and the dust of their passing in his eyes, and there is this bus and there is that bus and there is the bus he intends to fall underneath, that one, the dirty brown one coming out of the bus station now. Swami can see everything in his head, the precise moment and character of his tumble under the wheels, and still there is nothing going on in his emotions that is much different to how he has been for days: that he ought to be dead, that he longs to be dead, that he will be dead.

What is this hand on his arm that he doesn't feel? This voice in his ear that he doesn't hear? A youngish man grabs hold of him from behind, and hisses, "You dirty bastard son of a prostitute, this is your last chance, stay out of the white man case or you're finished," – and shoves Swami. It is not a vigorous shove. It is the kind of shove that could hardly fell a child, but Swami is not noted for being steady on his feet – and down he goes, like a stone off a ledge, there at the side of the teeming street, inches away from the thundering bus he'd set his heart on falling under. His good arm comes out instinctively to cushion his landing, and then he's lying on his back, looking up at the complicated network of legs that are stepping over and around him.

I can't even kill myself.

But maybe he is jumping to a premature conclusion. For on that dusty patch of sweltering street, as the crowds barge over him and kick against him, there is a sense of overwhelming doom coming from somewhere he doesn't recognize; it is building up within him like some peculiarly appalling and terrifying form of indigestion, he can feel it taking a hold of him from the outside and filling him up on the inside, and he is fighting it; it is too terrible, he does not want to be overcome by it. A stroboscopic effect of light passing through gaps in the swarming people above is assaulting him, the shock of finding himself on the ground and yet alive is oppressing him, and it is at this moment – when the tightness around his heart sets in – that he has a split-second vision of the white man passing from life to death. The word *Rama* is there, enclosing everything, and at the same time that his body starts to thrash out a relentless, last-ditch panic for life, his mind goes under peacefully.

9

The bus that Swami had intended to expire under is roaring away to Palani in its regular hourly fashion, tailgated by another that is going to Cuddalore. They pass within a metre of him, and passengers inside press their faces against the greasy bars of the open windows, straining to see the man lying face-up in the dirt road. Swami also sees himself. *Who is that?* he is wondering. There is a sense of idle curiosity and irrelevance to the question, such as might occur when solving a puzzle in a lazy hour during a time of sleepy contentment. He waits for a time, looking at his own body from above. Two men are now crouching next to that body, buffeted by the crowd. They put it in the recovery position, so that one of its arms flops over, and while one of them bends down to place his ear over the chest, listening for life, the other one is wafting a newspaper in front of the face. Swami is more amused than surprised to realize that the chest they are listening to, the face they are wafting air over, belong to him. He places himself higher, to get a better view of himself, and sees the whole picture: how his own body lies there, tended by a middle-aged man who has a ring of sparse and unkempt hair circling a very large bald spot, and who has a dirty mark on the back of his otherwise spotless white shirt; and there is another man, much younger, perhaps the son of the middle-aged

fellow, a lanky youngster who now stands up and looks
mournfully at the spectacle at his feet. There is a growing
circle of onlookers jutting into the road on one side, to
the anger of passing drivers in cars and buses and taxis
and autorickshaws, all honking their horns violently and
brushing against people as they try to nudge their way
past. In the commotion, a decision is taken to move the
body. Swami is distantly pleased to see three or four people
pick him up and lift him – rather roughly, but he forgives
them – away from the traffic. The circle of onlookers
quickly forms again, while around it Mullaipuram carries
on, its people shoving at the edges and shouting complaints. Swami is getting used to his new condition now.
*Why are they bothering with that body when I'm not even in
it?* Nevertheless it is interesting to see the body picked up
once more and carried, with some urgency, to a taxi. And
now Swami finds that he knows what people are saying.
His impression is that their words – compared to his own
understanding – are pitifully inadequate signals, tragic
misfirings of cosmic incomprehension; one day they will
cease to speak so uselessly, he knows, and he wishes he
could let them know how ineffectual they are being.

Meanwhile a negotiation is taking place over the going
rate for half a mile in the back of a black-and-yellow
Ambassador taxi.

"Saar, that fellow is dead," the taxi driver is pointing out
indignantly as he turns the ignition, "it is not auspicious
to be having the dead man in my motor vehicle."

"Very well, don't take him, you miserable son of a
louse, we will get out immediately!" shouts the middle-
aged fellow who has taken it upon himself to get Swami
to hospital; he is a professor of chemistry, and he has no
idea why he's involved himself in this business. On any
other day of the week he might have stepped over the
body with a curious glance. He mops at his balding pate
as he struggles with Swami's inert matter.

"But Saar—"

"Enough!"

"But Saar—"

"Enough!"

"But Saar, maybe you are working in an office, but are you wanting a stranger dragging a corpse inside that office without a word of warning? Even a highly respected gentleman like you, Saar. Answer me this, Saar!"

"Enough, desist, cease!" shouts the professor, who has been struggling all this time to pull one of Swami's feet into the back of the car, "we will not deign to use your miserable, ungodly taxi, which disgraces Lord Ganesha and the goddess Lakshmi who are residing on your filthy dashboard, we are getting out without delay!" As he barks the words he succeeds in banging shut the back door at last. "Okay, go."

"Saar, I didn't say I wouldn't take him," the taxi driver says sulkily, setting off.

"Doesn't matter," the professor shouts, as he and his son arrange Swami across the back seat of the taxi. "It doesn't matter what you say you'll do, and it doesn't matter what you say you won't do, we don't want to travel in your miserable, godless taxi, so if you say another word then you can stop the car immediately and we will get out now!"

"Saar, don't be angry with me," says the taxi driver, "I have children to feed and clothe like any other man, and I can't have a dead fellow in my taxi for less than three hundred rupees."

"Three hundred? To go to the hospital? It can't be costing more than fifty! You louse, will you take advantage of a dying man?"

"Taxis are for the living, Saar. If you want a vehicle for the dead, call an ambulance."

"I order you to stop immediately!"

"Two hundred and fifty, Saar, that is very best and very lowest discount fare in Mullaipuram for dead people!"

With negotiations and arguments at this extremely gentle, early and delicate stage, the taxi struggles through a sluggish river of traffic, and relentlessly honks its way towards the hospital. "You louse!" says the professor, "we are getting out immediately, stop this car!" he declares at each juncture in the haggling process. Meanwhile the professor's son sits in the back with Swami's head and torso lying across his lap, scowling, nursing murderous feelings of resentment against taxi drivers and men who drop dead in public.

"Appa," he hisses sulkily, "we should never have got involved in this."

"Don't lecture me, boy," barks the professor, furious – furious not merely because he does not want his authority questioned in front of this insolent taxi driver, but also because he knows his son is right. What has possessed him to get involved like this? It can only be some small cosmic alignment beyond his comprehension.

"You crazy sonovapig!" the taxi driver abruptly yells out of the window – there seems to be a man out there who is guilty of riding a bicycle while exhibiting insufficient terror of taxi drivers. The professor slumps back in his seat, exhausted by anger, confrontation and the deaths of strangers. One hundred and twenty-five rupees, that is where negotiations are stalled. This is at least twice as much as the going rate, but after all, thinks the professor, there is some logic in the driver's argument – the man lying across him appears to be dead, as dead as a drowned snake chopped in two and both halves thrown on different fires; such a freight ought to carry a premium, given that the taxi driver probably sleeps in the back of his taxi six nights a week.

"All right, you cheating wastrel, one hundred and twenty five," he agrees gruffly.

"Oh very good Saar, thank you Saar, we are reaching fairest and very best excellent agreement!"

The professor nurses Swami's folded legs against his chest, and – in that lurching taxi with a cheating driver and a furious son and a dead man – concentrates on achieving the calming vision he always relies on in times of acute stress. It involves beautiful chemical formulae, and the Nobel Prize for Chemistry, and splendid shawls being draped over his shoulders by worthy dignitaries, while an audience of international big shots – amongst whom is the President of India – looks on admiringly.

Swami doesn't know and doesn't care whether his self and his matter have separated. Maybe an analgesic hallucination is occurring in his dying brain that can account for his current experiences, but why should Swami care? It is clear to him that worrying at the reasons and causes behind things is a choice made by living men, every one of them. Dead men such as Swami have no interest in all that nonsense. He is currently experimenting with where to position himself in relation to his body. It feels too cramped, too human almost, to rest below the roof of the taxi, but he still feels slightly attached, almost by some physical bond, to these three men with their pitiful emotional outbursts, the deluded sallies of their redundant language, and he wonders as to the outcome of all this, so he drifts in and out of the taxi as it forces its way through the centre of town to Mullaipuram Anna District General Hospital... until, abruptly, he finds himself no longer attached at all, not to that world he'd been alive in, with all its taxis and all its people. Not to anything.

There is the darkest tunnel stretching ahead of him, of the most profound and compelling aspect, such as no one who has seen it could refuse to enter. Though its appearance and aura is ominous and something to be mightily afraid of, yet he knows that its purpose is irresistibly beautiful, and as soon as it opens up in front of him he enters it willingly, losing every link to the mortal world.

In a dilapidated resuscitation room in the over-stretched Accident and Emergency wing of the hospital, while an exhausted doctor rips Swami's shirt open and checks for signs of life and clamps an oxygen mask over the breathless mouth and nose, and while a second exhausted doctor hooks the body up to a monitor and shouts "VF" and applies salmon patches to the chest and shouts at a nurse to set the defibrillator at 150 – and scolds her, too, with a "Well don't leave the mask on", because the first doctor has forgotten to take it off – there are still some moments to pass before the two defibrillator paddles will deliver their surge and try to shock the useless flailing chambers of Swami's heart into pumping blood. Swami is far away from such trivial matters, passing without bodily form down that vast, noisy dark tunnel, at speeds outside description, towards a warm, yellow glow that becomes exponentially brighter and more compelling until he hurtles into it with a sense of inexpressible relief and gratitude.

"So this is it," he calmly tells the figures who come to greet him, in a medium beyond speech, these four black naked wordless guides. It is surprising to notice that the messengers are armed with clubs, and surprising, too, that they take hold of Swami brusquely. But it is not alarming. The light that surrounds Swami and that extends in every direction without variation is overwhelming, it hugs the higher self with a loving peacefulness, and in the grip of these guides he feels safer and more accepted than he has ever dreamt of. They lead him through an infinite chamber that is thronged with indescribable forms, all of which Swami can communicate with and recognize, though he feels no need or compulsion to do so. Certainly his mother is here, he can feel her presence simultaneously distinct from all other presences and merged with them into one absolute presence; also his ancestors since time began, all of them, every dead loved one and acquaintance is here, and not just as he knew them, but in a distillation of all their incarnations, so that they are every aspect of themselves that they ever were. They are emanating a love that is so universal as to be beyond the meagre attributes of the personal; the personal seems so meaningless in this place that it no longer exists, and Swami can no longer recognize it. Swami – we shall continue to call him this, although now he is something far greater that can't be adequately described – is infused with contented peace and has no fear as the guides calmly transport him through the time and space that lies beyond time and space to a great god. Swami knows him, of course: it is Yama Dharmarajan, the King of the Dead.

The god is small and naked and withered. He seems monumentally bored. He sits on his high wooden chair and gazes at Swami over his beard with an inscrutable look. To one side, sitting cross-legged on the floor, is his helper Chitraguptan, who has an immense book open in front of him. Behind Chitraguptan a mass of clerks and scribes are endlessly engaged in transcribing records of lives and deaths. And behind them, stretching far, far away, is a long narrow series of antechambers lined on both sides with books and scrolls and records.

"Here he is," Chitraguptan tells Yama Dharmarajan, in his utter wordlessness. Yama Dharmarajan doesn't react.

Swami has never felt such downright relief as he says to Chitraguptan, "Yes I'm here now."

No one replies.

"I didn't know," Swami says wonderingly, to Yama Dharmarajan. "I didn't know." He knows that Yama

Dharmarajan knows he didn't know. He knows that Yama Dharmarajan knows everything. Life after death is so simple and beautiful.

Yama Dharmarajan yawns.

This is the most blissful moment of Swami's death, as he stands in front of the yawning King of the Dead, knowing that he is merged with something great. But – and this sometimes happens – it seems there has been a mistake. Chitraguptan is frowning and scratching at his bald head, just behind his right ear.

"He's not R.M. Swaminathan the grain trader," Chitraguptan murmurs lugubriously, so interjecting – with a meticulous attention to the demands of an infinite bureaucracy – a strangely unexpected sour note into what had seemed to be the blissful site of the afterlife.

"No no, I'm R.M. Swaminathan the police officer," Swami says, after a moment, very eager to please, and aware more than ever of the ineffable beauty of being here, under Yama Dharmarajan's heavy, bored gaze, as that great King of the Dead emits another long, slow, indolent yawn.

Chitraguptan doesn't acknowledge Swami. Frowning again, as though there is something in the enthusiasm of Swami's reply that doesn't add up, he scratches at his head once more, this time behind the left ear, and gestures minutely to two or three notaries. They scuttle over to him. There is a short, furtive consultation, before the notaries rush off to instruct further notaries and clerks and archivists and registrars and scribes – all the pen-pushers of the afterlife who inhabit the smaller chambers of rippled infinity. There is much riffling through books and decaying papers, and Swami sees great clouds of dust rising up all around, from uncountable numbers of rarely thumbed tomes, and he has the definite impression that this is not how it should be, for how can there be dust in paradise? He starts to feel, even in this most glorious of places, some stirrings of unease. No longer does he feel as though he is harboured in the universal presence of everyone who ever existed, and that they all make up one single organic consciousness and universality – of which he is a vanishingly small, infinitely significant part. Though he is trying to fend off a strange new idea – it is called fear – he is starting to be aware of the meagre, the small and the personal...

A wrinkled clerk comes hobbling down a long corridor carrying a scroll wound around two femurs. The clerk places the scroll in front of Chitraguptan, and methodically unwinds it to the correct place, pointing. Chitraguptan looks down at the scroll, shaking his head as though there has been a ridiculous procedural error.

"We didn't ask for R.M. Swaminathan the police officer, from the Vanniyar community," Chitraguptan explains to Yama Dharmarajan. "We asked for R.M. Swaminathan the grain trader, from the Goundar caste. We need the other one. This one will have to go back, he's still got work to do."

"I don't want to go back," Swami says, but Yama Dharmarajan is unconcerned as to what Swami wants, he is still staring impassively, naked on his high wooden chair, and already the four black messengers have Swami in their grip and are speeding him away from the King of the Dead.

"Isn't there some work for me here?" Swami begs Yama Dharmarajan.

But away they go, down the vast chambers, Swami struggling violently and impotently – the guides have hold of a limb each, and now they grip their vicious-looking clubs in a threatening way, as though they are worried Swami might somehow break free and become part of the afterlife before it is ready for him. Swami feels everything blissful leaching away, until all that remains of his insight into universal peace is a ragged sense of a few individual presences; and here is his mother again, an unsatisfactory fragment of her, a shred that has torn itself away from the absolute whole in a fruitless attempt to try and soothe him; and there he is, the white man from Mullaipuram, this time Swami can see him in a corporeal form, tanned, clothed like an ageing hippy at a Goan beach party, making ridiculously human apologetic gestures.

"They're taking me back!" Swami cries, "Oh God, no, don't let them take me back!"

"You have to go," says the white man, "don't struggle, it will be okay. There's a reason."

But it is not okay, Swami doesn't want to go back, it hurts, he screams in agony as the black messengers hurl him contemptuously down, down, flailing back down the awful tunnel; the yellow light, that had wrapped around him like swaddling clothes, falls away and away from him. Like some man tumbling from the heavens to the paltry earth of human smallness he sees his body far below – how pathetic and uninviting and contemptible it seems, that useless agglomeration of cells – and he notices the doctors around it, monitors flatlining, shouts and instructions, and on the fourth application of the CRU paddles Swami hurtles back into his shell screaming in horror as his body spasms violently – and the doctors, gazing at the jumping line on the monitor, simultaneously crow, "Got him!"

"Sinus rhythm. Looks like an MI," says one of the doctors, "we'll try some thrombolytic stuff."

The paddles are replaced in their holders, the nurse is inserting a drip, the oxygen mask goes back on, blood samples are being taken, and here is an anaesthetist to put a tube down the windpipe of Swami – who was dead, and is alive.

10

It is dawn in Mullaipuram, after a night with no moon and little movement in the air. The stars are fading as quickly as the sun is rising, and many people in the town are ahead of the light, washing and stretching, performing their devotions and their ablutions with the same methodical care. Jodhi, Kamala, Pushpa and Leela are on one side of a bed in the Intensive Care Unit. On the other side are Amma and the twins she had to give away two years ago, Suhanya and Anitha, who have just arrived with Uncle Kandan, Swami's brother in Coimbatore, after travelling overnight. Half the members of this unhappy family are ceaselessly snivelling, and the other half seem frozen and expressionless in their distress. Amma, with the twins slumped against her breasts, slowly counts – again – the tubes and pipes that are sticking out of her husband's unconscious body: five. Now that she has counted them again, she counts them again *again*, as though next time the answer could be four, or six – and as though such an outcome might matter – but no, it's five, always five. She follows the snaking path of each one, from each aperture in her husband, natural and contrived, to its source, and invariably ends up looking in incomprehension at some piece of gadgetry such as only the Mohans of this world could possibly understand. A great surging sweep of powerlessness and ignorance has her in its grip. Her brother-in-law holds her by the arm tightly, as though propping her up.

Outside, the world carries on carrying on, and Jodhi hears it with some resentment, its junctions building up to the morning gridlock, its street vendors preparing to sell their wares, its drivers honking their horns to win their minute and trivial advantages over one another. She wants to run out of the hospital and into the town, screaming at everyone and everything, "Please be stopping all this at once! Stop it now!" – then, in an ensuing silence, she would explain carefully that today is a day that is different to all the other days, and that is why everything has to stop.

"Amma, Appa!" the twins are whimpering at random intervals, and in unison, in a way that might be explained by the dynamics that apply to schools of fish turning all at once, to flocks of birds wheeling round together. They do not go into specifics – moaning "Amma" and "Appa" seems sufficient. The two girls burrow into Amma's soft breasts, inadvertently wiping their runny noses on her sari.

"Why did we go to Coimbatore?" says Anitha.

"We shouldn't have gone to Coimbatore," Suhanya adds.

"What has Coimbatore got to do with any of this, you foolish girls?" says Uncle Kandan in irritation.

"Yes Uncle."

"Sorry Uncle."

"There's one now!" Leela hisses, as a white-coated man glides past in the corridor outside and stops to speak with a nurse. All through the long and unbearable night they have been trying to talk to a consultant about Appa, but Amma's courage fails her now that one is standing close by. She looks towards the fellow with an urgent longing. Amma is in awe of doctors.

Uncle Kandan goes over to the man sombrely and murmurs respectfully. The doctor comes over at last.

"I am Dr Pandit," he tells Amma. "You are Mrs Swaminathan," he adds, as though she might have overlooked her own identity. He is a pale fellow from the north, speaking Tamil with a Hindi accent. He doesn't even have a moustache. What is a North Indian doctor doing in this place, Amma thinks. How can a man without a moustache be a good doctor? But she says, "Yes Doctor," and immediately bursts into tears, which sets off the whole family, so that the ones who weren't crying before start crying now, and the ones who were crying before continue to do so, with more vigour.

"Yes yes, all right, stop crying, I am begging you," Dr Pandit says, "it is not helpful. Hasn't anyone spoken to you about your husband yet?"

"No, Doctor. Only about medical fees," Amma gulps, her shoulders heaving up and down in distress – 12,000 rupees is the going rate for a day in intensive care. It is more than a month's income. Whatever happens to Swami, Amma knows it's all up for her family. They will be indebted for generations, and all her daughters' lives are ruined – no wonder she's so upset, what does the fancy Hindi doctor expect?

"Your husband is scoring a three or a four on the Glasgow Coma Scale," says the doctor, "but there's no evidence of significant myocardial damage. He was clinically dead, but they got him back within ten minutes of dying. That is not too bad – anything longer than that is difficult. He may or may not be waking up soon, it's too early to have a clue. We've no idea yet if his brain is affected – speaking frankly, it might be fine, it might be chutney, it might be some place in between. If he's showing no change in a week, we should do a brain scan, but it's expensive. Also, the longest time you can afford to keep him in intensive care the better – if he goes onto a general ward he'll probably get a chest infection and he might not survive that. I'm very sorry," and with that Dr Pandit pads away.

There are many configurations in which six daughters and their mother can look at each other fearfully, and most of them happen now as the women snivel and sob and hold on to one another. Amma lowers her head onto Swami's thighs and cries "My husband, my husband!", which sets the rest of her family off again, and there is a short period of unfettered grief and howling – Leela boo-hooing like a six-year-old, her arms rigid at her sides and tears racing one another down her cheeks, Kamala attempting to speak as she sobs but succeeding only in uttering incomprehensible moans and gasps – until they start to pull themselves together, with Uncle Kandan saying "Come come" uselessly from behind his weeping red-rimmed eyes.

The sun has risen, and Pushpa draws back the thread-bare curtain of the hospital room to let natural light come in. Its aspect is kinder than the strip light that had illuminated Swami like a corpse on a slab of stone. Now the family keep watch over Swami in a calmer way. They attend to every move of a nurse who comes in to monitor his data and to shift his limbs into new positions. After the nurse has gone, they crowd round again.

"Sooo peaceful," Jodhi whispers, gently holding her father's hand.

"Appa is very handsome," Kamala says, smoothing Swami's hair into place.

"Wake up Appa," says Leela.

The day passes interminably, and not a flicker of consciousness disturbs the brow of Swami, no matter how intently his loved ones search for it. By late afternoon, his wife and daughters have been awake for thirty-six hours, and one by one they fall asleep. Amma fills up a red plastic chair with her buttocks, leaning to one side with her head against the wall, her cheek hunched awkwardly against her left shoulder. Each one of her long, far-apart snores sounds like an elephant being forced backwards through a wind tunnel. The twins sit on the floor at her feet, their arms intertwined across Amma's lap, their heads resting on their arms. Pushpa and Kamala are on the floor on a thin pale-green mat, sleeping on their sides in almost identical positions; at their feet, on another mat, Jodhi and Leela hug each other like sleeping lovers, Leela mumbing in her sleep. Only Uncle Kandan is awake. Now that all the women are sleeping he keens to himself gently, terrified that his brother is going to die. He kisses Swami's bare shoulder and says, "Wake up!" helplessly, then walks away, out of the room, in search of a bidi to smoke and a place to smoke it, one of Amma's hair-raising snores following him through the door.

Is it the broken catch in Uncle Kandan's wretched, grief-sodden voice that does it, or the tickle of one of Uncle Kandan's hairs against Swami's ear? Is it some deep dream that is only dreamt by men in comas, or just a random intrusion of misfiring neurons, signifying nothing? Swami groans, croaks "super-computer" and then sinks back down into the even murkier depths of unconsciousness that lie in whatever deep-down dark and mysterious dream world he's lost in.

A nurse comes in to shift the position of his arms and legs, but seeing the whole family fast asleep she thinks better of it; it can wait an hour or two. She gazes at the family group, struck at so much unconsciousness around the unconscious patient. Very distinguished face, she tells herself, looking at Swami. Looking very peaceful as anything, she thinks.

* * *

A further day passes before Murugesan visits Swami in hospital, and let it be said immediately and very firmly – during the passing of those twenty-four hours there may or may not have been a miracle in Mullaipuram Anna District General Hospital.

Murugesan had left for his night shift after Swami had disappeared on his final, fatal walk, and afterwards he had gone to sleep at home, unaware of the tragedy through all the long hot day. His wife had woken him in the afternoon. He had shouted at her and made her cry. "Why didn't you tell me earlier?!" he'd yelled, which was unfair because she'd woken him as soon as she'd found out. Murugesan had gone straight to the police station to raise a collection from his colleagues, and had gathered over 3,000 rupees; there were different degrees of shock and guilt and unease and sympathy behind the giving of each contribution. Then he had headed for the Mariamman Temple, made some offerings of fruit and money, and paid for the blessings and prayers of a temple priest. Finally he had gone to the shops to buy a few gifts. Only now is he lurking awkwardly at the door of the Intensive Care room, self-conscious and embarrassed, as though seeking permission to do something not entirely permissible. He's not sure why he feels as guilty as he does – rationally, he cannot find much of a link between his own behaviour and his friend's misfortune – but remorse has him in its clammy grip and isn't letting go. He feels miserable and worthless.

"Brother, come," says Amma softly, when she sees him.

All the daughters are there, ranged around the bed like lovely guards, keeping vigil over their father. There are a few gaudy cards from well-wishers on the window ledge – *Be Hopeful and Happiest*, one of them declares, over an image of a blissfully content hospital patient eating the finest South Indian titbits under the gaze of an adoring and ecstatic family, while being comprehensively cured of the trickiest fatal diseases by a crack team of consultants in a vast and luxuriously appointed medical facility. It seems a far cry from this shabby cube of Intensive Care, with its well-used apparatus crowding the family members.

Walking in, Murugesan feels discomfited. Something is not as he would like it to be. Amma and her daughters seem too... He gropes around for the right word as his gaze flicks from Swami to Amma and from Amma to the girls, then back to Swami again; too *contented*, he realizes. Kamala is smiling at him sweetly, almost as though this is any old regular happy occasion.

"So?..." he says gruffly, looking around at them all. "What is the news?"

"Come, Uncle," says Jodhi, giving up her chair for him, "please sit."

Murugesan sits, uneasily. He is staring over Swami's face to Amma at the other side of the bed, and what he sees does not make him feel any more comfortable: she seems criminally peaceful – where is her wifely distress? He focuses on his old friend's profile, the firm thrust of the nose, the tiny rise and fall of the chin, the fractional movement of the tube entering a nostril as Swami breathes in and out, and as the pillow gives under his head. Then he refocuses, looks at Amma again, looks into her eyes and tries to understand. Something, he feels sure, is not right: it is not right that Swami's womenfolk are so peaceful and assured, it is not right that there is no grieving or worrying in this place. Look at her, he is thinking, look at her – as though there isn't a care in the world! He leans down and starts taking things from a plastic bag.

"Card," he says, passing it across to Amma, who takes it and nods, "and this is something towards medical expenses," he adds, handing her an envelope. "All the police officers in Mullaipuram are contributing large and small. And there's this," he finishes, holding up some fruits – mangoes, jackfruits, bananas – and feeling inexplicably foolish. "Fruits," he says feebly.

"Thank you Brother," Amma says, smiling at him too kindly, so that he feels more uncomfortable than ever.

"Uncle," Pushpa says earnestly from the foot of the bed, "Appa is very happy you have come."

Murugesan stares at her blankly, then looks at the evidently unconscious Swami.

"What is his prognosis?" he asks Amma.

"Everything is with the gods now," Amma tells him. "I have left everything to the goddess Mariamman and Lord Murugan," she adds, as though it is the easiest thing in the world to detach oneself from one's troubles in this world and leave their resolution to the gods.

"But what do the doctors say?" Murugesan persists, irritated.

A nurse enters the room, rather shyly, and looks at Swami in a curious fashion. Murugesan waits for her to do whatever she is going to do. The nurse hesitates, smiling all the time at Amma.

"What is it?" Murugesan says, brusquely. He has his uniform on, he feels authoritative. "Please do your work."

The nurse smiles awkwardly at him and then looks towards Amma, saying, "Sister, what I mentioned to you before, here it is." She takes a large bundle out of a plastic bag, and from several grubby cloths she unwraps an elderly camera. "My husband has brought it to me," she says. "The picture..."

Murugesan sits back in his chair, looking around him in an exaggerated fashion as though everyone else must surely feel as bewildered and irritated as himself at this bizarre behaviour.

"Come," Amma indicates, "please, yes, you must be having the picture."

To Murugesan's beggared belief, the nurse steps up to the end of the bed, frames Swami in her viewfinder, and presses the shutter. A flash goes off.

"But what is this?" Murugesan asks, looking between Amma and the nurse. "What kind of behaviour is this? When a man is in, when a man... what is the meaning behind this?"

"Brother, please be calm," Amma says.

"But what is happening?" Murugesan asks.

The nurse touches Swami's feet through the bed sheet, then brings her hands together reverently.

"Thank you," she says, and rushes out.

Touching his feet? Murugesan, shaking his head slightly, one hand smoothing the hair down on the back of his head, waits for any hint of sense or reason to manifest itself, as his old friend lies unconscious next to him.

"Uncle, please be happy," one of the twins says.

"She took a picture and touched his feet!" Murugesan bursts out.

"Uncle, Appa is walking with God," the other twin informs him, gravely.

* * *

A short while after Anitha – or is it Suhanya? – informs Murugesan about Swami's cosy ambles with the godhead, Murugesan is standing by the Sugam Tea Stall just outside the hospital gates. The Sugam Tea Stall, manned for seventeen years by a five-foot, 40-kg ex-convict and toddy-distiller called Pugal – known as Hairy Pugal, on account of his extreme baldness – is commonly perceived to brew the finest roadside tea in the town of Mullaipuram. The stall itself is in deplorable condition – an ancient rotting wooden cart on four seized-up broken wheels – but the tea... Many patients and doctors at the hospital swear that Hairy Pugal's concoction is an important component of their medical regimes. He is never short of customers, which explains why so many beggars lie in the sun nearby, like a row of decaying fruits. Hairy Pugal lets them get so close, but not any closer – any closer than where they are and he thrashes them.

Murugesan watches the renowned tea vendor brewing up a battered old urn of strong milky tea. He has been drawn here by a hankering for familiarity. The incomprehensible burblings of Swami's womenfolk disturbed him, and he had stalked off with ill-disguised impatience. He likes predictability and the everyday known. Against the arbitrary buffeting of large events beyond his comprehension, he derives immense comfort in small certainties. He likes to be told in advance by his wife what food he will be eating later. He enjoys his own subtle expertise in interpreting the many different ways in which she can hang his pressed uniform from the handle of the great metal wardrobe in their house, and he likes the small unspoken rituals that punctuate the tasks of his working life – an ancient joke often repeated with this colleague here, an old trivial problem chewed over with that one there. What he doesn't like is the everyday known slowly transmuting into something no longer known nor everyday – and this is how it has been with his old friend Swami for some time now. How did Swami change from being a regular guy to being an outsider? From being a close friend to a wary acquaintance? And how did the fellow's womenfolk, so sensible and down-to-earth, turn into the kind of people who claim a desperately sick man is not sick but walking with God? When did all this nonsense start? Was it when the white man fell on Swami? Or was it afterwards, when Swami started to investigate the white man's death? Or was it long before then, when he suffered his stroke? Murugesan doesn't know. All he knows is that when it comes to Swami, each day has seemed slightly more peculiar than the last, to the point that today seems very strange indeed. And if this is today, what of tomorrow? Murugesan pulls several faces in protest at what the future might bring.

Hairy Pugal, satisfied that the concoction in his vintage tannin-black urn is hot enough to scald a turtle, pours Murugesan's tea from one glass to another in tall and daring parabolas, to cool it down slightly, then presents it to his customer. Murugesan takes it without a word or a glance and turns to the street, sipping at it quickly. Staff and patients and relatives are standing around the stall in ones and twos, out of reach of the beggars in the dirt, drinking tea and smoking, pawing at the dusty road with the soles of their sandals, staring into the passing flow of traffic and pedestrians and thinking about death. But there is nothing more comforting on the face of this earth than drinking Hairy Pugal's sweet milky tea by the roadside, and then smacking one's lips and banging the empty glass down on the vendor's dirty tray – that is a truth that Murugesan learnt some fifteen years ago. So he polishes off the tea, and smacks his lip, then bangs the glass down noisily – and belches too, as a bonus. Hairy Pugal's eyebrows rise fractionally as though to say, "Yes, I am a skilled artisan in the craft of making tea, one of the best you will ever encounter, and the tea you have just consumed is amongst the finest tea ever concocted since the art and practice of tea-drinking was first developed. It is super-tea."

As Murugesan contemplates entering the post-tea world once more, he notices a doctor arriving at the stall with the words "Consultant Cardiologist" on his name badge. Murugesan watches the man receive his glass of tea, then approaches him.

"Doctor, I am Sub-Inspector K.P. Murugesan."

"Yes?"

"It's possible you have treated my colleague, retired Sub-Inspector R.M. Swaminathan?"

"Yes yes, I saw him immediately after my colleagues brought him back and stabilized him."

"Yes Doctor. Doctor—" Murugesan gestures in the air vaguely, not knowing how to put his question.

Dr Pandit, sipping his tea, watches him with very little curiosity or interest, as though something like this happens every day, as though he has heard every permutation of query for every conceivable sickness and situation, and now merely awaits confirmation as to which permutation this one will prove to be.

"Doctor," Murugesan tries again, "this fellow, my friend, R.M. Swaminathan, Sub-Inspector, retired..."

"Yes?"

"He was acting very strangely for some time before this heart attack, his whole character changed..."

"Yes?"

"...and also a white man fell on him..."

"Yes?"

"...ever since when, he seems to find things out without my really knowing how..."

"Yes?" Strangeness, white men, psychic prowess – Dr Pandit is not easily impressed.

"...and you see, now he has died, and he has come back from death, and his family say he is walking with God, and with my own eyes I saw one of your nurses entering the room and taking his photograph, Doctor..."

"Yes?"

"...and touching his feet!"

"Yes yes," says Dr Pandit decisively, finishing his tea and banging it down on the tray with the special authority that comes with being a cardiologist, "and you're not knowing why?"

"I have no idea," Murugesan says. "I cannot get any sense from his womenfolk, they've all gone crazy, that is why I am asking you."

"Well now," said Dr Pandit, "it is quite simple. In the night, as two nurses were changing his position, he said 'Rama, Rama, Rama' – three times he said it, like that. One of the nurses ran out of the room, and the other decided she was with a patient who was walking with God. You see? I've seen it before, this kind of thing. It happened like this with a patient in Pune, his whole village started worshipping him. And you see, true or false, the rumour spreads like wildfire. Of course," says Dr Pandit, fiddling in his pockets for three rupees to give to Hairy Pugal, "the other day your Mr Swaminathan also said 'slum biscuit' in a very powerful and impressive manner, I heard it myself, with my own ears."

"Slum biscuit, Doctor?"

"Slum biscuit."

"What is slum biscuit?"

"I have no idea. But he is showing signs of lightening, Sub-Inspector—"

"Lightening?"

"—coming out of his coma... but on that occasion, that slum-biscuit occasion..." Dr Pandit raises an eyebrow "...on that occasion, no one decided he was walking with God."

"So he's not walking with God?"

Dr Pandit shrugs. "I didn't say that. That is something I am neither saying nor not saying. How am I knowing if he is walking with God or not? I know about his heart. I know that life departed from his body and then returned to it – who knows where it went to in the meantime? These near-death experiences are not understood. More tea!" he raps at Hairy Pugal – Dr Pandit drinks oceanic quantities of tea – leaving Murugesan to scratch at the stubble on his neck, deep in thought.

11

Having learnt that her husband said "Rama, Rama, Rama" while in a profound state of non-being, Amma has started to emanate an irritating serenity. She has taken to smiling beatifically at startled innocents on the smallest premise, and to walking more slowly down the hospital corridors so that she doesn't huff and puff in front of curious onlookers. Huffing and puffing in front of curious onlookers would be inappropriate in a woman who is the wife of a man who is believed to be walking with God.

For all Amma knows, Swami's brain might only be notionally more useful than a plantain stepped on by Mrs P – but if God is taking care of Swami, what does it matter? So she sits in the centre of her serenity in Swami's hospital room, as complacent as a tired elephant being scrubbed down by a conscientious mahout at the end of a long day's logging.

For five days Swami has been adrift in a strange untellable tale that does not belong to the ordinary lives of his wife and his daughters, to his town and to his lived experience. He is not dead, but nor is he completely alive. He exists, like a machine that has been plugged in but not turned on. As for his family, the panic of the first few days after his death and resuscitation has eased away. The girls are almost getting used to him like this.

At the moment Pushpa is reading Agam poems to him from the Sangam literature, as Leela executes dance exercises in the corner of the room. Jodhi and Kamala are at home, looking after Suhanya and Anitha.

> *"Bigger than the world,"* Pushpa reads,
> *"higher than the heavens,*
> *more unfathomable than deep waters*
> *is this love for this man*
> *of the mountain places*
> *where the bees make their sweet honey*
> *from the kurinci flower*
> *with its black stalks."*

"Amma," Leela says again, abandoning her exercises, teasing at her hair idly because she is restless and looking for something to do or say or imagine.

> *"In no place, and not among the festive warriors,*
> *not with the girls dancing closely in twos,"* Pushpa recites,
> *"in no place did I see my dancer."*

"Amma, Amma..." Leela says; finding anything worth doing or saying or imagining is a struggle.

"Stop it Leela!" says Pushpa, from the other side of Swami. "Stop Amma-Ammaing all day long!"

Leela directs a scornful glance at Pushpa, and tugs at her sleek coconut-oiled hair as though combing it for ideas.

"Amma," she says abruptly, "I need to be alone with Appa."

"What is that, Daughter? Alone with Appa?"

"Why are you wanting to be alone with Appa?" Pushpa asks, frowning in suspicion.

Leela closes her eyes with an air of mystery, the better to trawl through her boredom for a plausible reason.

"Appa is wanting this," she says, experimentally.

Amma and Pushpa turn to look at the freshly shaved face fronting Swami's unconsciousness, and then swivel back round to contemplate Leela.

Always this youngest daughter of mine is like this, Amma tells herself, moving her happy head side to side fractionally in the manner of an enraptured connoisseur at a fine concert... *Think of the things she is always saying, look at the way she can dance like candle smoke without even knowing it...*

"Amma!" Pushpa explodes, from a deep well of envy, "she is telling an untrue thing!" – but Amma is already rising, splendidly.

"Come my daughter," she says to Pushpa, and "be quiet," she adds, ominously, as a half-syllable of protest escapes from Pushpa's lips. She exits the hospital room, a sullen Pushpa trailing behind, to be received with wide-eyed curiosity by the handful of hangers-on who are loitering in the corridor outside. On the way out Pushpa glares at her youngest sister, but Leela, alarmed at what she has just done, is unwilling to meet her gaze. She keeps her eyes tight-shut, in an approximation of someone who is involuntarily partaking in mysterious bouts of cosmic wisdom. Only when she hears the door shutting does she peep out from her eyelids, to stare open-mouthed around a room which now seems fearful but for her father in the middle of it, in all the strange and horizontal mystery of his situation. The recurrent wheezing and whirring that emanates from his lower legs – mechanically inflating pulsatile stockings on his calves are minimizing the risk of blood clots – takes on a louder and more sinister tone.

"Amma, Sister," she calls softly, frightened that her daddy will die and that it will be all her fault, "come back!" But when nobody comes she doesn't call again. She walks around the bed, to where Pushpa had been sitting, and picks up the book of Agam poems. "Appa," she tries, with an edge of panic to her voice, "shall I read to you as well, Appa?" And so she finishes the poem Pushpa had started:

"My pride, my love, I am dancer.
It is for his love that these shell bangles
slip off my wasted hands."

Elsewhere, in the corridors, in the wards, in the hospital compound and in the streets beyond them, the conscious human world is going about its business in all its fractious, noisy ways. Leela starts to feel a little calmer. She places the book on the bed, by her father's legs, and holds him by the hand.

"Appa, when will you wake up? Appa? When will you talk to me again?"

But the only answer is the whirr of the apparatus and the hum of Mullaipuram.

Leela picks up her father's limp and heavy hand and lowers her head to it, defying an urge to weep as she brushes her lips against his hairy wrist.

"Please don't die again – one time is enough."

In another part of the hospital D.D. Rajendran is advancing uneasily. The patients' relatives thronging the corridors are parting respectfully to let him pass unhindered – everyone knows who DDR is – then turn around and watch him from behind, puzzled, as though he is an unusual vessel sighted in unlikely waters. As he walks, DDR is deep in thought.

He is a man who takes his spiritual life seriously. His devotion to the guru Sri Sri Dravidananda Gurkkal – whose silence has penetrated to the starting point of the centre of the spiral of all knowledge – has granted him a certain amount of self-acceptance over the years, but now he is troubled, and his faith in Sri Sri Dravidananda Gurkkal is not helping him. His growing

foreboding is that although he doesn't understand why
this limping fellow R.M. Swaminathan has entered
his life in such a disturbing fashion, yet everything
is developing in such a way as to suggest that there
is some meaning behind it all – that it is all going to
make sense eventually, but in ways which might not
prove comfortable for himself. The rumours sweeping
Mullaipuram about R.M. Swaminathan returning from
death to walk with God have thrilled him and appalled
him. Yes, DDR is becoming sure of it, there's something
of the indefinable-infinite-everything in this fellow's
experiences – the fellow's disability and suffering, the
way a white man fell on his head and expended his death
gaze on him, his strange way of talking, the numbers
he spouts, the breakdown, the falling silent for a week...
and then death, and then life, and then, maybe, God.
Aren't these *exactly* the kind of events that happen when
a man's earthly existence and cosmic fate are leading
him beyond the merely human towards a glimpse of the
universal? Always, DDR reminds himself, always this
is the way – it is not the priest, it is not the scholar, it is
not the initiate who truly glimpses God. It is the ones
you don't expect. It is the madman who stands under
a tree for fifteen years, being beaten and laughed at;
it is the ten-year-old girl who has fits and visions and
manias and is locked away and starved and thrashed;
it is the limping, spluttering, urinating, silent six-
daughtered imbecile who half-brains himself courtesy
of a plummeting white man – these are the ones who
are granted glimpses of the godhead... I am involved
now, DDR muses, both fearful and flattered – I brought
him to my house, he urinated on my marble floor, he
fell apart in my presence, he entered upon silence after
I told him about the silence of Gandhi, the silence of Sri
Sri Dravidananda Gurkkal...

"Oh God, why did I end up shouting and bellowing

at this holy fellow?!" he blurts, to the discomfort of a sweeper woman who is watching him stride past her.

Dabbing at his moustache as he walks, still sunk in schizophrenic cogitations as to the meaning of all this what-not and what-all, he reaches the little knot of people outside Swami's hospital room. He glances with disdain at the hospital porters stationed at the door. They are under instructions from the hospital management to prevent any unauthorized access.

"Shall I go in?" he says, to one of the men – who nods minutely and steps aside. Everyone knows who DDR is and what he looks like. Everyone but Leela.

Inside, the machine powering the pulsatile stockings gives a great heaving groan and then falls silent. The curtain is three-quarters drawn against the fierce light outside, granting a warm subdued glow to Swami and his daughter. Leela is hunched over the bed, resting her cheek on her father's chest. She has placed her left-hand palm downwards on Swami's forehead, while her right hand rests lightly on his thigh. Her hair is splayed in a black, glossy fantail across his bare torso, so long and full and thick that it covers his chest without a gap or a chink. *What is this?* DDR wonders, moved by such a vision of beauty and devotion – and as he stands there gaping, the most beautiful child he has ever laid eyes on lifts her head, her hair gently rolling off Swami's chest and sweeping down over her shoulders.

"This is my Appa," she declares.

He gently closes the door behind him, and nods. From his immaculate appearance and bearing, Leela can see that he is a VIP.

"Saar, do you want to touch my Appa's feet?" she whispers, conspiratorially.

DDR shifts from one heel to another, unwilling to cede power to such a young girl, but wondering, too, if this is some kind of test to which he should submit.

"Maybe," he admits. He can abruptly feel his heart knocking against his chest wall, and feels irritated with himself. "Maybe later."

He approaches the bed and looks down at Swami, nervous and melancholic. There is a faint whiff of stale urine in the air, because a bag is nearly full, a detail which DDR notes with distaste. And there is a fly in the room, whose flight he follows for a few seconds from the corner of his eye, until such a point as the little creature lands on the very feet that have been the subject of so much respect and speculation, as if even the smallest of God's beasts feels compelled to touch the feet that may be walking beyond the earthly realms. What does it all mean, DDR grunts to himself miserably. Do these, do these and other signals, mean that the fellow is at one with the godhead? He gazes with longing at Swami's face.

"Which daughter are you, child?" he asks, without looking at the girl.

"I am Leela, Saar. I am the youngest daughter."

"Where's your Amma, my Daughter?"

"I told her to leave," Leela says, with a flash of pride.

"Hm. Not the words of a dutiful daughter."

"Appa wanted to be alone with me," Leela explains, with a dash of resentment.

DDR arches his eyebrows, impressed despite himself. "Why is that?" he breathes.

"Because, Saar," Leela says, "because, because..." She wonders who he is, and realizes she feels frightened. He is looking at her too urgently.

"Because?"

"Because he knew that you were coming," she gulps breathlessly.

He pulls a chair up to the bedside, next to Leela, and they both gaze at the unconscious man's face.

He turns to her, as though he expects her to say

something else, and so, for want of anything more imaginative, "Touch his feet, Saar," Leela implores him, "touch them."

DDR is sorely tempted. He looks down at the small peak in the sheet at the bottom of the bed. But he is not ready to submit. There is something holding him back.

"When I met your Appa, he said something which I didn't understand. I've been wondering about it ever since."

"Yes Saar?"

"Do you know what it is?"

"Yes Saar."

"What?" He turns to her in dismay. His question had been purely rhetorical. "You're saying you know what it is that he said to me?"

"Yes Saar," Leela repeats.

Half doubting her honesty, half longing for her truthfulness, he gazes at her dubiously.

"Well?"

"Yes Saar?"

"What is it? What did he say to me?"

"Saar, you already know what he said to you."

"Yes yes, *I* know what he said to me – but do *you* know what he said to me? That is the question."

"Yes Saar. I'm already telling you I did," Leela points out.

"Yes yes, that is all very well," DDR answers her irritably, "but I'm telling you to tell me *what* he said to me."

"But Saar, If I know what he said to you, and if you know what he said to you, why do you need me to tell you?"

He leans back in his seat, eyes blazing, abruptly convinced that he is being taken for a fool, and that the man lying prone in front of him is no more walking with God than hanging out with monkeys in the trees.

Leela senses his dangerous temper flashing, and her eyes fill with hot tears.

"I'm very sorry, Saar. Please forgive. But Saar, I am believing that Appa told you a number, didn't he..."

"What what?"

Leela stands up and goes to a pile of three or four books under one of the plastic seats. She extracts one and starts flicking through the pages.

"Tell me the number, Saar, and then you will understand. What is that number?"

"What is that book?"

"*The Sacred Couplets*. Appa was trying to communicate a wisdom to you. What number?"

"Ninety-five, my Daughter," says DDR, submitting to her. Once again his heart is knocking in his chest.

So Leela reads:

"Sweet words and humble conduct are the greatest jewels; no other kinds of jewel exist."

"Now do you understand, Saar?" she asks him, simply.

"Oh God," DDR moans, sinking his head in his hands – "I am bellowing and raging at your Appa, who is unearthly wisdom personified, like the mighty Tiruvalluvar himself, revered author of our famous *Sacred Couplets*, and he deigns to educate me in the error of my ways – *and I do not even hear him!*"

He walks around the bed and reverently places the tips of his fingers on the guru's feet.

"You can pray if you want to," Leela says.

12

Today, in Mullaipuram Anna District General Hospital, Swami is coming back to the world.

One wife, six daughters, one brother, two grandparents, one friend, one sister-in-law, three neighbours, two nurses, and four relatives of indeterminate provenance are crowding into the room. Granddaddy regards life and death as roughly equivalent, and of little interest to anyone with half a brain, including God. He is sitting cross-legged in a corner and playing his flute – now there is a man whose insights deserve to be heeded by anyone in this world intent on attaining spiritual enlightenment. Naturally no one takes a blind bit of notice of him. Everyone is crowding round the bed in three rough tiers of homage. Amma and the girls comprise the first row, while the least influential people peer from the third tier at the bottom.

Swami's lightening has been picking up in pace, his eyelids have been flickering for half a day, at uneven intervals, and he has occasionally issued deep, uncomfortable moans. At times a small spasm judders his cheeks.

"Come back to us now, my husband," Amma breathes to him, squeezing his hand. "Wake up."

"Wake up Appa," Leela pleads.

"In his own good time, he is coming," says Dr Pandit,

as Jodhi strokes her father's temples and prays for his eyes to open.

Dr Pandit has become annoyed by the growing status of this patient. After all, he reasons, the fellow's accomplishments only stretch to being unconscious. Day by day, however, rumours about Swami's spirituality have been generating spontaneously on the flimsiest of premises, have been self-replicating and mutating: some fantasists claim that to fall asleep in Swami's presence while touching him is to be granted a weak but tangible insight into walking with God; it has also been said that terminally ill patients are clamouring to be wheeled up and down Swami's corridor, convinced that proximity to his aura will extend their lives and reduce their sufferings; and it has even been claimed that Swami helpfully levitates when the nurses give him a bed bath. Such speculations are creating havoc, as far as Dr Pandit is concerned.

"Appa, wake up, wake up," Kamala urges gently.

Yes wake up damn it, the doctor thinks, looking at his watch, *wake up and get better and go home as soon as possible; I've had enough of this nonsense.*

"Can't you stop your respected elder from playing that terrible music?" he asks Amma irritably.

"Nobody can stop Granddaddy from playing his flute, Sir," Amma replies with dignity, "though many people are trying."

Dr Pandit sighs to himself; what a family!

* * *

Outside the hospital, Mr and Mrs P are among a great throng of well-wishers massing by the main entrance. A loose cordon of police officers holds them back. Mrs P is sweating profusely, despite the black umbrella she uses for sheltering from the sun. She is not used to standing around in the sun feeling excited – although there was that one day on the lawns of Senate House in Chennai, six months ago, when a stand-in for the Tamil Nadu Deputy Minister for Information Technology had presented her son with the whopping great cheque for the *Sri Aandiappan Swamigal Tamil Nadu Information Superhighway Endowment Scholarship*. She mops her brow, panting like a mule. The umbrella above her cannot generate a zone of shade below her that is large enough to shelter her body. Golfing umbrellas are yet to become the next big thing in Mullaipuram.

A hundred excitable conversations are taking place among Swami's new devotees.

"Levitated," some skinny, wrinkled, middle-aged man in a dirty dhoti is affirming to anyone who will listen, "just rose up like a gas-filled balloon!"

"Adaa-daa-daa!" someone exclaims at the miracle.

"Rose up like a balloon," the man continues, "for the convenience of the nurses, granting them first-class easy access for full bed-bath washing!"

All through the growing crowd people are debating the extraordinary powers of their cherished Sub-Inspector of Police (retired), Mr R.M. Swaminathan.

"Medical expenses come to lakhs of rupees," someone is declaiming, "family can't afford to buy an out-of-date aspirin, and yet all medical expenses mysteriously paid from mystical high sources!"

"What rubbish," someone disagrees, "what is this mystical-high-sources nonsense? The gods and saints are having bank accounts now, is it? Medical expenses are being paid by DDR, everyone knows that by now!"

"Exactly!" spits his conversational combatant eagerly, "that is exactly what I am saying. Who can explain why D.D. Rajendran would pay such a bill? Truly it is a miracle!"

Further back in the crowd a schoolmaster from a nearby village is holding court:

"When the white man from the sky died at our guru's feet," he pontificates to a knot of family and friends around him, through spectacular bucked teeth and loose spittle-flecked lips, "when the white man expired there at his feet," he adds, for he has a rhetorical bent, "oh yes, my Brothers and sisters, then I was knowing something godly was up, praise be to my saviour Jesus and Lord Krishna if you like and also Sai Baba! Some people were mocking Swamiji that day—"

"Some idiots were really taking Swamiji to pieces!" an onlooker agrees, indignantly.

"—yes Brothers, it's true, to the shame of the whole Mullaipuram District and every Taluk and village in it, to the shame of Tamil Nadu and all South India..." – this fellow is wasted as a hopeless schoolmaster, he would make a first-rate terrible pastor – "...there were some who were not wise enough to recognize the true import of events. Always it is like this with these holy men and saints, with my Lord Saviour Lord Jesus Lord Christ himself it was like this too, Lord Jesus was mocked and spurned and denied, but as for me I knew straight away—"

"Not just levitated," another fellow nearby is gleefully fibbing to a small circle of grimy, green-shirted sceptical bus conductors, as his ten-year-old son pushes and shoves to stay within the circle, enthralled; "actually turning round in mid-air, rotating full 360 degrees!"

"Appa Appa, why is he rotating?"

"Why? Son, where is your common sense? For all-over bed-wash!"

He repeats his cry ecstatically, and it carries over the heads of the crowd like a call to worship – *For all-over bed-wash, bed-wash, bed-wash!* – mingling with other attestations and magnificences, as the sun beats down on everyone's brains while some three hundred metres away, in a small room now guarded by police, a man is coming out of his coma.

"Why won't they let us in?" Mr P is saying to his wife grumpily outside the hospital entrance, offended by all the common gossip swilling around. "We're practically family."

Since the marriage of Mohan and Jodhi was first posited – a lifetime ago, it seems, and in a superseded world – Mr and Mrs P's views on the suitability of the match have had their ups, their downs, their arounds and their every-which-ways. "Not looking like best available option," Mrs P had told her sobbing boy genius, in the hours after Jodhi's father had been abducted and all the fellow's womenfolk had thrown themselves to their knees on the dirty road in a crazy bleating heap. "We have had enough of these sob-story crazies, forget about this girl." And Mr P too, though retaining a liking for the disaster-prone Swami and his pretty daughter Jodhi, had agreed that paternal abduction was an eccentricity too far in a would-be's family.

Their blockhead wonder-boy, adamant as he is that Jodhi is the only woman he will marry, needs a miracle to sway his parents' decision. But maybe a miracle is what he is getting.

* * *

One of Swami's eyes opens fractionally, and quivers under the assault of the light. As Jodhi hears herself take in a sharp intake of breath at her father's tentative lurch into consciousness, the image comes into her mind of a wobbly newborn calf struggling to remain upright.

"Husband!" Amma whispers, and she starts sobbing in a wretched way, hunched over him, cradling his face between both hands.

Swami's other eye opens. All his weeping womenfolk are holding on to him fiercely, as though frightened that the gods might take him back at any moment.

"Husband, you have been sick, you have been sleeping, you have been with God!"

There is gentle commotion from everyone crowded into that small room; there are tears and there are praises to God; there are great sighs of relief and noisy harrumphing vibratos of excitement; and there are whispers and prayers and exultations.

Swami looks around, confused. He can just about recognize his wife. Who are all these others? He has a headache, a painfully dry mouth, and there is a noise reverberating around his mind which he does not understand, an eerie, distant call, like an echo of the sounds of another world. He feels as though he knew that noise once, in another time... What is it? But no, no, he can no longer recognize it. It is like trying to cling on to the narrative of a fading dream. He closes his eyes as if to evade the sound, slightly surprised that he is here and that he can perform such feats as eye-opening and eye-closing. Then, with a greater awareness of himself and his context coming to him steadily – *my daughters, my daughters* – he attempts an experimental licking of the lips. But his mouth is so dry that his tongue sticks to his skin. It stays there, stuck out of his mouth and to one side, in a manner that looks neither dignified nor godly.

Amma seems in two minds over whether to pick the tongue up and put it back in, but the nurse is already dribbling a little water over Swami's lips and tongue. The tongue slides back in of its own accord. Swami opens his eyes again and looks at his wife and daughters, attempting to smile, but failing comprehensively.

"He's going to speak," Leela pronounces. "Appa, what is it?"

"Don't trouble him, my Daughter," Dr Pandit says in a kindly way. "Mr Swaminathan, you've been in a coma, now you are awake, but please be taking your time, please, you are all right and your family is all right and everything is all right, don't be frightened, don't worry."

"But he *is* going to speak," Leela says, apologetically.

"Husband, what is it?" Amma says, watching her husband swallowing and working his lips.

Everybody strains to hear the first conscious words that Swami will utter since his sojourn with the gods. Swami's gaze flickers between his wife and his daughters. A flash of irritation animates his face for a moment, taking them by surprise, for he has just come to a revelatory understanding of the mysterious and unearthly noises that are resonating around the chambers of his cranium.

Damn father-in-law, damn flute, he thinks... *Doesn't he ever stop?*

"Speak, my husband," Amma begs, beginning to cry again.

Swami nods slowly on his pillow, twice, and bares his teeth experimentally.

"T..." he says.

"Husband?"

"T..." Swami tries, "t... t..."

At that moment Granddaddy – having transported himself to a higher realm through the portal of the beauty of his playing – is cavorting through his most incredible vision yet: he can see the young Lord Krishna playing *his* flute and gallivanting with big-bosomed gopis, playing tricks with them, teasing them, and being amorous... It is a wondrous vision, and for a few seconds that seem to last for ever but that he will never recall afterwards, he is so lost in the sacred landscape his meditations have led him to that he even forgets to wheeze into his flute; the slobber-saturated scrap of wood sits limp in his gnarled old fingers, half hanging off his lips.

In the brief silence that marks Granddaddy's spiritual

ecstasy, Swami's family and friends hear the first profound declaration of their Swami, who has cheated death and come back from the gods to share it with them.

"Tea," he says.

Granddaddy, shaking his head in complacent wonder at the beauty of his own visions, begins to blow again.

13

"Daughter, tea!" Amma orders urgently, to any or all of her daughters.

Jodhi gets to the door first. Crying with relief and gratitude that her daddy has come back to her, she bustles out of the room and goes scurrying down the corridor, as the hangers-on outside the door shout in surprise.

There is no way that Jodhi will suffer her father to drink the weak and tepid brew of the roaming hospital tea vendors; a daddy who has been unavoidably deprived of tea by an eight-day coma deserves the very best tea available, and the very best tea available is made by Hairy Pugal. Clutching at the scarf of her *chudidhar* to stop it from flailing behind her, she runs for the street outside. Fixated by her commission, she barely registers the throng of people outside the hospital as she scoots past the policemen guarding the entrance. Her body plunges into the pulsating ranks. "Swamiji's eldest!" someone cries, as she goes barging through, and the people in her wake start following her excitedly, while the people in front of her surge forwards to meet her. Within a short time she is the unmoving centre of a circle of people that is forever getting smaller and denser, as everyone crowds in on her.

"Let me through!" Jodhi cries, dismayed, "Tea, I must be having tea for my Appa, Appa is wanting tea!"

"Swamiji is awake!"

"Swamiji lives!"

"Swamiji drinks tea!"

The throng surges in, packing the people even more closely towards the centre. Umbrellas are knocked out of hands, a few ladies are wailing, some individuals gasp for breath, and all the time Jodhi is crying "tea, tea!" and trying to scrabble through the people in front of her.

K.P. Murugesan has just come on duty and has taken over the supervision of the police at the hospital. During his long service with the Indian Police Service in Tamil Nadu he has policed many overcrowded gatherings, and he has a perhaps overdeveloped sense of how easily they can degenerate into stampedes. So he blows his whistle and takes his men into battle, leading by example in the noble art of thrashing the general public, just in case it is the right thing to do.

Yells break out as the dozen policemen wade in, striking out with their lathis. They make quick progress, burrowing into the crowd even as the people break up in panic. Within a minute a panting Murugesan and his men have rescued Jodhi. There are a few casualties nursing bruises and bitter grievances, but in the circumstances it has been an effective action.

"Tea, Appa, tea, Appa!" Jodhi is insisting, despairing that her father has asked for tea and that tea has not materialized.

"All right, Daughter, come," Murugesan says, in his kindly way, panting from his exertions, and he leads her to the Sugam Tea Stall. Behind him his men fan out, still waving their lathis at the sullen crowd that has been forced back.

"He's awake? He's okay?" Murugesan asks.

Jodhi nods blindly.

"Thanks to God," Murugesan says.

The Sugam Tea Stall stands where it has always stood,

shabby and decrepit, its paint peeling onto the patch of dirt it occupies. A great vat of hot milk simmers over a gas flame, the vat's dented tin lid flapping gently over the rising steam. Yes, the tea stall is there, almost as important a fixture in this part of Mullaipuram as the hospital itself – but where is Hairy Pugal? As Murugesan looks around in irritation, the fellow appears from the back of an autorickshaw, where he'd been sheltering.

"Tea!" Murugesan shouts, "Tea! Swami is awake!"

"Yes Saar!"

The master starts to brew his famous potion.

A large man and a larger woman are making their way tentatively towards Jodhi and Murugesan, negotiating clumps of onlookers and hostile policemen. "No no, let us pass, parents of the girl's would-be!" they are pleading, hands held up submissively whenever a constable impedes them.

"I am the mother-in-law!" Mrs P claims.

"We are the family members, let us pass!" her husband shouts.

They get to Jodhi more or less unmolested, and Mrs P, bypassing the awkward male authority of Murugesan, instinctively hugs Jodhi to her breast. Jodhi starts crying, and does not protest as most of her head disappears into the superabundant across-the-board immensity of Mrs P's bosom.

"Parents of the girl's boy," Mr P explains to Murugesan, with a dash of pride.

Mrs P, fat, hot, sweating profusely, her heart beating like a drum at a wedding because of all this excitement and expenditure of energy, strokes Jodhi's hair protectively.

"Not to be worrying," she says, over and over and over, between her pants, "not to be worrying."

Hairy Pugal is determined to create the best super-tea he has ever brewed up in his life. "Hurry up hurry up!" Murugesan sometimes urges, but Hairy Pugal is a great artist fulfilling the most significant commission of his career, and great artists will not be hurried up. It is another few minutes before he is ready with a battered aluminium jug.

"Saar," he says, "the tea that I have brewed is not for pouring in this dirty spot and then carrying in a glass to Swamiji in there, skin will be forming on top, Saar—"

"Yes yes, never mind that, just—"

"—this tea I only am taking to the hospital, Saar! This tea I only am pouring inside the hospital!" Hairy Pugal's eyes are shining religiously as he holds up his tannin-stained vessel in one hand, and two battered glasses in the other.

"Yes yes, all right all right," Murugesan says. He barks a few orders at his men, and Jodhi – under the care of Mr P and Mrs P – is escorted back into the hospital by Murugesan. The tea vendor walks in their wake, bearing his tea as though it is the nectar of immortality from sacred couplet number Eighty-Two.

Swami is propped up on his pillows when Jodhi returns with not just his tea but with a tea vendor, and Murugesan, and a full complement of potential in-laws. She hurls herself to her knees by his bedside.

"Forgive me Appa, big crowd is outside and I am getting stuck like anything."

Swami blinks benignly.

"Appa!" Jodhi blurts, ecstatic and overcome by his mere sentience.

Swami smiles weakly. He is not used to sentience. Ten minutes of the stuff have left him plumb-exhausted.

Mr and Mrs P shuffle forwards awkwardly, behind Murugesan, who is lifting his hand in a wordless and shiny-eyed greeting to his friend Swami.

"How is our respected Brother, Sister?" Mrs P whispers hoarsely to Amma.

Amma, taken aback by their presence, doesn't know what to say for a moment. She gapes and smiles at them, then looks at Jodhi as though the girl must have hidden depths – how else could she land the parents of the prodigy while buying tea?

"What about Appa's tea, Amma?" Jodhi says. "The fellow there has it, Amma."

Hairy Pugal steps up in his dirty shirt and lungi, sheepish and proud.

"Just the tea Appa is asking for, Daughter, not the fellow making it."

"Yes Amma, sorry Amma."

"Madam," says the tea vendor, "fault is all mine, I am insisting Swamiji has freshest, best-brewed, most professionally attended and lovingly administered quality super-tea! So I am pouring freshly Madam, please to observe."

Swamiji? Swami is thinking blearily, as his mouth fills with saliva at the sight of the hot sweet steaming tea that is being poured into a glass.

Hairy Pugal pours the tea back and forth from the first glass to a second glass, hypnotically, some three, four times, holding the lower glass at waist level and the higher one above his head, until he deems the temperature of that graceful arc of tea is optimal for a sick man who has just been hobnobbing with the gods.

He passes the precious vessel to Murugesan, who carefully delivers it to Jodhi, who solemnly places it in Amma's outstretched hand.

"Tea, husband," she says, and Swami nods feebly as she holds it to his lips.

One small sip of that famous concoction is all it takes to reconnect Swami to the here and the now and the wherewithal of his life in a full and meaningful way, not just for the first time since he has come out of his coma, but for the first time in two whole self-pitying, depression-deluded years. He smacks his lips, weakly but appreciatively, and someone towards the back of the room – some cousin of who knows whom, some fellow who shouldn't really be there but has somehow got in – shouts "Adaa-daa-daa-daa!" rather loudly.

Swami takes a larger gulp of tea, gazes at his wife and daughters, and smiles at them beatifically, because they exist.

He falls into a deep and peaceful sleep.

Book Two

1

Mullaipuram, which lies like a stunned and sitting duck in the unforgiving central plains of Tamil Nadu, is blasted all year round by its three seasons: the wet, the cool and the hot. The wet, lasting from October to December, is unbearably hot and torrentially wet; the cool, lasting from January to the middle of March, is unbearably hot and bone-bleachingly dry; and as for the hot, which occupies all the months left over... the furnace blast of its insufferable forty degrees centigrade scorches the will to live out of every breathing beast the plains can muster, and anything that foolishly continues to exist is made doubly miserable by a sweat-hoovering 100% humidity.

Some two months after Swami emerges from his coma, the hot season takes Mullaipuram in its vicious grip. Mange-riddled dogs lie on their sides in any patch of shade they can claim, holding their legs straight out in big "W"s, lolling their tongues across the dirt. Wincing taxi drivers with itchy heat-rash buttocks hunch in front of their melting dashboards, nosing the searing air from portable fans wired up to the car batteries. People with nowhere to go and nothing to do are spontaneously catching buses in despair, spurning the seats inside to cling to the roof or hang off the sides – they close their eyes in delirious relief to feel the moving air circulate around their hottest bits and pieces.

In these intolerable conditions, and under the stewardship of Amma and Mrs P, the uncertain romance of Jodhi and Mohan is taking another hesitant step. After weeks of maternal arbitration, the young couple are – at this very moment – sitting side by side in the flea-bitten auditorium of Mullaipuram Theatre Palace, watching a film called *When I Saw You I Knew*. They are chaperoned loosely enough to encourage a certain degree of intimacy, and yet tightly enough to foreclose any hint of impropriety. Negotiations on the identity and function of the chaperones were time-consuming and complicated, with the two mothers campaigning for as many chaperones as possible (to maximize the impression of respectability), and with Jodhi campaigning against Amma being one of the chaperones under any circumstances (to minimize the possibility of mortification). Mohan campaigned neither for nor against any detail of the much-awaited great day, on the grounds that no humiliation is too much trouble for him. The end result is that the happy would-bes have Pushpa sitting to their left, while to their right are Devan and his wife, and then an empty seat which Anand is supposed to be occupying; to the disappointment of Pushpa and Jodhi he has not shown up.

Everyone in this cinema sweats like a roasting pig. Chubby Devan squirms in his sodden shirt and trousers on his grimy half-sprung seat. The petite and delicate Mrs Devan moans under her breath, fanning her face and panting for oxygen in the fetid dark. Pushpa and Jodhi sit with their heads close together, as far away from Mohan as possible – even in near darkness he is visibly leaching sexual excitement from every clogged-up pore of his body. The two girls can feel the sweat under their arms spreading outwards into saucers, into small plates, into large plates that eventually meet and form giant, drowned butterflies over their breasts. They are trying not to cry in boredom and discomfort. It is a three-hour film and there are ninety minutes to go.

This is *great*, thinks Mohan. Drops of sweat are rolling off the tip of his nose as though from a dripping tap. His left hand is carefully edging towards Jodhi's right hand at a speed of one millimetre per minute.

Mohan has an ideal of how the date might pan out, an ideal he has lovingly and obsessively tended over the long nights of waiting for the negotiations to be concluded. In this heart-warming vision, he is sitting next to Jodhi in a dark and luxurious auditorium, thigh-to-straining-thigh with his Jodhi in the dark, their hearts hammering for one another, the very hairs on their arms sticking straight out of their eroticized goose-fleshed skin and yearning to touch and tingle as he senses her hand nudging closer to his, closer, closer, as he edges his hand closer to hers, closer, closer, and he feels – oh yes, oh, oh this is it, oh – he feels her hand *merging* with his hand, like a, just like a – oh yes – as though it's a, like, like...

Curiously the vision often falters at this juncture, when what is required is a powerful and inventive simile to summon up the incomparable beauty of young love.

...like eight fingers and two thumbs, comprising ten digits in total, all interconnected, Mohan thinks.

Ninety-one minutes later, five sopping-wet and exhausted individuals exit the dusty foyer of Mullaipuram Theatre Palace and stand blinking under the canopy of an electrical goods shop. They are all dispirited, even Mohan, whose testosterone-fuelled clammy paw – when it had finally met with the delicate fingers of his beloved after two-hundred and forty-five minutes of digital stalking – had caused Jodhi to jump out of her seat.

"Thirsty," Pushpa gasps, to Jodhi.

"Bad thirst," croaks Mrs Devan, to her husband; he is standing a little to one side, legs apart, discreetly fanning his private parts with a newspaper.

"I want to die," Jodhi tells Pushpa.

She catches Mohan looking at some rather personal highlights of her anatomy, which her drenched *chudidhar* is clinging to obligingly, just as in all the obligatory monsoon scenes in all the films Mohan has ever seen, and so she turns away from him sharply.

"Friends," Mrs Devan is groaning, inexplicably, to Jodhi and Pushpa, to her husband, to God, "Friends, Friends," and she heads across the road, still saying, "Friends, Friends."

"Friends, oh my God, Friends!" says her husband, following her, "that is not best value for money, wife, some other place, not Friends, wife—"

"Only place," she calls from the other side of the road.

"Friends!" Mohan exclaims to Jodhi and Pushpa rapturously; this is an unexpected bonus, surely his Jodhi cannot but fail to be impressed by Friends? "I am only going there once before, for my sister-in-law's birthday! Please be coming," he tells them.

Friends is Mullaipuram's one and only western-style café. It is located in Mullaipuram's top hotel, the four-star Hotel Sangam owned by D.D. Rajendran. If you are visiting Mullaipuram for some obscure reason known only to yourself – and if you are a VVIP, or a VIP, or an IP or even just a P – then you are recommended to stay in the Hotel Sangam. Jodhi and Pushpa have never been inside such an opulent establishment. They stick closely together as they follow Devan and his wife through the garish marble atrium, past businessmen in western business suits who are smoking and talking in loud voices on black sofas that are very far apart, one sofa to each businessman – and enter the wholly unfamiliar environment of Friends, with its soft armchairs and peculiar *objets d'art*, its foreign newspapers and cultural magazines, and the underwhelming élite of

Mullaipuram who comprise its clientele. Mohan trails in the wake of the two sisters, limping because of the unfortunate lie of his underpants as he watches their buttocks.

The party sits down on facing sofas, Jodhi and Pushpa on one sofa, Devan and his wife and Mohan on the other.

"Coolness," says Mrs Devan, with relief.

It is indeed nice and cool in Friends. The air conditioning in here could keep milk fresh for a month.

"Ayyo-yo-yo," says Devan, flapping his damp shirt over an ample, glistening belly.

Jodhi and Pushpa stare blankly ahead. They have never experienced air-conditioning like this before. They are already freezing, they feel their wet clothes turn from clammy to chilled.

"Refreshments," Mrs Devan says – it seems she only speaks in nouns – as a waiter arrives with menus. Jodhi and Pushpa hunch over the menu proffered to them, and try to keep their eyes from popping out and bouncing all over the place: *Tea, Rs.45, South Indian Coffee Rs.50, Cappuccino Rs.75, Skinny Latte Rs.75, Coca-cola Rs.50, Lassi Rs.70, Mango Juice Rs.60.* Neither of them has ever paid more than fifteen rupees for a tea or a coffee or a coke or a fruit juice, and then only as a special treat. Hairy Pugal's super-tea only costs three rupees...

"Don't be worrying, I am settling this," Devan reassures them, queasily. "What is your refreshment?"

The two sisters look at each other dubiously, signalling all manner of mutual miseries by the uneasy fractional adjustments of their expressions. A waiter stands in attendance.

"We will be taking what you will be taking," Jodhi says at last.

In the book *How to Attract Women*, a well-thumbed copy of which lies inside brown wrapping paper in a blue plastic bag under a pile of *Computer Programmer Wow!* magazines in Mohan's metal cabinet, it is confidently asserted that no woman can resist a man who makes her laugh. Mohan has read the relevant sentence dozens of times, so he knows it off by heart: "Where is the woman alive who can resist the charms of a man who makes her helpless with laughter? If only you can find her laughter button, and keep pressing it, then we guarantee she'll be putty in your hands!" This dictum has made a lasting impression on Mohan. *Putty in my hands!* he is always thinking, shaking his head in wonder. He has been desperately waiting for his opportunity to locate Jodhi's laughter button. He intends to press it, vigorously and repeatedly, till she spasms with uncontrollable hilarity – and this is the moment, he judges, to strike.

"We are all having Scotch on the rocks!" he shrieks hilariously, capping the joke with an ear-splitting "Ha Ha Ha" for good measure. He adds a late and sound-barrier painful "HA!" to finish off.

Jodhi, Pushpa, Devan, Mrs Devan, the waiter, other waiters, the manager, the table boys, a visiting inspector from the Mullaipuram District Board of Food Preparation and Hygiene, and all the clientele of Friends stare at him; businessmen in the atrium turn their heads and frown at the wild shouting; distant strangers in the furthest reaches of the hotel – lift boys between two floors, a honeymoon couple behind locked doors, chefs in busy subterranean kitchens – pause for an instant, cock their ears, wonder if they heard something.

"I am having coffee," says Devan, after the longest conversational pause in recent history, scrutinizing his younger brother sadly; Mohan's tragic mouth is still open, having been petrified by the excruciating shock of being unfunny beyond current scientific thinking in this field.

"We will be having coffee also, isn't it Pushpa?" Jodhi

says, now starting to shake with the cold, wrapping her scarf around her neck more closely.

"Yes," says Pushpa, and then, "Oh no," in the tone of voice of someone who cannot believe that things can get any worse.

"No? Yes?" Devan says.

What is Pushpa talking about? Of course things can get worse. Isn't that why things were invented? Everyone looks to where she is looking, and here comes Amma plodding into Friends, looking exactly like the hard-working, coarse-skinned, unsophisticated, financially burdened, self-sacrificing, rupee-careful, daughter-obsessed, marriage-fixated, lower-middle-class overweight Indian housewife that she is – though newly empowered by having a husband who is reputed to have walked with God. She is dragging Leela by the hand.

"Just happened," Amma says, attempting to breeze in nonchalantly, "just happened to be passing cinema after you came out! What a happy coincidence! Saw you all jolly as anything coming here!"

"Most welcome, Madam, please be sitting," Devan declares gravely. "How is your respected husband Swamiji?"

"Yes, seat," Mrs Devan adds, gesturing.

"Yes thank you," Amma says, thrusting an annoyed-looking Leela into Pushpa's side and lowering her rear into an armchair. She has never sat within such accommodating padded luxury before, it takes her by surprise. She tips backwards inexorably, like something toppling off a wall, and for a few undignified moments her legs are cycling the air. Everyone watches with some interest.

"I tried to stop her," Leela whispers apologetically to her sister, who nudges her to be quiet.

"Husband is very well," Amma is saying, as she struggles with the furniture, "he is still recuperating in the mountains. Trying to keep low profile, but everyone and all is coming to him for spiritual bliss!"

"When he comes back to Mullaipuram, everyone will be going mad," Devan predicts.

"DDR is having very big plans for husband," Amma boasts, "DDR says he is going to—"

"Amma!" Jodhi pleads, embarrassed at these boasts. It is an open secret that DDR is funding the family now, from Swami's stay in Thendraloor to the girls' educations, but there is no need to crow about it.

"Yes yes Daughter, be quiet, just for a moment I am stopping by, stop worrying. What a very beautiful coffee house!" Amma is wearing a sari, and has no scarf to pull closer around her neck. She is already shivering. "How are we liking the movie?" She asks Mohan hopefully.

"Not very best quality," Mohan admits, still crestfallen at his failure to locate Jodhi's laughter button and pump it till she had begged him to stop.

Amma glares at Jodhi; it must be her fault.

"Please be choosing refreshments," Devan says, in a faint voice, passing Amma a menu – this is proving more expensive than in his worst nightmares.

Amma's eyes lock onto the menu. A vein starts throbbing on her goose-pimpled neck. At home she could supply some of these drinks at twice the quality and a fiftieth of the price.

"Nothing for us," she says, on the back of a repressed choking gulp, "just stopping by."

"Pushpa," Leela whispers, "I am very very cold."

"Shush," Pushpa whispers.

"Cold?" Amma says, approaching deep-frozen, her teeth just about chattering. "Not cold at all. Very refreshingly cool," she claims. "Well then..." and she directs a piercing gaze at Jodhi, and threatens her: "...having very wonderful time?"

Everyone looks at Jodhi, who fakes a grisly smile and implements two and a half nods.

"Pushpa," Leela hisses, "Jodhi is liking some other boy, isn't she?!"

She says it a little bit too loudly; she says it during an unfortunate gap in the western muzak; she says it with horrifying conviction and revelatory relish, even though she has made it up. Before anyone can fully comprehend, Jodhi – already embarrassed beyond endurance by every wince-rich detail of this date – lands a stinging slap across her little sister's face. They stare into each other's eyes and share a second of intense mutual shock, then Leela splits the airwaves with inconsolable howls, and Jodhi throws her head into her hands, sobbing.

Devan and his wife sit limply agog at yet another pre-engagement meltdown, a monstrous marriage implosion. Even Mohan – instinctively exploiting the unexpected, narrow window of opportunity that is Jodhi's high neckline by glancing down her *chudidhar* as she hunches forwards – can't help wondering, as he strains for a glimpse of that heavenly bra, what it is about this family...

2

Two thousand metres up the jungle-cloaked Vadapra-desam Hills of the Western Ghats – a mountain range that snakes down the southern states of India – lies the hill station of Thendraloor. Founded in the early nineteenth century by hot-tormented American missionaries and British administrators, its temperate climate gave them relief from the scorched dust bowl of the plains. Every April, during the first seventy years of the settlement, a sweating army of coolies and packhorses would guide, tow, push and carry colonials and the Indian élite up the winding, perilous mountain tracks. An even bigger army was entrusted with lugging up the essential bits and pieces which this privileged band couldn't possibly do without: Persian rugs, mahogany davenports, fruit trees in vast urns, looted stone artefacts from village temples, silver tea sets, marble busts of Charles Dickens, iron baths, formal wear for every style of occasion from balls to pig-sticking parties, harmoniums, three-cylinder mangles and other essential little knick-knacks. After a meagre four months' rest and recreation, the privileged interloping indolents and all their multifarious paraphernalia had to be transported back to Madurai, Madras, Tiruchirapalli, Cuddalore.

The town's appeal and facilities grew rapidly. By 1916, British civil engineers had designed and built a fifty-mile road from Thendraloor to the railway junction at Kodai Road – although a pedant might be minded to challenge the description "designed and built", given that the British ingeniously utilized legions of bonded labourers to do all the work. The settlement developed into a full-blown English town from the Home Counties, complete with boating lake, golf course, churches of three denominations and a Rotary Club, as well as its own tally-hoing hunt, which rode out to hounds three times a week – through the pastures and dolmens and centuries-old middens of the surrounding stone-age tribal peoples – to harry astonished wild dogs and hyenas. After Independence in 1947 the Indians embraced Thendraloor enthusiastically, even the fox hunt, which is still going strong. These days tens of thousands of holidaymakers descend on the town every year by car and bus and luxury coach, overtaking each other on blind hairpin bends just because they can. It's true that the town itself is not very relaxing any more, given the Indian genius for enhancing any quiet un-spoilt beauty spot with vast concrete viewing platforms, immense heaps of stinking refuse and speakers blaring out distorted film songs, but anyone who chooses to can still find a sort of quiet in the outlying villages, and a peace in the nearby dense jungle, and awe on the mountainsides.

It is just after dawn in the Vadapradesam Hills; the sky is mostly clear and the temperature is slightly chilly, but not uncomfortably so. A man is watching the sun rise in the present tense, which is to say, with much attention and not much thought. He squats on a wide ledge on the hillside, one hand clutching a sapling that grows from a cleft in the rock, the other hanging limply by his side. He is looking out over a great valley to a series of verdant peaks. Thin strips of cloud below the peaks are changing in hue, from orange-edged black to bruised purple to – as the sun outstrips them – translucent wisps

of white. Swami grunts involuntarily. He has started
coming here most mornings, without really knowing
why. He was never much of a nature lover, but since his
death and rebirth he no longer feels much interest in
the consolations of books.

Kamala accompanies him. She is waiting in an
autorickshaw parked a hundred metres away, at the
end of an intermittently navigable track. The driver
of the auto, a well-meaning but overeager fellow with
a streak of impertinence, is struggling to contain his
curiosity about her father. He sits in the front of his
vehicle, imploring her to tell him all about Swamiji's
enlightenment in Mullaipuram, when it is said that
no less than seven curd-faced devils bearing evil
talking giant *rudraksha* beads flew into the town
spreading malice and misfortune, but were repulsed by
Swamiji's innate and burgeoning saintliness – Swami's
story gets a different mangling in different parts of
Tamil Nadu. Kamala is not in the mood for this kind
of thing, and she gets out of the auto. She is interested
in looking after her father's material needs – cooking
his food and washing his clothes and facilitating his day
and being his human walking stick. She walks some
of the way towards him, then stops next to a bleached,
lightning-blasted tree trunk, and squats, and waits.

Swami finds it easy to attend to the rising of the
red sun and nothing else; only when it crests the
highest peak might any strong thoughts kick in. He is
sometimes aware of that feeling of transition between
the two states of not-thinking and thinking. When he
is not thinking, he cannot think about not-thinking;
and when he is thinking, he can think too much about
thinking. But when he is moving from one condition to
the other, he can not only understand intellectually that
thought is the source of all fear; he can for a few brief
moments feel its truth, with all the heft and texture of a

rough stone weighed in the palm of the hand. And then there is a trick he has learnt – to let it go, that undiluted experience. Trying to hang on to the feeling it grants is to submit to the fear of losing it.

There is the sun, moving higher, becoming too bright to look at as it abandons the mountains below it, and now here are Swami's thoughts kicking in.

Many people have firm ideas about what Swami should think about. Amma thinks he should think about Jodhi's marriage. D.D. Rajendran thinks he should think about certain ambitious plans that are being formulated on his behalf. Jodhi thinks he should think about saving her from Mohan. Pushpa thinks he should think about his health. Leela thinks he should think about going home and cuddling her. The least fortunate people of Thendraloor and its environs think he should think about their diseased limbs, their sick children, their dirty wells, their crippling debts and their miraculous hopes. The spiritually excitable think he should think about explaining his enlightenment. Only Kamala and Granddaddy hold few views on what Swami should think about. Kamala is fulfilled by serving him, and Granddaddy is not big on thinking.

Swami will never attain Granddaddy's purchase on the present tense, but sometimes he comes close.

I want my breakfast, Swami thinks.

A serpent eagle soars easily in the distance. Some jungle beast – a common langur – is screeching in the canopy. Without warning Swami briefly slides into the dream world that comes to him on occasion – the one with the white man. Sometimes the white man can just appear next to him, like an imaginary friend conjured up by a small child, but at the moment the white man is more of a warmth, communicating elementally in units of acceptance. So the two of them just hang around together for a few moments, and then the white man is gone.

Whether Sub-Inspector (retired) R.M. Swaminathan has inadvertently accessed some spiritual plane beyond ordinary human experience is an excellent question. Don't ask – that is the best advice. Isn't it enough that he's at peace with himself in a way he has never known before? This is the way of it for many people who have died and come back. Now that Swami possesses the power of being at peace, he is wielding a force that is irresistibly attractive to people near and far. They crave it, that peacefulness of his. Because they do not have it, because they know they cannot buy it, because they rarely encounter it, their souls would suck it out of him, if they could.

He gets up from his haunches, laboriously – the shooting pains down one side are far less intense than they used to be – looking at Kamala as she starts walking towards him up the rocky path. When they meet he rests his hand on her shoulder and allows her to guide him back to the auto. With his new beard streaked with bars of white, his crisp green kurta, his confident way of inhabiting the fettered motion of his own body, and his silent devoted handmaiden at his side, he looks every inch the living saint that some say he is.

The auto driver sits up straight as his passenger approaches. His starving, junk-fed inner life longs to sink its teeth into Swami, but the man is too shy to put his questions to him directly. Eager to please, he wrenches the starter cord of the auto's cacophonous two-stroke, proud of his youth and his strength, proud of his passenger. The engine ignites on his first attempt.

"Ready Saar," he says.

Kamala helps her father into the back seat and gets in besides him. The auto swings round, and the driver makes a slow and careful zigzag along the uneven, rock-studded track. He expresses his respect for the guru with a series of blindingly obvious one-word commentaries on their journey.

"Rocky Saar."

They drive for half a mile, veering and lurching up and down and left and right, the jungle thick on both sides, until they reach a junction with a minor road.

"Junction Saar."

The auto heads off left up the skinny strip of tarmac. They crest a hill. The driver cuts the engine – "Cutting Saar" – and they free-wheel down the other side, accelerating to a flat-out rattling full-whack speed that couldn't be improved upon even if the engine were running. They are making for Highlands, an isolated stone cottage overlooking a hillside break in the jungle, some five miles out of Thendraloor. DDR has rented the place for Swami's recuperation, after the doctors advised that Swami shouldn't stay in the baking plains at the peak of the hot. The cottage was built – in much the same manner as the Thendraloor road was built – by a long-dead tax collector from Madurai, a Scotsman who derived enormous satisfaction during his retirement years from studying the abundant and fascinating fauna of the Indian jungle from the comfort of his own verandah, and then shooting it.

After a couple of miles they are climbing again. The driver pulls at the starter cord and the engine judders into life.

"Engine Saar!"

All the people they come across are travelling in the other direction, mostly on bicycles, going from the outlying villages to their jobs in the hotels and eateries and shops and businesses of Thendraloor; they free-wheel down at breakneck speed, two and three and occasionally four people to each bicycle, many of them waving and shouting respectful greetings when they see Swami.

When the auto is not far from the turn-off to High-lands, a man looms up ahead of them, walking up the hill. He looks behind him at the sound of the auto and steps to one side to let it pass – then jumps out at the last minute, shouting, forcing the driver to lurch to a veering halt.

"Stopping Saar!"

Swami's and Kamala's bottoms rock forwards off the back seat and then fall back again, heavily.

"Hey, you dimwit donkey!" the driver shouts at the man in the road, but the man takes no notice.

"Swamiji Swamiji," the fellow is moaning, rushing up, "I have come to see you, I must see you!"

He is a young man, short and heavily built, unshaven for two or three days, with a proud and slightly over-the-top moustache.

"Not to be bothering Swamiji like this!" the driver yells, and he gets out of his seat saying, "Get lost, get out, get away from here you son of a dog and a donkey!"

More by accident than design, for Swami is already indicating that he will speak to the fellow, the two young men engage in a complicated and uneasy wrestling match, neither of them fully committed to fighting, but neither willing to concede to the other.

"Wait," Kamala pleads with them, "what are you doing?!" – but they take no notice, and now their four-legged stand-off gets more serious, and they begin to lurch around perilously.

Swami has been struggling to lever himself out of his seat without Kamala's help; once he manages it he steps out of the auto and says "No no" to the two young men. They start to disengage, gradually, over three or four de-escalating stages. The intruder, panting from his exertions, hanging on to the driver's shoulders more out of comradeship than aggression, pleads, "Swamiji, you are knowing me, Swamiji?" When Swami nods, the man blurts, "Forgive me!" and bursts into tears, dropping to his knees so that he can kiss Swami's feet in respect.

"Come," Swami says.

Raising his hand to Kamala and the driver, to indicate that everything is all right, he leads the visitor down the road a short way – and waits to see what this is all about. He knows the visitor by sight: a young constable called Apumudali, a recent recruit on probation with the IPS.

Swami is becoming less and less taken aback at the way people are seeking him out willy-nilly – but still, what is this man doing here, so far away from his duties, crying on a mountainside?

"Swamiji, you know what I did, Swamiji—"

Apu wrings his hands and casts tortured glances at Swami, at the surrounding forest, at the sky, at Swami again.

"Swamiji, how can you be so calm after what I have done? I have come here before you, my fate is in your hands, Swamiji—"

The man is hysterical. Swami waits for him to come out with his terrible problem or his awful guilty secret. His wife has left him? He has monstrous debts? His brother has a brain tumour? There are all manner of terrible problems and guilty secrets killing any number of people right now, but the tear-stained Apu cannot bring himself to say what his particular terrible problem or guilty secret might be. Perhaps it's pretty bad.

"Swamiji, Swamiji – Swamiji..." Apu squats down on his haunches, rocking on his feet, shaking his head in self-disgust.

Swami feels hungry, and wonders how long this encounter might take. He raises his hand slightly to his watching anxious daughter, as if to say "don't worry", and shifts on his feet, settling down to wait for Apu to spill the beans in his own good time – and is taken by surprise when Apu's own good time is now.

"Swamiji, mighty Swamiji!" and the fellow hurls himself on to Swami's feet and starts pawing at

Swami's legs in a pathetic fit of hysteria, shouting "I killed Swamiji... I was the one, it was me... forgive me, Swamiji!"

Swami rocks back on his heels, almost falling over.

He's crazy, Swami realizes – but Swami is wrong. It is true that Apu killed Swami. He was the fellow who pushed Swami over in a busy Mullaipuram street and hissed "You dirty bastard son of a prostitute", precipitating Swami's fatal heart attack. In fact, if he's not careful then he's going to kill Swami all over again, but here are Kamala and the driver running over, shouting, and as the driver pulls Apu away from Swami, Kamala tends to her father. She gets him steady on his feet, and brushes him down solicitously, and takes control.

"You must not be behaving like this with Swamiji," she lectures the sobbing young police constable, who is now being held loosely by the driver.

"Sister—"

"Come and sit with him in the hour of silence, at three o'clock – then you will find peace."

"Sister... Swamiji—" Apu watches as Kamala leads her now passive father back to the auto. She helps him into the back. Apu remains kneeling in the road, still shedding tears.

As the vehicle phut-phuts away, Swami takes a final glance at the wretched Apu. *What does he mean, he killed me?* Just before Swami's head lurches back and the auto zips away, he and Apu exchange glances, and Swami can read the words that the crying man is mouthing: *forgive me, Swamiji.*

3

Swami's elevation from derided cripple to possible spiritual guide is playing havoc with the consciences of more than one Mullaipuram policeman. At lunchtime Murugesan arrives at Highlands. Unlike Apu, at least he is expected, and in control of himself. This is the third time in six weeks he has sacrificed a day off from work to endure fourteen bone-rattling hours on a bus, seven torturous hours each way – and all so that he can sit with Swami for a while and feel a kind of peace within reach, and yet wholly fail to say what is on his mind. Each time he comes, he finds evidence of Swami's spiralling status: the respect of the locals; the daily "hour of silence" in a jungle clearing near Pambarpuram village, at which first dozens and now hundreds of devotees are said to attend; and the most effective evidence of all – Swami's imperturbable aura of calm.

They sit in wicker basket chairs on the verandah of Highlands, staring out at a vista of scrub and jungle. Just being near to his friend affords Murugesan some temporary relief from the deep-seated anxieties that are plaguing him back in Mullaipuram, but he is not absolutely at ease. He has a natural resistance to small changes just as much as large changes. He has never sat on a wicker basket-chair before, for example, and he doesn't approve of starting now. As far as Murugesan

is concerned, too many new experiences have come
his way since that fateful day when a white man fell on
Swami, wicker basket-chairs being merely the latest.
Sometimes he wishes the rotation of the earth would
reverse, and he could go backwards in time to when his
certainties were unchallenged.

He is looking across at Swami, thinking, did he really
walk with God? Literally? Symbolically? Everyone is
believing it – but how does anyone know a thing like
that? Isn't it the case, he remembers, that in an earlier
time I held a mechanic's arms behind his back so that
Swami could punch the fellow in the stomach more
easily? – something to do with shoddy work on Swami's
scooter... Now, what kind of a guru is it that punches a
garage hand in the stomach? Would God walk with such
a man?

These are the kinds of doubts that assail Murugesan
day by day back in Mullaipuram, where he registers
the town's hysteria with bemusement. And yet... To be
with Swami is to feel one's doubts peel away. Swami is
indisputably emanating an aura of potent peacefulness
– everyone wants to be with him, and Murugesan is no
exception.

"Uncle," Kamala says gently, breaking his trance,
handing him a metal cup of cardamom tea; she pads
softly away.

Cradling the cup, Murugesan watches her go back
inside the dark, slightly chilly cottage. No matter that
its foreignness has been overwhelmed by India, there
is an alien feel to its architecture and atmosphere. He
observes Kamala through two doorways, as she sets to
work in the kitchen. She is now standing by a kitchen
sink, washing some utensils under a tap. A hundred, a
thousand times he has seen Swami's wife and daughters
washing utensils, and were they in some strange stone
foreign-built cottage on a jungle mountainside, standing

up, at a sink that has a tap? No. They were outside in the baked back plot of Number 14/B, squatting on their haunches under the hot sun of the plains, next to a red plastic bucket of water. Everything has changed, Murugesan thinks, rather vaguely; nothing is the same any more; I don't understand. But, there is Swami...

The two old friends look at each other with a mixture of affection and bemusement.

"Swami," Murugesan says – he is the only person left who still says Swami rather than Swamiji, and even he won't hold out much longer – "Swami—"

The calm, patient, almost vacant expression on Swami's face is exasperating to the sceptic in Murugesan. Why won't Swami respond? Why doesn't he smile, or nod, or speak? Why does he just wait?

"Swami, I have decided to become a better police officer."

It has cost him a month's anguish to grind out this oblique, preparatory, grudging, ambiguous and not overly ambitious declaration, but there is nothing much by way of a response from Swami – maybe his eyebrows rise fractionally.

"You know me of old," Murugesan says, "you know I'm not one of the worst, but – you know I'm not one of the best..."

Nothing. Damn him, Murugesan fumes, he is not going to help me one bit! He will force me to take this path all by myself. First he runs rings round us all over this dead white man, now he runs rings round my spiritual condition. Well, all right, if that is the way it must be...

Murugesan rubs his face in his hands, knowing he is coming close to telling Swami everything, everything about the white man, complete surrender and repentance. For that is the first and most difficult step. As Kamala clatters pots in the kitchen, he tries to work out what he will say, how he will say it: *Swami, I have obstructed the course of justice in this matter, please advise me...* he goes over various formulations in his head, nearly speaking several times but always drawing back, and marvelling to himself at the superhuman serenity of his old colleague.

"Swamiji, I did a bad thing, I—"

"Appa," Kamala calls from inside, "we must be getting ready."

Swami is already struggling up as she comes out onto the verandah. She helps her father to his feet as Murugesan looks on open-mouthed. *How can he be so passive, this great "Swamiji"?* That is his slightly scornful question. *How can he allow himself to be led away at this moment of my confession?*

Kamala takes Swami into his bedroom, where she helps him to wash and change – leaving Murugesan to stare into the scrub and the jungle beyond it, agonizing about what he might be doing wrong. *Surely Swami can see the process I am going through? Why would he walk away from me like that?*

* * *

Like most aspects of Swami's new existence, the hour of silence is a phenomenon that he neither foresaw nor intended. D.D. Rajendran – a frequent visitor of Swami's, now busy in Mullaipuram with ambitious plans for the future – would have rubbed his hands in glee at such a brilliant concept, and set to work on exploiting it. But the hour of silence came into being all by itself. During his first week in Thendraloor, Swami took to going on an afternoon walk. A relatively gentle jungle path leads to the village of Pambarpuram, and halfway along it there is a clearing by a mountain stream, where a shallow basin scattered with large smooth rocks creates a natural amphitheatre, at the centre of which is an impressive teak tree. It is here that he would pause for a rest. Within a few days curious onlookers were assembling, lured by the wild and escalating rumours about his spirituality, sitting in ones and twos and threes on the choicest rocks, squatting on the bankside, resting cross-legged under trees. After three weeks, there were more than a hundred – a motley bunch of proto-devotees, villagers, tourists, idlers, sceptics, well-wishers. At first they were waiting for something to happen. Nothing happened. Swami would reach the tree with his daughter; he would sit down and rest; after a while, ten minutes or two hours, he would get up and walk back to his cottage. But nobody was disappointed. They found their gossip and whispers tailing away into silence. If Swami rested for more than twenty minutes, all talk would have ceased, and many people were infused with a sense of spiritual rejuvenation. The word spread in Thendraloor and beyond, and the hour of silence was born.

Murugesan's eyes widen in wonder when he emerges from the jungle path into the clearing with Swami and Kamala – at least three hundred people are already waiting there, sitting in expectant knots amongst the rocks and shrubs. They observe Swami eagerly, watching his slow progress through their number, bringing their palms together in *namaskarams* and *vanakkams* as he passes them. Swami reaches his tree and sits down cross-legged at its base. And that is all there is to it. Though some new devotees or sceptical onlookers may start talking, they invariably cease in the end. The stream flows, the breeze passes, the shadows on the rocks shift gradually, the sun travels, the leaves of the trees rustle, the unseen beasts and birds of the nearby jungle call and kill and eat and die and fly and leap – and the people sit at the centre of this scene, silently gazing at Swami.

At the start, Murugesan wonders what lies at the centre of the process: is it peer pressure? Is it nothing more than the unremarkable comfort that derives from a joint endeavour in a setting of natural beauty? Or can only Swami engender this kind of response? For now, Murugesan doesn't know. After a while, he doesn't care. His thoughts are ebbing away. The longer the silence lasts, the more he becomes part of it. Only afterwards will he recall that all his problems left his consciousness, his very sense of self almost disappeared, and he experienced that intense level of living in the moment as is usually shown only by children.

And what is going on in Swami's mind as the collective will of the people submits to him? Much the same as is going on in theirs – a gradual letting go of almost everything, until only now is left. Before the hour of silence, and after the hour of silence, he may reason that there is some irreducible spiritual utility in what they all do together – they are claiming the present, because only the present exists, and to be in it is to be alive. Before the hour of silence, and after the hour of silence, he knows that any one of these accidental initiates could perform the role that he performs, if they only believed that they could; but during the hour of silence he just sits down and forgets everything.

Some forty minutes after the hour of silence started – after all, it wasn't Swami who named it and who claimed it was an hour – Swami shifts and yawns, and Kamala helps him up. A collective, satisfied, sibilant sigh emanates from his admirers. The hour of silence is over, and as people come out of their trances they smile and chuckle at each other, shake their heads in wonder; Swami is threading through them, his hand on Kamala's shoulder, and some of them are so elated that they prostrate themselves on the ground as he passes. As Murugesan watches, halfway between his own inner silence and his new outer awareness, he sees Apu for the first time, bowing down to the guru Swamiji. For a few seconds Murugesan feels a surge of peaceful amazement – Apu is here?! Swami is masterminding everything! But within minutes the anxieties attached to his everyday life and to his long personal charge sheet of small bad deeds seep back into him. Apu is here as well?! Apu, one of the very fellows I've perjured myself for, is also coming to see Swami? What is to be done?

* * *

"Yes yes, I was going to tell Swami everything," Murugesan admits, rather irritably, "three times I have come here to tell him everything, but something is always happening to stop me."

"That is how he is teaching you," Apu declares. "A guru is always using the ignorance of the disciple."

"Where did you pick up this rubbish?"

"It is definitely 100% true, I am reading about all the greatest gurus, again and again they are confounding their followers with completely illogical nonsense that leaves all baffled and unhappy – only later, when the followers are thinking about it very deeply, does the truth of what they were saying make itself clear."

"I am not a follower," Murugesan mutters.

"Look at how he has brought us here together. Everyday we are nodding greetings in Mullaipuram, but only here do we meet and talk."

"Why didn't you tell him everything already?"

"My everything is much worse than your everything," Apu answers.

"Yes, that is so."

"No no, it is much worse than you are thinking. You are not knowing everything I have done," comes the anguished answer.

"Of course I am knowing everything you have done..."

Murugesan is well-aware that Apu and a junior colleague, on encountering a rare white man in Mullaipuram, had harassed the fellow half-heartedly for a bribe. Later – off-duty and partly drunk and feeling their dignity impugned – they had tracked the foreigner down to his hotel and paid him a visit. They had got carried away, engaging in a few well-intentioned activities designed to encourage a man to acknowledge the error of his ways. After ten minutes of first-class entertainment involving cigarette burns and a heavy kick in the testicles, the white man had ruined everything by running at the window and jumping clean out.

Apu's lower lip begins to tremble.

"Brother, you are one of the many who covered up the truth about the foreigner—"

"Yes yes—"

"—but I am the one who kicked the harmless fellow in the balls – he drove us mad, he said, 'Don't blame yourselves...' – and watched him jump—"

"Yes yes, I know all that, it is *you* who don't know everything, for I am not only the dirty dog who lied to Swami to keep him off the case, I am also the dirty pig who told him the white man was a filthy rapist, God forgive me—"

"Brother..." Apu moans miserably "...Brother, this is nothing, I am even worse than you think, *I* am the disgusting, dirty lowdown snake who killed our beloved Swamiji!"

A sheen of dismayed disbelief comes over Murugesan's face, as Apu – snivelling and snorting – explains the fatal push that sent Swami sprawling to his death on a Mullaipuram road.

"What a dirty business," Murugesan whispers.

They walk the five miles to Thendraloor, side by side,

oblivious to the increasing traffic as they approach the
town, the coach parties of North Indians bellowing
Hindi songs, the foreigners in the backs of chauffeur-
driven jeeps, school parties crammed four to a seat in
fleets of shabby battered buses – the children shrieking
and emanating an almost continuous stream of sweet
papers and sick from the open windows. They pass a
church, a temple, a mosque, and they remain oblivious
to the cries of hawkers and beggars and guides. In the
dirty, litter-strewn wasteland that functions as the bus
stand, they agonize about what they should do.

"Full explanation and confession to Swami and facing
up to everything, however painful – that is the lesson,"
Murugesan argues at last.

"Telling Swamiji our bad deeds, not telling Swamiji
our bad deeds, what does it matter?" Apu is asking
miserably, sucking on a foul-smelling bidi as they wait
for the bus.

"What do you mean, what does it matter? Do you
want to cleanse the filth of your terrible actions or not?
The first step is confessing to Swami. That is common
sense! We know that is why we are drawn here..."

"You are not understanding anything, Brother. Swamiji
is not needing my confession, your confession, anybody's
confession. Swamiji is already knowing everything. He
is asking something else of us."

The temporary peacefulness that Murugesan had felt
when he was within Swami's aura seems very distant
now; he purses his lips, sucks up some saliva from the
back of his throat, swallows it, purses his lips again, as
he watches the buses coming and going. What is Apu
saying? He examines the younger man's melancholic
face.

"Something better than that, that is what he is wanting
from us," Apu adds, and he throws his bidi away bitterly,
saying, "I am going mad! He knows what I did. Why

doesn't he just report me to the authorities so that I can pay for what I did? Why won't he tell us what he wants us to do?"

Buses are roaring in and out of this place, turning in great roaring circles, gaining and losing passengers who hop on and off the steps of the moving vehicles. Murugesan looks up and sees a crow circling. The situation has become clear to him now.

"When people tell us what to do, do we listen, and do we do it?" he asks rhetorically.

"No, of course not, but people are not Swamiji. I would listen to him, and I would do what he told me to do."

"Yes, and the thing would be done, but you would remain the same. I am thinking, I am thinking..."

"What, Brother?"

No answer comes from Murugesan. He is thinking, *Now I understand. Swami is trying to guide us to reach understanding all by ourselves – only then will our actions mean anything.*

4

The sun beats down on Mullaipuram without mercy. It bounces its boundless heat around the small back plot of Swami's home, between the crumbling plaster planes of the surrounding bungalows and the walls which circumscribe that shabby area. Under its onslaught, a small, tentlike structure near the open back door of Number 14/B is swaying mysteriously – a pale-green shifting shape with three round talking bulges; Amma, Pushpa and Leela are peeling garlic together under the meagre home-made shelter of one of Amma's saris. They squat on their heels, in a triangle, systematically working their way through the garlic pile, depositing peeled cloves in a yellow plastic bowl. Amma is going to make three jars of pickle: one for her, one for a sister, and one to send to Kamala in Thendraloor.

Pushpa sticks her head out of the makeshift shelter of the sheet, sneezes into the sun-blasted air – all three of them have streaming twenty-four-hour colds, a consequence of their unaccustomed exposure to the freezing temperatures of Friends – then submerges herself back into the complicated, aggravating three-way combat that is taking place within the green light of the sari.

"You are looking incredibly stupid in those stupid things," she says to Leela, who is wearing sunglasses, "take those stupid things off, you stupid, no one can see you here but us!"

"Pushpa, that is enough!" Amma scolds, and the tent sways this way and that in the throes of her irritation. "She is just a little girl, let her play if she wants to. What is the matter with you, Pushpa?"

"Yes Pushpa, what is the *matter* with you?!" Leela repeats, with great satisfaction.

The slap from Jodhi yesterday has left no lasting mark, but Leela wants to signify her suffering. In western films she knows that when a handsome dissolute husband thumps his beautiful long-suffering wife, the saintly female partner takes to wearing a scarf and sunglasses whenever she leaves the house, to conceal the bruising; "I fell down the stairs," the wife says, if someone asks her what's wrong. So Leela is sporting sunglasses in homage to this glamorous ideal, and wears her scarf over her head. She has been roaming around the compound of police bungalows, longing for people to ask her what's wrong. "Jodhi hit me," she explains to anyone who asks. Her homage to the western model only goes so far.

Earlier in the day it had been Amma instructing Leela to take those stupid sunglasses off. But now she is pursuing a different strategy, and for the moment the sunglasses can stay. Stripping the garlic cloves at twice the speed her daughters can accomplish, dropping them into the bowl, she furrows her brow; she will have to be clever with Leela, to get to the bottom of the bottom of this Jodhi-and-Mohan business. Why did Leela claim that Jodhi is seeing another boy? Jodhi would never do anything as scandalous as that – would she? But why would Leela say such a thing, and why would Jodhi react so violently, if there were not a grain of truth in it somewhere?

One daughter of mine striking another daughter of mine in front of the boy's family, Amma muses disapprovingly. *What would my husband be saying about this?*

For a while the only sound is the rustle of garlic being peeled.

"I cannot believe my eldest daughter slapped my youngest daughter!" Amma complains.

"Amma, sometimes even you are slapping your youngest daughter," Leela points out, ambiguously defending Jodhi's blow.

"And your middle daughter," Pushpa agrees.

"All your daughters," Leela complains.

"I am your mother," Amma says; for twenty years she has employed the authority of this all-encompassing non sequitur to vindicate her very best mistakes.

"Yes Amma."

"I am slapping you for your own good."

"Yes Amma."

"Jodhi is not slapping you for your own good, she is slapping you because she is angry – because you are shaming her in front of the boy's family."

Silence from Leela; this is not a conversational direction which she is anxious to explore.

"And you are not seeing, Leela, how shaming it was for us?"

More silence. Pushpa pokes her head out of the tent to sneeze again, quickly followed by Leela, who sneezes three times in a row.

"Whoever heard of having a cold during the hot?!" Amma says, exasperated, as the two girls reappear under the covering; she blows her nose on the edge of her sari.

"Amma, don't do that!" Pushpa begs.

"That is how it was done when I was young!" Amma protests.

"It is not hygienic, Amma."

"And that dirty rag is hygienic, is it?" is Amma's answer, as she points at the drenched handkerchief in Pushpa's lap. When Pushpa doesn't reply, Amma gives a triumphant "Hmmph!".

"How many more, Amma?" Leela asks, pointing at the pile of garlic.

"All of them of course, you know that."

Leela sighs. She longs to roam around again, being romantically wronged and injured.

"So who is this boy Jodhi is liking?" Amma asks, in a guile-packed and deceptively conversational tone.

Leela bends her head and starts peeling garlic with extra attention. She has been evading this moment in her mind, the moment when she faces up to admitting she had invented the declaration; it is a depressing prospect. She strips a clove of its veined white skin, already imagining Amma shouting at her, forcing her to apologize to Jodhi. Her lower lip starts to quiver. A wave of reality washes over her, and she is just on the point of bursting into tears behind her sunglasses and confessing when Pushpa gets a dig in.

"She is a naughty dirty fat liar, Amma!"

"No I am not!" Leela is yelping halfway through this stream of unflattering adjectives, "you just shut up, you stupid!" She pulls the sheet off her head and delivers four explosive panic-induced sneezes, thinking *now what?* on each miserable atch-ooo.

"Pushpa," Amma scolds, "don't be saying these bad words to your little sister."

Leela fumbles her way back under the sheet, and glances fearfully at Amma and Pushpa.

"It doesn't matter, Leela, if you got a little bit carried away in that Himalaya of a hotel," Amma continues winningly, "no one is going to blame you or punish you, Leela, I am just wanting to know why you said it. After all, it didn't just come from nowhere – did it?"

Amma shreds the skin from the garlic cloves methodically, eyes on the job in hand, waiting for an answer. Now Leela longs for Pushpa to interrupt – even some more "naughty"s and "dirty"s would buy a bit

more time, even a "fat" wouldn't go amiss – but Pushpa
remains unhelpfully silent.

"Or did it?" Amma murmurs, into the silence.

It is make-or-break time for Leela. She stands at a
fork in the path of this matter, and contemplates which
direction to take: the *Yes Amma* of disgrace, repentance,
suffering and ultimate redemption; or the *No Amma* of
short-term relief and further disgrace. She is ashamed
of herself, but she also feels offended that Pushpa and
Amma doubt her story – what gives them the right to
think I'm lying, she asks herself furiously, even though
she is.

"No Amma."

"Well then," Amma says, her voice trembling a little;
it is costing her dearly to maintain this careful illusion
of self-control, she is more comfortable blurting out
whatever comes into her head. "Well then, tell your
Amma why you said – what you said – about Jodhi..."

The small, hot, sweaty germ-infested makeshift shelter seems as cavernous as the thousand-pillared hall
of the Meenakshi Temple at Madurai as Amma and
Pushpa wait for Leela to speak. Even Leela is waiting
for Leela to speak; she knows she is going to say
something, but what on earth will it be? Whatever it is,
it will need to be good, it will need to yoke together two
incompatibles and exhibit slippy semantic qualities: it
must make clear that Jodhi is not liking another boy,
while at the same time indicating that Leela is not a
naughty dirty fat liar.

"Amma," Leela whispers, conspiratorially, "Amma,
you see Amma, this is what I am knowing, the thing
is..."

Amma hunches down lower as she waits for the
revelation, stripping the garlic cloves at top speed; if
there were a world championship in garlic-peeling,
Amma would win it hands down with this kind of

performance, the stripped cloves are dropping into the plastic bowl at three-second intervals; Pushpa, on the other hand, has stopped working altogether. She concentrates on looking at the drenched handkerchief in her lap, wondering not so much what Leela is going to say, but whether on earth it will be true or not.

"Amma, somebody told me that somebody saw Jodhi wearing a pair of jeans."

Jeans! Amma thinks.

Jeans? Pushpa puzzles.

Jeans?! Leela asks herself desperately; where did *that* come from? But although the revelation has been dredged from a very small and obscure cranny of her back-to-the-wall imagination, it is by no means a bad effort. Hardly anyone wears jeans in Mullaipuram, maybe a few people who frequent Hotel Sangam and Friends, and some of the students at the Madurai University-affiliated college in Mullaipuram, young rich people who have been abroad.

Amma struggles to comprehend what a pair of jeans cladding the slender hips of her eldest daughter might signify.

"Must be at college she is wearing these jeans?" she says.

"At college," Leela confirms solemnly.

"Just one time she was seen or more than once?"

"Just one time Amma."

"Hmmph..."

Leela and Pushpa anxiously wait for her considered reaction. She is deep in thought and peeling cloves of garlic ever more effectively, her fingers a whirl of activity, her jaw working overtime as she ponders that small and enigmatic word, *jeans, jeans, jeans*, while the cloves of garlic drop, drop, drop into the bowl... No, she is not happy about these jeans; jeans represent a world she knows nothing about, jeans might be suspicious, jeans could mean anything from nothing to everything and all the terrible things that come in between – all the things that are much worse than nothing, and almost as bad as everything. These jeans could mean that Jodhi is blameless, but these jeans could mean that she is drenched in the all-out western decadence and moral degeneracy of – and Amma's eyes clench shut momentarily at the worst-case Chennai-bar-girl scenario – drinking and smoking and secret unsuitable boyfriends...

"And this you are knowing for sure, Leela?" she asks, thin-lipped.

"No Amma – I am just telling you what I am hearing, you can imagine what it made me think – but I'm not knowing if it is true or not."

"Leela, you are a very foolish girl! Very bad girl! Why did you imagine what you imagined in front of the boy's family like that?"

"Yes Amma. Sorry, Amma."

"Don't imagine things out loud any more!"

"Yes Amma."

"Do it in your imagination, that is the place for it!"

"Sorry, Amma. Yes Amma."

Clever Leela – she breathes more easily, knowing she has got herself off the hook as lightly as she could have hoped for.

"Don't be doing anything like this again!"

"No Amma. Sorry, Amma."

"Hmmph." Amma's scolding is automatic, she is barely attending to it, her overactive thoughts are racing around the situation of her eldest daughter. Is the girl wearing jeans or not, and if so, what is the purpose behind such disturbing and exotic behaviour? She turns it all over in her head, and misses Pushpa scowling at Leela, Leela sticking her tongue out childishly at Pushpa. What is to be done? How to get to the bottom of this business? How to do the best thing for Jodhi and land her that handsome boy-wonder for a lifetime of marital security and wifely status and unfettered shopping?

"Yes, just you keep out of it from now on, you naughty child."

"Yes Amma."

"You naughty…"

"Sorry, Amma."

"You listen to me," Amma says conspiratorially, leaning towards Leela and Pushpa, at last granting temporary respite to the remaining unpeeled cloves of garlic, "you just keep your eyes open for any more of this fishy jeans business, go with her when you can, be following her to college sometimes, be meeting her unexpectedly, be finding out what she is doing and who she is doing it with. Understand? If Jodhi is really wearing jeans, I want to know about it, I want to know when and where and who with!"

"Yes Amma."

"Yes Amma."

It will take more than a pair of jeans to prevent Amma from marrying Jodhi to the computer genius… She shifts from squatting to cross-legged, and gets started on the garlic cloves again.

"You girls, you listen," she abruptly chastises them, "not a word about these jeans to anyone, understand?"

"Yes Amma."

"Yes Amma, of course Amma."

"Not – to – *anyone!*"

The scandalous insertion of Jodhi's dainty legs into blue denim is an image that resides in these three heads and in no others – after all, it was only a few minutes ago that Leela made this nonsense up. And if, tomorrow, you interrogate any one of these three heads, all three heads will swear blind to sporting sealed lips, zipped lips, lips welded together with titanium rivets. What an incredible mystery, then, that within twenty-four hours the matter of Jodhi's deplorable jean-wearing activities is an open secret throughout Mullaipuram.

* * *

The P family home is a superior dwelling to Swami's dilapidated IPS-owned, British-built soldier's bungalow. After thirty-one years' employment with the Indian Railways, starting as a refrigeration mechanic and rising to the level of Assistant Station Supervisor, Mr P earns a salary double that of anything achieved by Swami. And notwithstanding Mrs P's pitiless efficiency in converting his hard-won cash into edible matter, he has been a careful steward of his earnings, putting aside at least twenty per cent a month since he was nineteen years old. These savings, and the sale of a small plot of land in his ancestral village following the death of his father, have recently allowed Mr and Mrs P to achieve a long-cherished ambition: they have moved into a brand-new apartment in Thenpalani's third most respectable area; it is a spacious four-roomer on the second floor of a gleaming-white concrete low-rise, just by a Tata Agricultural Peripherals Ltd regional office, with a balcony overlooking the Bharat Petroleum garage.

It is two days since the sweat-drenched and flesh-shudderingly awful catastrophe of Mohan and Jodhi's date. Mr P and his youngest son Anand are in the shiny new living room of their shiny new home, slouched on the considerably less shiny and far from new elderly plastic chairs of their old home, watching a test match on TV. The windows are open, and a single battered rotating fan stands on a table in front of them. They share its faint breeze, moving their faces in slow sweeps, left to right, right to left, to maximize its meagre respite from the stultifying heat.

India and England are battling through the third day of the test in Nagpur. England's strong position has not been worrying them unduly, but now Sachin Tendulkar has been clean-bowled for three in his second over, and the father and son are awash with the disappointment of seeing their god unmasked as a man.

"See that big, hulking, clumsy bowler there, what is his name again?"

"Hoggard."

"Yes him – what is he doing, bowling out Sachin? Doesn't he realize Sachin is our best player?"

"Appa, England are trying to win."

"That is the problem with these foreigners coming to India. Wherever they are going in India they are abusing our hospitality. This Hog fellow, now he is ruining my day completely! As if we don't have enough to put up with, with that weeping lover-boy in there, mental-break-downing all over the place!"

"Yes Appa," Anand says wearily. As it happens, he's not feeling too good himself, he rather feels like doing what Mohan is doing.

Mohan is much too busy to watch the cricket. He is engaged in the laborious and time-consuming activity of lying face-down on his bed for sixteen hours. He has risen only twice during that time – once to urinate, and once to hurl *How to Attract Women* out of the window and onto the large flat roof of the Bharat Petroleum garage, where it will lie – bleached and baked by the sun – for many months, until the next wet sweeps it away and turns it into pulp.

"Come on, my very own Rajah, my King," Mrs P is murmuring at his bedside, stroking his hair, caressing the back of his neck, "don't be sad, everything will turn out all right, don't upset your Amma like this, Mohan." In some despair she looks at her middle son's prone body; he is flat out, head turned away from her, face buried in his arms, beyond her reach. She has appropriated two of the household's three fans and trained them on his unmoving form, so that in his desolation he doesn't overheat. His shirt collar flaps in the breeze.

"Mohan, Mohana, Mohan *kannu*... See, my pet, what very best snacks I have for you! How hungry you must be, my life..."

Mohan is refusing to eat, even though his mother has assembled an ever more tantalizing and comprehensive array of titbits to tempt the lovelorn loser out of his sullen self-pity.

"See, look at what I've got for you—" and she dangles some home-made halva over his head, saying "Mmmmmm" and – who can blame her, it would be a shame to waste it – she pops it into her mouth. "Delicious, baby, don't let Amma eat it all! Amma will get fat," she suggests, thirty years too late.

Can nothing ease Mohan out of his face-down hunger strike? Not even the most lip-wetting sweetest luxury nibbles? Not even the sound of Mrs P ripping into them like a combine harvester going through a ripened crop?

"Mohan *chellam*, you cannot be lying down here like this for the rest of your life."

From the living room comes a commentator's glum pronouncement – "He's out, he's out, another wicket tumbling!" – and groans of dismay from Anand and Mr P, and then a frustrated "Wife, leave that stupid lover-boy in there alone!" from Mr P. "Stop humouring him, wife! He'll get up when he's hungry!"

Poor Mohan; his passion for Jodhi is of boundless extent, but he knows that when it comes to her passion for him, boundless is not the first word that trips off the tongue. Is it any wonder that he just wants to lie face-down and die? His every hope with her keeps getting dashed, and all because of her father receiving a white man on his head, being abducted, dying and living again and becoming God – how can a young girl concentrate on falling in love, even with the holder of the *Sri Aandiappan Swamigal Tamil Nadu Information Superhighway Endowment Scholarship*, when the father is pulling off amazing stunts like that? Mohan groans aloud just thinking about it all. It's been downhill ever since he ecstatically walked Jodhi to the Tamil Nadu Milk Board outlet during their first pre-engagement meeting, and pointed out that a goat was a goat. The romance and sweet intimacy of that brief walk is something he still cherishes every sleepless night of his life – and in the traditional manner – as he lies awake in bed thinking of his true love. Since then, Jodhi is evading meetings; Jodhi is complicating negotiations between the parents; Jodhi isn't answering most of his long and passionate emails, and is replying with brusque two-liners to the rest...

"Come now, my brave King, my eyes, help your mummy-amma help you, talk to amma-mummy."

"Amma, she's not going to marry me," he says into his pillow.

"What? What's that?" Sixteen hours of silence and now she misses it, she couldn't catch a word, she leans down close and strains to hear.

"Not going to marry me," Mohan repeats flatly.

"Mohan, why are you saying this? What are these worries? Everything will be fixed, only yesterday I am speaking to the mother, you know how much she likes you; it is the mothers who decide what happens, my son, not the daughters. I will have a daughter-in-law in a few months!"

"Likes another boy."

"What Mohan? What's that?"

"Other boy."

"No my Son, all this is cleared up, I am telling you this already, the younger sister is a very naughty girl, she is making it up."

"No Amma."

"Yes Mohan."

"No Amma."

"*Yes* Mohan."

"Jeans."

"What's that, my darling ?"

"Jeans."

"What's that?"

Mohan spins round and shouts, "*Jeans!* She is flying around here and there and everywhere with other boys in jeans, Amma! Everyone knows it! She is trying to make complete fool of me!"

5

Having shaved their chins and trimmed their moustaches with extra-scrupulous care, and having chastised their wives to iron their shirts with extra elbow grease and backbone, the off-duty and impeccably turned-out Murugesan and Apu are about to make contact with D.D. Rajendran. They are speeding along on Apu's scooter, bouncing over the potholes of the illegal road that DDR has built to connect his house to the main road more directly. They arrive – rather apprehensively – at the mansion on the outskirts of town. Murugesan steps off the back and smoothes down his trousers as Apu parks the bike nearby. Two guards greet them at the compound gate of Mullaipuram Mansions.

"He's at home?" Murugesan asks; he thinks he knows one of these guards, the fatter one with the badly stitched-up harelip. Murugesan racks his brains – he's sure he arrested him once, yes, for assault, three or four years ago. The fellow was sentenced to nine years, but Murugesan is neither surprised nor disappointed to see him now; it attests to DDR's extrajudicial influence.

"Yes Saar."

"Give him this and find out if he can see us – we'll wait here."

"Saar," the guard says, taking the envelope from Murugesan, "you can be coming inside and waiting there."

"No, here is fine."

Murugesan steps into the shade of the high wall of the compound and squats down on his haunches, looking at the horizon – Mullaipuram's tatty skyline – across a mile or two of wasteland, fields, scrub, building plots, light industry. Apu joins him.

"So hot," Apu complains.

* * *

This is a time of great flux and personal development for DDR. With his slack pot belly in his lap and his snorting paraplegic dog at his side, he is sitting at a snooker-table-sized desk in his office, fiddling with Bobby's ears as he flicks through some paperwork. Bobby grunts ecstatically, sounding not unlike DDR's mysterious and reclusive wife on those rare occasions when DDR grants her some physical attention.

If this year had gone as expected and planned and financed, DDR would at this very moment be campaigning in the state elections for a seat in the Legislature. Yes, he would be hitting the dusty election trail in a fleet of honking, tooting, speeding 4x4s, he would be standing on the backs of Maruthi vans in godforsaken hellholes, declaiming his promises to slack-jawed villagers: lower taxes, bigger subsidies, less corruption, cleaner water, cheaper gas, better crops, better cricketers, better politicians, fewer potholes, more happiness, computer access for all, supplementary nuclear weapons and victory in Kashmir. There would be free ghee today and tomorrow and the day after tomorrow for old people, children, newly-weds, widows, married couples, pregnant mothers, educationally deprived fathers, the disabled, the backward classes, the scheduled classes, the middle classes, the advantaged classes, the jobless, the workers, retired freedom fighters, reformed criminals, tribals, pensioners, students, farmers, landless labourers, women, men, eunuchs and livestock. During such soaring flights of oratory – which will now never take place – his henchmen would have been distributing pens and sweets to excited squabbling children, while his senior team would be in some village elder's house, drinking tea and buying votes with hard cash. Sometimes the backing of a village leader or a dominant family or a revered matriarch with a face like a jungle bison could sew up every available vote in the entire village. Sometimes even more favourable results can occur: one astute local politician of DDR's acquaintance is known to have secured the votes of 746 people from a village with only 545 registered voters – now *that* is the kind of supercharged very best special turbo democracy that could once make DDR's heart swell with pride: the democratic process in action, such as the heroes and freedom fighters of India's Independence fought for and suffered for and died for. And so, somewhere on this earth or elsewhere, there is a small and misty-eyed avatar of D.D. Rajendran that regrets sacrificing his political aspirations – either for the TDTTM Party or the DTTTM Party, he was never quite sure which one he'd plump for – for the sake of Swamiji.

But only a small part. Since a long time ago, even before the coming of Swamiji, the starved and monobrowed inner ape of DDR's conscience has been making guttural protests about its filthy living conditions, jumping up and down angrily and evolving in crude leaps towards a new morality. One could argue that this new morality is as rank as a rotting fish in the hot, but at least it represents an improvement on DDR's old morality, which was as rank as two rotting fish in the hot.

From where does such affecting moral improvement spring? Perhaps it is from DDR's metaphysical anguish. His deeply credulous inner longings have been tormenting him for a couple of years with irksome physical manifestations: sleepless nights, a spotty back, and hard, knobbly, once-a-week stools. The doctor cannot explain these ailments – and DDR doesn't expect him too. DDR knows they are symptoms of his mental corruption. Sometimes he finds himself looking long and hard into Bobby's blameless eyes as if to fathom how a paraplegic dog in a wheelbarrow, a dog without the wherewithal even to wag its own tail, can be as happy as Bobby is – and with such frequent and unproblematic bowel motions.

The result of all this is that DDR has reached a stage in his life when he can hardly be bothered to get richer and more powerful. To most observers this might seem an obvious manifesto for less anguish, more meaning, better happiness and extra fun, but if you consider the tiny proportion of rich and powerful people that tends to implement such a common-sense policy, then you may wish to concede that DDR is a veritable saint among the filthy rich.

The coming of the guru Swamiji has advanced and accelerated the ramifications and intensity of DDR's life changes. He has visited Swami five times already in Thendraloor, and experienced with his own mind the blessed peace of the hour of silence – and a racing imagination afterwards. He has sought, and believes he has been granted, Swami's permission to develop the outline of a kind of spiritual business plan for the guru to follow in his teachings and dealings with devotees. He has sat down with an overawed Amma and sketched out these plans – the way forwards, the ashram, the social work, the short-term steps, the long-term vision. He has not felt so energized and excited for years.

What about his old guru, Sri Sri Dravidananda Gurkkal? Pah, says D.D. Rajendran, Sri Sri Dravidananda Gurkkal is an ordinary human link to the godhead – good fellow, tries hard, but anyone can get a funny tattoo and claim to have penetrated to the starting point of the centre of the spiral of all knowledge... being with the Guru Swamiji is in another realm of experience entirely. DDR sits back in his chair and sighs like a lover; to be with Swamiji is to know, however briefly, that the truth behind things is peace in the present tense.

There is only one fly in the ointment. A white man was abused by the police in one of his hotels; he launched himself from a window on the seventh floor, and died in the street below. Anyone who is serious about following the Guru Swamiji will, sooner or later, have to confront this little difficulty. For DDR, it is sooner.

* * *

He looks up at the two off-duty police officers standing respectfully in front of him as they stumble their way through an incomprehensible preamble. After a time he looks back down at the note that they had written to him:

Respected Sir,
We are friends and devotees of the new guru Swamiji. We wish to talk to you in confidence about important super-extra-special matter.

Sub-Inspector K.P. Murugesan
Constable S.P. Apumudali.

"...is when I knew he was guiding my journey from afar," Apu is saying.

"Guiding from afar?" DDR asks.

"Sir, I am ashamed to tell you my guilty action in full, what I did to Swamiji, but I have been going backwards and forwards and here and there and everywhere in my head, wondering what it all means, wondering how to confront Swamiji with my filthy black deeds, how to pay for the deed I did, and then I started to understand, Sir."

"Yes?"

"Yes."

"No – I mean, what is it that you started to understand?"

Apu puffs himself up in a kind of vicarious pride for Swami.

"That there is no need for me to tell Swamiji anything like this – he is already knowing, and guiding me towards correct resolution."

"What resolution?"

"Sir, I am not fully certain yet," Apu admits, "but I know Swamiji is leading me closer and closer to it. That is why I'm standing in front of you now."

"And the same with me Sir," Murugesan chips in. "I was not comfortable with my conduct in relation to the guru, and several times I am seeking him out and trying to tell him, but all the time he is knowing my situation better than myself, and is guiding me towards my decision in very best direction."

"But – what decision?" DDR asks

"I am not completely sure at this precise minute, Sir," Murugesan admits. "We are coming here today to talk to you about this..."

DDR rests back in his chair, twiddling the tips of his fingers together lightly, glancing from Apu to Murugesan and then back to Apu again. There is much he doesn't understand about this, and something he doesn't like. What has any of it got to do with him?

The three of them remain silent for a while, Murugesan and Apu standing in front of the desk uneasily, DDR looking up at them. At times Apu can't help flicking his glance towards the bloated hound marooned in its wheelbarrow next to D.D. Rajendran; and Bobby, as though to register a dirty protest at the arrival of these visitors who have distracted his master from tickling him, distends his jaws in a foul-smelling yawn, which triggers certain processes within, so that a small coil of excrement extrudes from his back passage at a slow and regular speed. DDR watches it – rather enviously – then shouts "Boy!" – and Bobby's boy runs in immediately, wraps up the turd in scraps of newspaper, cleans up the wheelbarrow, washes Bobby's bottom with an old rag and a plastic beaker of water, and exits. He feeds two TB-riddled parents by such skills. The policemen watch with a morbid fascination.

"But – I am just not understanding why you are coming to me to tell me all this," DDR says eventually, after the boy has disappeared.

Apu rubs at his chin, says "Yes Sir" and "Well Sir" and "The thing is Sir" and falls silent.

"It is about the white man, Sir," Murugesan offers, at last. "That is how this began, that is what connects us all, isn't it..."

A frown steals across DDR's forehead, narrowing his eyes. His heartbeat gets faster without him knowing why. "What about the white man? What has he got to do with anything?"

"Sir, this white man..." Murugesan hesitates – and yes, it is true that a seasoned observer of his moustache would detect the makings of a twitch – "...this white man, his unfortunate death was creating the problems for me, and for Apu, and also for you Sir, little bit..." No answer from DDR, who seems suspended between an admission and a denial, so Murugesan presses on. "Sir, we are feeling very anxious that we are risking your angry feelings, but this white man, this white man who fell on Swamiji on that fateful day, his unfortunate case is not just a matter of right and wrong and what-all – that is what I am coming to understand through my meditations on the guru Swamiji—"

For DDR, it had seemed as though the white man ceased to be a problem long ago, when the heat of the case cooled down and the authorities lost interest; since Swami became Swamiji, he has hardly thought about such ancient history, he has been absorbed in plans for the future. Are the repercussions of that white man plummeting from his second-worst hotel still reverberating?

"I am not sure how or why," Murugesan is saying, when DDR shows no signs of replying, "but right from the beginning I was seeing something I was not understanding about Swamiji and this white fellow, Sir. When Swamiji was Swami, I just hoped it was all a damn-fool business, I couldn't understand why my old friend and colleague was becoming troublemaker to us all for the sake of this dead foreigner. But now, when we know that Swami became Swamiji, well, if you think about it, and if you know what we know..." – he gestures at Apu and himself – "...then—"

"Then what, Sub-Inspector?" DDR asks, although he wishes he could be spared the information. "What do you know?"

"Sir, Swami started becoming Swamiji not when he died, but when the white man fell on him. There is some special link, sir. We thought we were trying to stop him from troublesome investigations – but we were hindering him from his spiritual path. Death of white man and death of Swami linked together in cosmic pattern," Murugesan says, as Apu nods with conviction. "Everything is in the pattern!"

"But – get to the point!" DDR blurts, exasperated. "What do you want? Twenty minutes you two have stood in front of this desk and mumbled about this and that."

"Yes Sir."

"Most sorry Sir."

"Just tell me what you want from me!"

"Sir, you see, when we were all trying to stop Swami from poking about in these matters, Apu is taking very bad and specially extra-worse step. Brother, tell Mr Rajendran..."

Apu's eyes start watering, and a perfect tear tops the rim of his left eyelid, races down his cheek, hangs around on his chin for a few moments. It drops onto his left shoe.

"I killed the white man and I killed Swamiji too, God be forgiving me, Sir."

"You? You killed Swamiji? How did... how did you kill Swamiji? Swamiji had heart attack in the street!" DDR says, appealing to Murugesan.

"He is giving him a push and warning him off the white-man case," Murugesan explains. "He is pushing him to the ground and setting off the heart attack."

"Oh my—"

"Yes Sir," Murugesan agrees, putting an arm around the snivelling Apu, while DDR gazes at the younger man as though he's a leper. "But Sir, everything is in the pattern, in one way Apu is killing Swami, but in another..." – a series of nods and grimaces and unusual facial expressions precede Murugesan's thesis – "...if Swami hadn't died, then Swamiji wouldn't live. Because of this, we have talked and talked, Sir. We have examined everything that has happened, every way in which Swamiji is teaching us, and we are believing he is guiding us to see for ourselves that the number-one very best, most noble action is to make amends, Sir – but if we make amends, Sir, we are dragging in everyone involved in the abuse and cover-up, small and large. Like you, Sir. That is the difficulty."

DDR's head sinks lower over his chest, and his back hunches. So that is what this is about. He has never willingly faced up to a bad deed and paid the price. Is this what the guru wants of him?

6

In an obscure side street off Periyar Road in Mullaipuram, in the permanent shadow of the 120-year-old Church of St Xavier and St Sebastian, sandwiched between a failing travel agency that organizes temple pilgrimages to Chidambaram, Srirangam, Kumbakonam and Thiruvaiyaru, and a DVD-rental store that only opens when the owner's psoriasis is easing up, lies a portal into a strange world beyond Amma's comprehension. It is called Anjaneya's International Internettings.

Anjaneya's International Internettings comprises one super-tiny room divided into eight cubicles, each cubicle containing one chair, one table and one computer terminal. The tap-tap of fingers on battered keyboards goes on until late at night. Street dust and bidi stubs litter the corners of the room, fraying posters hang off the walls, and a naked light bulb hangs down at waist level. It is not one of the more popular or well-run Internet cafés in Mullaipuram, with its slow connection speeds, dreadful coffee and virus-afflicted machines, but it is a wise choice of Pushpa's to bring her mother to this out-of-the-way place. The task they are about to undertake is of a delicate nature.

Elements of Mullaipuram are awash with talk that Jodhi has been gallivanting around in jeans with boys; yes, in jeans and in who knows what else – tight

195

T-shirts, diaphanous *chudidhars* – for there is no limit to the depravity people require in others when they are not getting enough of it for themselves. Some people are on the brink of going into open season on Jodhi's sluttish failings, so thank God that Amma is unaware of the worst gossip doing the rounds. Nevertheless, a fraction of those preposterous whisperings have reach-ed her ears. She has been informed that Jodhi, despite ongoing marriage negotiations with her peerless boy, has advertised herself without her parents' consent on a matrimonial matchmaking site on the Internet.

Furtive youths peer over the tops of their scruffy par-titions as the two women enter the Internet shop; left hands are slowly withdrawn from below the table line, and right hands click on mouse buttons with some alacrity. Pushpa grabs a spare chair from an unused cubicle and sets it down for her mother. For the first time in her life, Amma sits down in front of that mysterious inanimate god of modern life, the computer. She is po-faced and solemn, like a child in front of a doctor. She watches blankly as Pushpa searches for Indian matrimonial sites.

"What are you doing?" Amma complains. "Just look in the computer and see if it has Jodhi inside."

"Amma, this is number-one Tamil matrimonial site, we'll try this one first."

Amma watches, still bewildered, as Pushpa starts searching on www.tamilbrides.co.in.

"What are you doing, Daughter?"

"Amma, be patient, I am putting in correct age and height range and weight range and location and education details of Jodhi, then if she is there she will appear on screen."

"Ayyo-yo!" Amma exclaims, as a column of earnest faces appears in front of her. "Look at all these girls! What are their parents thinking of, letting them be displayed like fillets of fish on a slab! As if a computer can find a good boy!"

"It is just the modern way, Amma."

"It is the job of the parents and the matchmaker."

"Now the computer is the matchmaker."

Pushpa scrolls down a page of photographs and short excerpts from written profiles, and Amma can't help locking on to the write-ups.

22 years, 5'2", 46 kg, wheatish complexion, slim, M.Sc. Marketing, Brahmin, caste no bar—

"Desperate," Amma sniffs.

22 years, 5'0", 48 kg, slim, very attractive, NI. Tech Services, divorced, marriage annulled on grounds of groom unable to consummate—

"Ha!" Amma says.

22 years, 5'1", pleasant-looking, 75 kg—

"Water buffalo," Amma points out.

For nearly an hour they sit hunched over the keyboard in Anjaneya's International Internettings, scouring www.southindiamatrimonials.co.in and www.vanniyar-mates.co.in and www.wife-to-go.com, but their chances of finding Jodhi here are about same as their chances of stumbling across her in the street in a pair of jeans – which is to say, on the slim side.

* * *

Anyone with a background in diagnostic medicine may be wondering if Amma suffers from NSwF syndrome, a degenerative brain condition affecting the synapses and neuronal pathways. The full medical term for this syndrome is No Smoke without Fire. We can see the debilitating effects of this illness in Amma right now: her failure to find any evidence that Jodhi is advertising herself on the Internet has no bearing whatsoever on her fears that Jodhi might be doing so. Only if Amma had stumbled across a website called www.jodhi-not-up-for-grabs.com, complete with cutting-edge Flash presentation of her eldest daughter renouncing denim and declaring her undying commitment to Mohan, would the symptoms of her NSwF have found relief at this time. A fruitless hour in Anjaneya's International Internettings has only exacerbated her anxieties, and she returns home to Number 14/B on the warpath, trailing Pushpa behind her. In one way or another, the storm is about to break.

"Jodhi!" she cries, bursting through the door, "Jodhi? Jodhi! *Jodhi?! Jodhi!*"

Jodhi and Leela, having come to an uneasy truce about the slap, are in the bedroom watching TV together; they look at each other, hearts sinking. From the timbre, volume and quantity of Amma's "Jodhi"s it is immediately clear that their mother is in one of her least reasonable, most excitable moods.

Jodhi emerges from the bedroom, Leela behind her. Pushpa comes and stands by them, and the three girls watch Amma jostling around the little bungalow as she deposits her plastic shopping bag here and her silk money purse there and her bad mood in every place. At last she turns around, and at the highest pitch of frustration, she's off:

"Just tell me, Daughter, is it true?"

"Amma?"

"Don't Amma your Amma, just tell me now, is it true what they are saying?"

"Amma, what are they saying?"

"Jodhi, you know what they are saying!"

"No Amma!"

Amma glares at her eldest.

"You two," she tells Pushpa and Leela, without looking at them, "go and sit at the front!"

The younger girls troop the three yards to the verandah, shutting the front door behind them; this is not so much to afford privacy to Amma and Jodhi, which would be impossible given the size of the bungalow and the loudness at which Amma can shout, but merely to lower the volume a little. Pushpa sits down on the top step, sighing heavily.

"This is all your fault, you dummy," she says.

Leela doesn't reply. She knows that Pushpa is right. She sits down next to Pushpa, and they both gaze at the nearby bustling road, where India is getting on with being itself. An egg-seller on a bicycle is passing by, pulling off his ordinary everyday miracle, riding slowly down the street with a five-feet-high stack of six-by-six egg cartons wobbling on the back of the bike. On a moment-by-moment basis he must deal with the anarchic traffic, the treacherous road, the reckless pedestrians, and so he sways left and right minutely in the small moving arena of space that is granted him on the busy street, he slows down and speeds up fractionally, adjusting and compensating, forever modulating, keeping the precarious swaying stack on a vertical axis even when the bike is not. The girls' eyes lock onto him as the most interesting spectacle available, and follow him as he progresses down the street.

"How is he doing that?" Pushpa sighs, as if this unheralded feat of balancing symbolizes a difficult life sensibly negotiated, all pitfalls and traps avoided with high skill and wisdom.

They watch him turn a corner – where, unknown to them, a feverish cow with an infected foot makes a sudden lurch into his path, and for the first time in several years he goes crashing to the ground with his eggs, all 900 of them, most of which smash. Within minutes, a medium-sized crowd is watching a pack of stray dogs snapping and snaffling over a mud of raw egg and road dust, as a weeping egg-seller cycles away with a stubby stack of only 200 eggs on the back of his bicycle.

Inside Number 14/B, things are hotting up too.

"Look me in both eyes, you have advertised yourself on internetting marriage site, haven't you!" Amma is barking at Jodhi; Jodhi is so amazed by this accusation that she can't reply immediately. "Well?!" Amma raps.

"No Amma! Of course not! *Who* is telling this rubbish!? *Why* are you believing it?!"

Amma is used to being at least slightly right sometimes, even when she's notably wrong; but Jodhi's reaction is so clear and bold that even the most limbic reaches of her unreasonableness take a heavy hit. It is only many years' experience in maintaining her position in the face of all opposition, logic and justice that help her to limp on for a little while longer.

"A perfect boy! Ready and waiting! Parents not even bothered about dowry any more! And this is all because of my hard work, Daughter! And instead of thanks all I am getting is jeans and dirty Internet doings and gossip all round the town!"

"Amma, please, what are you *talking* about?"

"What everyone is talking about, that is what I am talking about!"

"Amma, please, stop believing every gossip and tittle-tattle you hear!"

"How will I marry my five other daughters if my first daughter disgraces us all in her jeans?!" Amma continues, gamely, like a card-player with a weak hand going for an all-or-nothing bluff.

"How will I survive another day if my mother keeps treating me like this!" Jodhi complains, with some feeling. "Amma, I am only ever doing what you and Appa are telling me to do!"

They stare at each other, sharing the horror of a good Indian daughter and a loving Indian mother reduced to a bitter stand-off. Amma's chin and lower lip start to tremble, followed shortly afterwards by Jodhi's lower lip and chin, and within a few seconds they are both weeping on either side of the void between them, not knowing what to do. Jodhi turns and runs into the kitchen and out into the backyard.

"Daughter," Amma mouths helplessly and soundlessly, "I'm sorry, please forgive."

Here is Leela, being pushed into the room by Pushpa at the open door. Leela herself is not looking too good at the moment in the trembling-chin and lower-lip department of life, now that she is finally going to admit to Amma that she has been cobbling up a whole heap of rubbish about Jodhi, and that it is all her fault.

* * *

The retired tax collector who built Highlands died of a very bad mood in 1947, mainly to register his fervent disapproval of Indian Independence. Little of his thirty years' occupancy remains. Successive Indian owners of Highlands have stripped the cottage of its colonial past. One of them even installed a puja room complete with bronze statues of four notable gods, which is exactly the kind of thing that would have made the tax collector very angry indeed. But at least there is something from the tax collector's days that has survived. It is the desk that Swami is sitting at. It is a large sloping desk, with deep drawers and two long-empty inkwell holders, and it stands on the verandah of Highlands, its rich veneer in tatters, disintegrating. The tax collector used to write letters of indignation on it, and keep his private papers in the drawers, and conceal a small collection of ethnic erotica – of a distinctive Victorian stamp, and of a mostly pseudo-scientific character – in a secret internal chamber.

It is 10 a.m. The sky is clear. The jungle is pristine after an overnight rain, and langur monkeys are gambolling under the verandah and in the long-abandoned gardens of Highlands, sizing up a raid on the kitchen where Kamala is preparing *parotas* and a potato kurma. Swami sits on the verandah, Amma's latest letter on the desk in front of him, reading, pausing, reading, pausing, watching the monkeys, reading, pausing. He is not a natural writer of letters, and as for Amma, who is a burst waterpipe of words in any medium, she wields a pen with all the control of a baboon using a fire-hose – but letters are all they have for as long as he is in Thendraloor.

Swami has written to Amma that he is okay to go back to Mullaipuram for the last couple of weeks of the hot, and has mentioned to her that sometimes he wonders if things are getting out of hand on the guru side of things – but Amma is adamant that he is a first-class very best gem of a guru, and has told him so repeatedly in her letters. And today, it is true, there is a kind of spiritual afterglow about him on account of a now unremembered incident from early in the morning. The white man came to him. Swami had been getting up after a rest, and Kamala was about to help him wash, when the man just came walking into the room with a calm smile on his face, and sat down in a chair. Swami, still unwashed as he was, had sat down next to him. They didn't speak out loud, they just accessed a few aspects of each other – it's less effort like that. *You're in two places*, the white man had suggested. *I never think about it*, Swami had replied. The white man didn't respond. *They suffer more than they need to*, he had observed at some point. Shortly afterwards he got up and left, and Swami went to the kitchen to find Kamala.

"Appa, half an hour you are sitting there hardly blinking, I was frightened."

But Swami had already forgotten. He has lost that human urge to cling on to anything. People, however, are clinging on to him. No matter how much they seem to benefit from his calmness when they are with him – in the hour of silence, during informal sessions – they are desperate to have more of him when he is not there. They hope he can solve their practical problems, they pray that he'll cure their sick relatives, they arrive at Highlands at all hours imploring his blessings, worshipping him, breaking down...

It's always like this – isn't it? – when some poor devil gets a fistful of the spiritual rammed into his life. Everyone else wants it too, and in their desperation to get it they trample dirt all over its essence – because that essence is far simpler than they can see, and much more limited than they are prepared to accept. Swami, for sure, does not possess the incredible powers that people impute to him. For example, he lacks the basic supernatural skills claimed by even the most run-of-the-mill charlatan, and so remains unaware that the tax collector's hidden cache of erotica is only eighteen inches away from the tip of his middle finger, which is currently tracing Amma's anarchic grammar and semantics in this morning's letter. He would hardly know what to make of that tight bundle of dodgy nineteenth-century sepia images, tied up in scraps of jute sacking, undisturbed for sixty years – those front views and back views and side views of bemused four-foot-six tribal women forced to stand naked next to a measuring rod held by a big white hairy hand amputated by the edge of the photograph. Amma's letter – fifteen pages long and rather light on content – is more than amazing enough.

...husband definately you are the guru you are coming back from the death isnt it you are dying and living husband and the comon people are beliving in you you dont want to diserpoint the people and anyway husband fourgive me but whatever and all you are thinking on this matter is

not importent you are simple pure guru of course you are
humble and thinking you are not the god but it doesunt
matter because every one is knowing you are the god they
are feeling it imedeeatly in your presense and bowing down
to you because they feel the god in you...

Maybe she's half-right. Maybe she's half-wrong. But
which half is right, and which half is wrong? Swami
doesn't know.

...and look at D.D. Rajendran husband he is spending the
lifetime cheating bullying swindling he is caring only for the
fat wallet and the bulging bank and the dirty doings and
then he is incountering you and what is he doing I will tell
you what he is doing he is becoming best reformed caracter he
is giving up filthey cheating ways and devoting himself to the
good works isnt it husband and all Mullaipuram is talking
about this and saying how can this happen and they are
ansering that it is you the guru who is making this happen
because DDR is feeling your aura every body is feeling your
aura every body is knowing that DDR is devoting himself to
you now husband he is making very big plans and now he
is paying educashun fees of all dauters husband so what are
you thinking of when you say you are not sure if you are the
guru of course you are the guru you must be the guru or why
else would DDR be doing all this husband...

Swami's default condition these days is passive
– more than likely, god lies in the reception and not
in the commission – but when he thinks at all about
DDR's activities, then he feels ambiguous. Five times
already the fellow has been visiting, with a legion of
retainers, and once with the owner of a tea plantation
who – unknown to Swami – was excited about making
a big donation towards DDR's plans for an ashram, but
understandably wanted to sample the new guru's aura
first of all, just like he did with tea. But Swami is not so
sure about this idea of an ashram. What about Number
14/B and his ordinary life?

...and what about the dauters husband they were in number one worst posishun no dowries no chance no good boys no anything husband and during very first pre-engagemunt meeting white man is falling on your head in extra special spirichual way and in second pre-engagemunt meeting DDR is taking you away for the higher reasons and then you are dying and then you are walking with God and then you are living and before I know it parents of Mohan practiculy giving us dowry for Jodhi now what is this husband if not power of your godlyness now we have no dowry worries with or without very fastest scooters what is that husband if not a miracul so now we are knowing why we had no sons husband so try to realize your humble guru nature makes you too modest but whatever you say or do the people are knowing you are the guru and so do I husband I am proudest wife in all Mullaipuram I never thought that when you died it would be very best thing that ever happened to me...

At page eleven of Amma's letter – which is remarkably similar to page one and page four, and page ten – Swami is interrupted by a wailing; there is some kind of commotion at the front door of Highlands. He gets up from the desk and limps slowly into the cottage, as Kamala goes rushing to the front to peer out of the window.

"Appa, it is a woman with a baby bundle, and there is a man beating the earth. They look like tribals."

Swami sighs. Another stillborn child. How can I make a dead baby live, he asks himself? Surely I am not this god they say I am. I don't even remember walking with God. I am just a man who is no longer in despair.

7

Perhaps Leela's guilty conscience has cracked just in time, because today a pained Mr and Mrs P are visiting Number 14/B, bringing with them a panoply of aggrieved expressions, half-hidden hurts, multifarious doubts, and some second-best-quality Sri Lankan tea. At first Amma is not very worried. If they had visited yesterday – before Leela had confessed to her every assault on truth's citadel, from her lessermost random dabblings to her utmost inspired gossip-mongering, then who knows how Amma might have handled this difficult encounter? Even a woman who can draw on all the authority that comes with being the wife of the Guru Swamiji might have struggled for equanimity in such circumstances. But now, for the first time in weeks, Amma feels as though she has an understanding of the Jodhi situation. She might be exhausted after a night of recriminations and tears with her youngest and eldest daughters, she might be feeling hard-done-by because of the obstacles placed in her path, but at last she feels as though she is in control: Leela has admitted to all her mischief, and Jodhi has unambiguously reaffirmed that her daughterly duty is to marry the person whom Amma and Appa deem appropriate.

The conversation in the living area of Number 14/B has been delicate but substantive in its treatment of the jeans, and has now come to a halt. Mr P sips at his tea in a parsimonious fashion, and smoothes down his moustache with his free hand, gazing glumly at the cement floor of the bungalow, at the bright but worn home-made mats – Kamala's handiwork. Mrs P is not interested in the floor. For some reason, she has taken the opposite tack, and with her head thrown back is earnestly scrutinizing everything above her, taking in the curious exposed rafters of this old British-built house. Amma gazes with some appreciation at the way those three chins of hers arrange themselves on the exposed neck, like fleshy garlands.

"Well well," Amma says, sighing; she thinks she is home and dry. "So many sorries and apologies and what-all," she offers, so that Mr and Mrs P cease their mysterious musings and return their attention to her; "all this confusion and the many gossipings, one day we will all be laughing!" she trills gaily. "Please be understanding," she sums up, "Leela is a little girl, she is not knowing all these serious consequences of getting carried away with silly stories!"

Why do Mr and Mrs P seem so strangely unconvinced? Mr P has shunted his buttocks to the edge of his white plastic chair, and sits with his elbows on his knees and with his chin on his fingertips, nodding non-committally at Amma's reassurances. Mrs P, who has no wish to challenge the fundamental constraints of her personal physics by shunting her buttocks towards any perilous edges, is conveying her unease by planting both forearms on the armrests, and by failing to partake of a plate of fried banana wafers that is well within range.

"You see," says Mr P at last – scratching his nose, tweaking his ear, smoothing his moustache, slicking back his hair, pursing his lips, crinkling up his eyes, raising his eyebrows apologetically, lowering his eyebrows decisively, raising them again rather less decisively – "you see, the thing is – Madam, this is very delicate matter, please be forgiving me but – the thing is, what it is necessary to say, at this point in time, at this juncture, at this moment..."

Hasn't he molested his own body enough? But look at him, he is still scratching and tweaking and pinching and rubbing things in embarrassment.

"Dowry situation?" Amma asks, puzzled.

"No no no, this is not about dowry, let us not be worrying about dowry situation."

"Dowry situation is now excellent," Amma boasts – choose your scooter, she is tempted to say. She knows and they know that an alliance with a family that is now intimate with D.D. Rajendran is not to be sniffed at.

"Not about the dowry," Mr P repeats.

Amma is frowning now, and no longer feeling quite as serene as she did ten minutes ago. She finds herself in one of those rare situations in her life when she cannot even hazard a guess as to what to think – so she remains silent, looking between the husband and wife. Mr P smoothes his moustache for the umpteenth time and glances at his wife, who drums her fingers softly on the armrests and glances at her husband, who breaks into an ominous and apologetic smile and glances out of the window, and—

Just as he is about to come out with it – whatever the damn thing might be – the front door opens and Jodhi walks in from her day at college.

"Oh – greetings Sir, greetings Madam!" she exclaims, in about as excellent an imitation of pleasure as could be hoped for from a woman who is facing marriage to their middle son. "How are you?" She looks around the room apprehensively, as though Mohan might spring up from somewhere at any moment and identify a goat.

"Hello Jodhi," says Mrs P awkwardly.

"Returning from college, is it?" Mr P says; he has come out in a sweat.

"Returning from college, yes..."

Jodhi looks at these three middle-aged faces and understands that her future is on the line; but during the night she has resigned herself to the worst the future can hurl at her.

"Daughter, while we are talking about this and that, take some money and go and buy the vegetables."

"Yes Amma."

Jodhi goes into the bedroom to deposit her books, comes back into the living area, and with a degree of self-consciousness so acute that it threatens to overwhelm her ability to walk, she finds Amma's purse on the shelf, extracts thirty rupees, goes into the kitchen and gets the shopping bag. Mr and Mrs P watch her.

"I'll go and come back," Jodhi says, almost inaudibly.

"Yes, go and come back," Mr P says in a kindly way, and turns back to Amma as the front door clicks shut.

Poor Mr P – now he has to go through his repertoire of nervous gestures and aborted gambits from the beginning, which is a time-consuming procedure. Amma is thoroughly on edge by the time he has scratched the stubble under his chin for the very last time and is ready at last to spill the beans.

"We are hearing everything you are telling us, the jeans, the Internet, the gossip, the dear little sister creating troubles, yes yes, the naughty little monkey..."

"Yes, that is not the problem," Mrs P chips in.

"There has been all this gossip, that is so, but we can see Jodhi is a good girl, it is not as though we are thinking she is doing any bad thing..."

Amma smoothes her sari down over her thighs.

"...but the thing is, she is not seeming so very enthusiastic," Mr P points out.

"Not 100% keen," Mrs P suggests.

"Almost as though," Mr P says slowly, "almost as though she is not liking Mohan."

Amma rocks back in her seat in an approximation of horror at this amazing allegation.

"Not liking Mohan? Not liking Mohan?" Her hands are flailing up, in the manner of a woman flabbergasted that such a trifling impediment could be the source of all this bother; after all, how could anyone not like a boy genius who is fully expected to go straight to the top of the Indian IT sector? "Let us not be worried by this – yes yes, of course she is liking Mohan, who could not like your splendid son!"

"She is seeming little bit... reserved," Mrs P says delicately.

"Yes yes, she is little bit reserved, this is the young girls for you, of course they are little bit shy, who would want it any other way?! When I was introduced to my husband first few times, oh!" exclaims Amma, and she laughs with a desperate gaiety, fingering the edge of her sari anxiously – but curiously fails to develop her theme, mainly because when she was introduced to Swami the first few times, and saw his proud gaze and bristling moustache and ceremonial police cadet uniform, she had been subject to such disturbing bodily sensations that she had nearly fainted.

Mr P's shoulders rise and fall heavily. This is not proving easy. He had hoped that Amma would meet them halfway in facing up to the problem, but she is proving intractable. What is he supposed to do now? There is scarcely a protuberant aspect of his corporal matter that he has not tweaked, pinched, stroked, patted, tapped, rubbed, fondled and pawed; but at last he brings his hands in front of him, extending the thumbs towards each other; he connects the two tips of his thumbs together, and gazes at the connection as though it might short-circuit the impasse.

Amma's chest is heaving up and down. She senses that the parents of the boy have something terrible to say, that even now they are wheeling its monstrous engines out into open view. She swallows. She can hear crows squabbling on the red tile roof above her, cawing and flapping, and from somewhere outside she can hear children chanting and squealing as some adult carries them around like gunny sacks, playing the same game that she had played as a child:

"Does anybody want to buy my salt?
Does anybody want to buy my salt?"

"You see, Mohan is worried..." Mr P says.

"Yes?" Amma says. "What are these worries of Mohan?"

"I am very sorry for my frankness, please do not be misunderstanding me, I have best interests of both the young people at heart, but he is worried..." – the thumbs break apart, waggle in circles, cease waggling, connect together again – "...that she is having the sweet feelings for another boy somewhere, somehow."

There, it is out at last, and all three of them can look at it – that very shocking possibility – with all the awe it can command.

"Oh!" says Amma, dismayed.

You could argue that this suggestion is not fundamentally different to her own anxieties until a few hours ago; you could claim that it is untrue; if you combine a modern outlook with a forgiving nature, then you might be tempted to say "so what" even if it is true – but wherever you stand in this matter, you cannot fail to appreciate how shameful it is to have the father of the boy touch his two big fat thumbs together in your own house and come out with it.

"Oh! That is... ayyo-yo-yo!"

"Forgiving me, please, I do not like to say this, but this is the impression Mohan is getting, so what can we do?" Mr P pleads. "We must make our enquiries."

"My Jodhi," Amma gasps, "eldest daughter of Guru Swamiji, and this, and this, and that is how you, and this is how I..."

Amma sits up straight in her seat, lowers her brow, juts out her lower lip pugnaciously and assumes all the dignity that the forty-odd years of life's battering have granted her, all the presence that her seventy-odd kilos of matter can afford her, and all the outrage she can chisel out of every available nook and cranny of her motherhood.

"Jodhi is best daughter in Mullaipuram, but if she is not good enough for you—" she bluffs.

At this moment, the best daughter in Mullaipuram returns from the market with her shopping bag of vegetables.

"Tell them," Amma commands her at once, "tell them that you are a dutiful daughter!"

"Amma?" Jodhi takes in the scene at once, sees that there has been a confrontation, sees that her mother is on the warpath, and her heart sinks; "Amma, let us be calm, I shall be making some tea..."

"Tell them! Tell them you are happy to marry Mohan – come, speak."

Jodhi looks at all three of them – the angered, anxious face of her mother, the half aggrieved, half apologetic expressions of Mr and Mrs P. All the lights illuminating the deep and hopeful chambers of her interior life start to go out.

"Yes Amma."

"There!" Amma declaims in bitter triumph. "Do you see? Jodhi, tell them you are the kind of girl who obeys your Appa and Amma in all things, great and small!"

"Amma..." Jodhi protests, embarrassed, "let us not become overexcited with our guests..."

"Tell them!"

Jodhi sighs. Her shoulders sag.

"Yes Amma. I am doing whatever my parents are telling me to do. I know you will make best decisions for me."

"You see?" Amma says to Mr and Mrs P, "you see? She is dutiful girl. Tell them, tell them you will marry Mohan!"

"Yes Amma, that is what has been decided," Jodhi replies, quietly and with great dignity, and she walks into the kitchen.

"You see?" Amma says, almost taunting her visitors now. "Tell them you are not harbouring the wrong feelings for another boy!" she shouts after Jodhi.

Jodhi makes no reply to Amma's demand. She takes a bunch of coriander from the shopping bag and places it on the wooden chopping block, and tackles a few of the tiny flies that are zipping around the fragrance of it, splatting them between her palms. Next she empties a paper bag of brinjal onto a sheet of newspaper and starts sorting them by size.

"Jodhi, tell them that there are no feelings in your heart for another boy!" Amma commands once more.

In the kitchen, Jodhi's head seems to be getting lower; the base of it is sinking into the top of her neck. As for her neck, it is retracting into her shoulders. Her shoulders would diminish too, if they could. Jodhi does not answer the question, not this time, not next time, and not even in a few minutes, when Mr and Mrs P – still apologetic and remarkably polite, given the circumstances – leave Number 14/B harbouring the gravest doubts about the viability of the marriage.

When Amma – calling from the verandah – fails to lure them back with promises about her husband's powers in this affair, she goes back inside and confronts Jodhi. They are both in tears. But Jodhi refuses to confirm or deny that she harbours feelings for another boy. She chooses not to respond to even the wildest and most destructive guesses at the putative boy's identity, and won't be bullied, provoked or tricked into discussing any aspect of the marriage with Amma.

"I will do what I am told," is her only comment.

8

D.D. Rajendran, Murugesan and Apu are sitting together in a dusty corner of the Mariamman Temple complex on Kamarajar Salai, in the shade afforded by a crumbling wall and a coconut tree. They are cross-legged on a low platform, not far from a woman sleeping on the bare stone with her child, and a stray dog that whimpers as it dreams. They bear ash on their foreheads, and they are bare-chested. They have just been through a super-deluxe, hour-long, 8,000-rupees purification ritual presided over by an old temple priest to the rhythm of kettle drums, as ululating women – bearing bunches of neem leaves in both hands, their long black hair soaking wet and their bodies smeared all over with turmeric paste – howled "Mahamayee! Maariaathaa!"

Other temple-goers who are engaging in their everyday temple life – clanging the bell as they enter, circling the inner sanctum, catching up with the gods – look across at the men curiously; what is going on with DDR now, they wonder. Why is he with those fellows in ritual clothes? Some of these onlookers settle down to watch, squatting down on their haunches under the base of one of the gopurams, or sitting on rocks between the pillars. And a reporter with the local rag, having taken some photographs discreetly, goes into the temple in search of an insider who will tell him what DDR has been doing here. Tomorrow a garbled account of spiritual regeneration, expensive Vedic rites and personal sacrifices will be on page two of the *Mullaipuram Murasu.*

Apu's chest is broad and smooth and muscled; Murugesan's chest is broad and hairy and strong and running to fat; and there is DDR's chest, which lies beneath sloping shoulders – the lightly haired, slack-toned, flab-layered pigeon-chest of a thin man gone to seed. He hunches over his stomach, round-backed, his slack man breasts quivering when he shifts position. His dark-brown nipples droop down and almost touch the pot belly lying in the trough of his lungi like a deflated football in a hammock.

"Thank you sir," Apu says.

"Yes, thank you sir," Murugesan agrees.

"Call me Brother, Brothers."

"Yes sir."

"Yes sir."

The mood they share is a mix of comforting and spiritual aspects: relief, resolution, redemption, catharsis. There is a certain dreaminess there, too, and who could be surprised at that? Wouldn't you feel the same, if an emaciated elderly priest in a loincloth – the son of a priest descended from priests stretching back into antiquity – had rubbed sacred ash on your forehead in that holy place, while reciting mantras that were first composed over three thousand years ago? Mantras that have been memorized backwards from one generation to the next to ensure that not a word will ever change or be corrupted? Mantras that have been recited millions and millions of times over thousands of years to hundreds of long-dead kings and thousands of long-dead artists and numberless long-dead ordinary Hindus? These are not some johnny-come-lately rites, tacking and gybing according to the prevailing cultural winds.

The decision to undergo a ritual purification ceremony is no light matter for the three men. It is a solemn preparatory step in the process that lies ahead of them, for they are going to face up to what they have done. At an appropriate time, they are going to hand in written testaments to the authorities about their various transgressions in connection with the death of the white man and the subsequent cover-up, and accept with equanimity the consequences. DDR will probably be the least affected. If his political aspirations had remained intact, then his strenuous efforts to deflect attention away from Hotel Ambuli could have been damaging. But what does he care now for the dazzling machinations of politics?

It is a different story for the other two. Murugesan's efforts to cover up on behalf of his colleagues risk a severe penalty – a demotion at best, possibly dismissal. As for Apu, the loss of his job is a certainty, and the prospect of prison is likely.

"Swamiji will be excellently pleased with us," Murugesan suggests.

"When shall we tell the guru?" Apu asks.

"When he is coming back, when he is rested, then we are telling him," DDR answers authoritatively.

They fall into silence again. Small children are racing around in the courtyard, squabbling and bartering violence. A lame old woman limps through their chaos with extreme difficulty, leaning on a wooden staff, muttering to herself. The three men watch her painful progress absent-mindedly.

"Swamiji is already knowing our decision," Apu says blithely. "Only the detail he is not knowing."

No one replies.

"I wish he would come back," Apu sighs. "It could be months."

"Don't worry about that," DDR answers, "he'll be back in days."

"Sir?"

"Please be calling me Brother."

"Brother, sir."

"I am speaking to his wife this morning, she is writing him the letters nearly every day, he is not listening to her advice, he is insisting he is coming back to Mullaipuram, to a normal life. So when he has decided the day, I will bring him back in a mighty convoy."

"Thanks be to God!" Apu says. He can hardly wait to confess his transgressions before Swami. Indeed, he fervently longs to turn himself in to the authorities, he yearns to bring shame upon his entire family, he's desperate to go to a hellhole of a prison where the inmates will persecute him, he's ecstatic about leaving his wife and child to struggle on without him – it feels like the least he can do. Such is the power of faith.

"Normal life in Mullaipuram," Murugesan muses. "That is not going to happen, Mullaipuram will go crazy when he comes back."

DDR has a strange look about him; the power and the responsibility of his new life are settling upon him, like a richly embroidered ceremonial shawl being laid across his shoulders.

"The Guru Swamiji is humble," he declares, "and does not realize his own power. He changes lives. He is like the most precious jewel," DDR suggests, with an impressive rhetorical bent, "which is forever unaware of its own fathomless beauty and value..."

"Adaa-daa-daa," whispers Apu, in admiration of this inspired poetry.

"Such a jewel," DDR continues, "is in need of a powerful steward to secure its destiny, and such a steward is in need of faithful guards to protect the jewel from, from... from hanky-panky," DDR says. Perhaps his impressive rhetorical powers have let him down a little bit at this point, but he recovers his position soon enough. "Such a jewel – the jewel we have been blessed with – requires a magnificent setting in which everyone can admire its awe-inspiring beauty."

 DDR's eyes close, and he breathes in the ecstatic oxygen of the right-hand man of the Guru Swamiji – he is imagining the glorious spectacle that will occur when he brings Swami back to his hometown. Meanwhile, the eyes of Murugesan and Apu widen; they have seen, for the first time, where D.D. Rajendran is coming from.

* * *

A few days later, at 6.30 a.m. in the dusty bus station at Thendraloor, Swami is sitting by the street stalls in a red plastic chair offered by the manager of a one-booth STD-ISD telephone outlet. Kamala squats on her haunches, one protective hand lying across their two suitcases. A crowd of onlookers and passers-by and snivelling devotees is building up, impeding the buses that are arriving and departing every ten minutes. For Swami is leaving his refuge at Highlands. He is abandoning the daily hour of silence in the jungle clearing, he is leaving behind his solitary dawn meditations, he is removing himself from the hopes and dreams of the ruined, the broken-boned, the withered-limbed, the cancerous, the beaten, and all those trusting individuals who are forever assuming he is on the brink of interceding in their miserable destinies.

"Appa, any water, Appa?"

Swami grunts a no.

"I hope the bus isn't late, Appa, too many people are here."

Some people are shocked that a man whom they believe to be a living godhead intends to board a common bus to transport his corporeal matter back to Mullaipuram

– how can such a dirty workhorse as a municipal bus be an appropriate mount for someone who has walked with God? A few of the most credulous are puzzled as to why Swami is bothering to engage with the tiresome constraints of time and space at all – why doesn't he just project himself to Mullaipuram instantly, via a handy astral plane? And while the majority of people wouldn't go as far as that, most of them feel that a more impressive vehicle is required. They desire their guru to be worthy of their awe. After all, the very biggest contemporary holy men swan around in fleets of air-conditioned luxury cars while police keep the roads clear of other traffic; during processions they repose in huge paladins carried by teams of human donkeys, as lackeys fan them down with banana leaves; on long-distance trips they charter their own planes, or are flown around in private jets lent to them by murky industrialists. And so while the devotees are impressed by the humble simple lifestyle of their guru, they wouldn't mind witnessing dashes of extravagant splendour, too, to set off his praiseworthy humility. A facility to entertain paradoxes with equanimity has always been a signal feature of spiritual sensitivity at the highest levels.

"Appa, maybe we can sit somewhere private, this crowd is definitely in strange mood..."

Swami doesn't reply. He intends to sit here while the bus is not here, and get on the bus when the bus is here. What could be simpler than that? But it's true that something strange is in the air. The crowd would like to sit at Swami's feet and have the freedom to wallow in his proximity, but there is no room or opportunity to settle anywhere for long, buses would mow them down, and the early morning's regular travellers are milling around everywhere. So an unseemly pulsing throng is pushing here and there according to the arrival and departure of the buses, and with increasing frequency people are yelling warnings: "Give the guru room," and "Sisters, Brothers, don't crowd Guru Swamiji!"

Oh dear, this throng is not happy with the guru's undignified predicament. There are dark mutterings about D.D. Rajendran; everyone knows by now that he is the guru's fixer, surely he should have taken this matter in hand and ensured that the guru's dignity is not abused in this way? But they are wrong to hold DDR at fault. DDR fully intended to arrive at Highlands on the appropriate day with three silver Mercedes, a Toyota Land Cruiser and a battered van of heavies, each vehicle bearing resplendent flags and very loud horns and supremely arrogant drivers. He had hoped to escort the guru back to Mullaipuram in a triumphant high-speed convoy – up to forty miles an hour at times – of non-stop tooting, parping triumphalism. It is Swami who has jumped the gun, travelling home of his own volition several days before he had intimated, thereby cheating DDR and Mullaipuram and the world of the splendour they require.

Or has he? You see, it starts when the bus arrives. Once the driver and the conductor have overcome their amazement at seeing the new Guru Swamiji hobbling towards their battered old vehicle – he is orbited by a semi-hysterical retinue of devotees, who squabble over the two suitcases that are being passed overhead – they help Kamala to manhandle the great man up the three steep steps and inside. Swami sits down with his daughter on a seat two-thirds of the way down the bus. Then the driver gets back into his seat, a little discomfited, and confers with the conductor who is standing in the open doorway, also a little confused. For there are no other passengers climbing into the bus.

"Mullaipuram!" shouts the conductor. "Mullaipuram Mullaipuram Mullaipuram Mullaipurammmmmm!"

He has wads of differently coloured tickets wedged

between the fingers of his left hand, and a leather bag at his waist full of coins, and pockets stuffed with low-denomination notes; he has seventeen years of experience, he can conduct a bus like a maestro can conduct an orchestra, he can thread through a swaying jam-packed bus from one end to the other and sell the correct ticket to every passenger without missing anyone or forgetting who is owed some change and who is in debt. He is a supremely accomplished bus conductor, and furthermore, this bus goes via the rail link at Kodai Road, and so is the means by which people can travel on to the large cities of Madurai, Chennai, Coimbatore. Finally, there are at least one hundred people in and around Thendraloor who got up very early this morning with the intention of barging and fighting and abusing their way onto this bus, taking with them their baggage and their sacks of grain and their chickens and, in one case, a goat with three legs.

Despite all these important details and pressing contingencies, no one is getting on the bus.

"Mullaipurammmmmm!" shouts the conductor, desperately, scanning the crowd that is gathered by the bus. If one person clambered in, surely the rest would follow? But it's no good – no one wishes to be the first to put themselves on an equal footing with the guru.

"Give us another bus!" shouts a young man with a pencil-thin moustache.

"This is the Mullaipuram bus!" shouts the conductor, exasperated, "if you people want to go to Mullaipuram, get on the bus, and if you don't, then go to hell! Mullaipurammmmmmm!"

Meanwhile the driver has walked down the bus to speak to Swami.

"Guruji saar, they are not getting on the bus because of very greatest respect for you, what shall I do saar guruji?"

Swami looks at Kamala, exasperated, then looks out of the window and down at a knot of people who are standing in solemn reverence below his window.

"Appa is definitely wanting everyone to get on the bus," Kamala tells the driver, and Swami nods his approval.

"Yes guruji."

The driver tramps up to the front of the bus, and interrupts the conductor, who is still cursing people willy-nilly – "How can you have another bus, you monkeys?" the conductor is exclaiming, "there isn't another bus, can I just summon up another bus because you monkeys are wishing it?! This is the bus!" The conductor cocks his head to listen to the driver's urgent advice, then turns back to the crowd. "Mullaipuram! Guru Swamiji says it is your duty to get on this bus, this is the guru's official position, he is not wanting you to stand there refusing to get on the bus! Mullaipuram Mullaipuram Mullaipurammmmmmm!"

It's no good. No one will get on that bus – not when an aspect of the living godhead appears to be sitting in it, as plain as a spot on the end of your nose; not even when the station supervisor comes bustling over, and gets mobbed with voluble complaints. He waves his clipboard around as though that might help – perhaps it does, in some situations – and mops his brow with a big handkerchief, and is helpless in the face of these demands to conjure up a second bus that will tail the first bus respectfully all the way to Mullaipuram.

"What am I?" he is shouting rhetorically, "what am I? Am I instant-bus manufacturer? Am I Managing Director of Tata Buses Supernatural Inc., Instant Bus Department? What am I?!"

"You are lazy stupid son of a prostitute!" someone shouts – he is furious that the bus company has not thought to lay on a second bus, given that it is only fair and proper that the guru should take the first. A scuffle breaks out.

The driver of the bus has seen enough. He revs up the roaring belching beast under his command, and with the conductor still shouting "Mullaipuram, Mullaipurammmmmm!" the bus sets off.

"Swamijiiiii!"

"Gurujiiiiii!"

"Guru Swamijiiiiii!"

Devotees are running along with the bus, beating on the side panels as they say goodbye. The bus turns out of the station calamitously, pursued by loping supplicants. A lazing stray dog doesn't get out of the way quickly enough – it yelps as the vehicle runs over its tail, and bolts away shakily. The bus picks up speed. Swami and Kamala are watching out of the window, Swami with his now trademark one-handed *namaskaram*. Then he turns to face forwards, a glum look on his face.

What to do? If people would just leave him alone, perhaps he would live in the present tense more often than not, without a thought in his head, without a care in the world... If people would just leave him alone, perhaps he could perceive his moment-by-moment experience with full force, never identifying anything with a limiting name or cataloguing its components or comparing it to other experiences... Something has happened to Swami that makes him receptive at times to a wisdom, the kind that the religions usually ignore, the kind that is known as it happens and then let go, rather than the kind with objectives to be analysed and clawed for. It longs to exist in a vacuum, which is why its purchase is so tenuous.

But Swami can't think anything for long. Thinking bores him intensely. Coming back from death seems to have altered his hard-wiring so that he naturally avoids thought where possible. Important strategic decisions are facing him – how to deal with Jodhi's marriage, how to live with his family in his new guise as guru,

and how to deal with responsibilities and structures
that are assembling around him without his input or
interest or comprehension – but his default condition
is acceptance. He clutches Kamala's hand. They watch
the passing scenes as the Mullaipuram bus negotiates
the messy outskirts of Thendraloor, admiring a grassed
area adorned by sheets that have been washed in the
river by *Vannaan* folk and are now drying in the sun.
Soon he isn't looking at anything much. He is like a
sleeping, helpless baby in a cot, whose overpowering
appeal feeds every action and anxiety of those orbiting
that small life, who can't help loving it, though it is
selfish and unaware.

The vehicle roars down the roads, through the jungle
of the Western Ghats, round the crumbling hairpins
that the British supervised, bearing, for the first time in
the history of the 6.30 a.m. Thendraloor-Mullaipuram
bus – it is a very small and distinct part of history, that
no historian has yet covered – only two passengers.
The driver sits straight-backed and portentous as he
contemplates his good fortune in being a chariot-driver
to the gods; this is a story that he will relate for the rest
of his life. He is intent on the perfect bus drive. If he
can help it, this will be a bus drive to surpass all others
– he has never accelerated and decelerated so smoothly,
nor taken corners with such remarkable efficiency and
finesse. Admittedly he ran over a dog, but that was at the
beginning, and since then he's been superb. Sometimes
he finds himself imagining he is in a film, undertaking
an important mission on behalf of the great will of
the universe that is Brahma, and at those times he
unconsciously looks out of narrowed eyes with a certain
swaggering arrogance. But as for the conductor, alas, he
does not derive such satisfaction. For a whole hour he is
lost in an agony of indecision: should he ask the guru to
buy a ticket, because the guru would prefer to be treated

as everyone else is treated? Or should he not ask the guru to buy a ticket – because, after all, gurus shouldn't need tickets, should they?

9

In one way or another, it is said by many people of most faiths that God moves in mysterious ways. This is a truism that D.D. Rajendran has encountered several times as his involvement with the phenomenon that is the Guru Swamiji has grown. This morning, too, he finds that God has moved mysteriously. For while DDR and Bobby are enjoying their morning massage side by side, a flunkey apologetically interrupts them with the news that Swami has set off from Thendraloor, early, and in a bus...

"Oh, no, oh no—" DDR moans, springing up and pushing his masseuse away. "A bus! What is the guru playing at, Bobby? What will the people think of him if he sits on a clanking bus next to a farmer whose behind is pressed up against a sack of millet?!"

Bobby doesn't seem to know.

DDR leaps into damage-limitation mode, getting his fleet of magnificent vehicles on the road within half an hour, with him in the lead car in a foul temper. The impressive convoy sets out to meet the bus on the road, honking splenetically and almost without cease for the entire journey as though to express DDR's feelings. He intends to transfer Swami into a Mercedes as soon as is humanly possible, for it is surely unthinkable that Swami should arrive in Mullaipuram in a bus.

The convoy intercepts the bus just outside a village about three hours from Mullaipuram. It is then, greeting Swami respectfully, that DDR comprehends the godsend that he has been granted... The guru and the guru's daughter are *alone* in the bus! He travels in the vehicle of the common people, and yet he is apart from them! He is both humble and magnificent... What a guru this guru is, DDR rejoices, nobody could come up with a better guru than this one, everything this guru does is gold dust!

He soon has things organized. Swami and Kamala remain in the bus, the driver and the conductor have a substantial amount of money pressed into their palms – it is their proximity to the guru which explains this good fortune, they agree later – and the bus starts on the next leg of its soon-to-be-fabled journey, only now it follows an escort of three Mercedes-Benz and a Toyota Land Cruiser and a lurching van packed with sundry flunkeys and bodyguards. Has there ever been a public bus journey like this one throughout the whole of India, even in North India, where all kinds of peculiar things are reputed to occur? What a bus ride – and Swami and Kamala haven't even bought a ticket.

* * *

"Oh," Swami says, as they approach the bus station in Mullaipuram.

This is the first word he has spoken in days. It is the last word he says for a week or more. It is emitted somewhere in the middle of a groaning sigh. So it is not true that the guru never speaks, as some like to claim, but it's certainly true that he doesn't speak much; only the extent of the anarchy going on at Mullaipuram Bus Station can explain his garrulous moment.

Who knows, perhaps people will denounce him as a

fraud in a week or a year, but today half the town is here, ready to greet their illustrious son. They all agree that he who was once their highly regarded and overwhelmingly beloved and super-intensely cherished Sub-Inspector (retired) R.M. Swaminathan is now their much simpler, their far greater, their very own Swamiji... The convoy and the bus are barely crawling, the police can hardly maintain a clear path for them, and the people are in a state of wild excitement.

"Swamijiiiiii! Swamijiiiiii!"

He makes his one-handed *namaskaram* to all and sundry in a respectful but weary manner, as the crowds beat on the panels of the bus and hurl blossom and sweets through the bars of the open windows.

"Appa!" Kamala cries – she had no idea it would be like this.

It is fully five minutes before the driver succeeds in parking his bus in the allotted bay without running anyone over, and the police have to beat some people almost senseless to clear a path so that DDR is able to board the bus and escort Swami and Kamala outside and to the waiting Mercedes; on that short walk, Swami is garlanded more times than is physically supportable by a host of local worthies whom he hardly registers, from politicians and priests to businessmen and a film boss. Two of DDR's men have to carry the offerings for him.

Swami and Kamala and DDR sit in the back of the most accessorized Mercedes, DDR beaming. *Ayyo-yo-yo!* Kamala is marvelling; she has rarely been in an Ambassador taxi before, never mind a Mercedes. She is in a state of shock at all these people, and at all this adoration and anarchy for her father. Her hands go gliding over the luxurious fixtures of the car.

"Very good," DDR is saying, "crowd is massive! Swamiji guru, you are not realizing the effect you are having! You are all humility. If I do not help you, what would happen? They are loving you so much that they would tear your arms and legs off."

The convoy travels at a crawling pace through Mullai-puram's hysteria, while garlands rain down on the Mercedes like some kind of supernatural hailstorm. Swami looks out of the window, his attention pitched in a very curious place, a distant contrary place of amazement and apathy. Onlookers are shrieking and shouting and crying. He isn't really taking in what DDR is saying. He is resigned to his fate.

"...not possible to go to your little bungalow today," DDR is saying.

"But – we want to go home now," Kamala says, plain-tively.

"Daughter, I understand, but look out of the window, Daughter! It is like this at your dwelling place also, there are thousands of people swarming there waiting for the guru. If we arrive there it will be complete chaos, they will rip your Appa apart out of their overwhelming adoration for him, we will never get you inside, and if we get you in we will never keep all these people out."

"But – we – I want to see my Amma and my sisters," Kamala protests, her eyes filling with tears.

"Yes Daughter, I know, don't worry, you are very good girl, but your respected Amma and sisters are not there."

"Where are they? Saar, where are they? Appa, where is Amma?"

"Please don't be worried Daughter, no no, no need for tears!" DDR laughs uneasily, as Swami's slow and undemanding gaze sweeps from his anxious daughter to DDR, and then out towards the throng they are press-ing through. "Daughter, Swamiji, your family members will be waiting for you at my house. Really, I was having to rescue them. Please understand the practicalities of this business, you have been away, you don't know how Mullaipuram is now, it is crazy for the guru Swamiji.

Life is not the same any more for the guru and his family."

"Appa?" Kamala pleads. She wants to go home; she wants to lie on the cement floor with her head in Jodhi's lap as Amma scolds them from the kitchen; she wants to sew a furry pencil case and show it to her father, gaining the approbation of his slow smiling nod, while Leela says that the pencil case is the most horrible pencil case in Tamil Nadu, and possibly in the whole of South India. But what can Swami do? It is obvious – even to a fellow who can go hours on end without a single thought troubling his holy numbskull head – that Number 14/B is not a viable option.

"Everything I am arranging," DDR reassures them, "please don't be worrying yourselves about any detail, already I have arranged for your family to be picked up, probably they are at my house already. It is secluded secure place, you will all be safe and private there. Very big place, please don't be anxious, I will provide best accommodation! Maybe in a few days you can go to your little house," DDR lies blithely.

Regardless of whether Swami is an aspect of the godhead or not – there seem to be indicators on both sides of the premise – has it got to the point of no return, this perception that he is? Can he go back to his ordinary life one day, and be a nobody again, even a laughing stock? If he tried, who would believe him now?

* * *

Amma, Jodhi, Pushpa and Leela are waiting outside Mullaipuram Mansions with thirty or forty other people of much more impressive standing – friends and acquaintances of DDR's who have been arriving at his house throughout the last few hours in order to be in on the action.

"Here he is, my daughters," Amma whispers to her brood, resplendent in her finest sari, as the cars come sweeping up the dirt drive, "imagine how he must feel!" She blinks some tears away.

"Amma, definitely Appa is in one of the big cars?" Leela whispers fearfully; she just wants to see her daddy. Like Amma, she is whispering because she feels self-conscious in this fine place with all these VIPs braying and milling around. Jodhi and Pushpa hold her hand, all family tensions being put on hold for this special time and momentous occasion.

Servants leap to the back doors of all three Mercedes and open them. A variety of impressive-looking personages are getting out of the cars.

Out of the first Mercedes emerges D.D. Rajendran, in his off-white Nehru suit, smiling broadly – "Friends... the guru Swamiji, he is here!" – and some North Indian dignitary can't help shouting "Wah wah!" – and everyone strains forwards to see the guru come out. There is something of an anti-climax as DDR turns around and finds himself helping Kamala out after him. She looks around her, warily, and sees her three sisters surging to greet her. Amma remains behind, conscious of her dignity. The girls embrace.

"Come and see Amma," Jodhi whispers.

"But Appa—"

"I will help him out."

So while all eyes await the imminent discharge of Swami from the Mercedes, Kamala goes up to Amma and touches her feet in the traditional way, and then embraces her, crying, while nobody notices or cares.

Swami still sits in the back of the car, not shifting. His mind is in its own faraway world at this moment. An image has come to him from nowhere, and this delays him somewhat. It would perhaps be instructive to record the profundity of this experience in its every detail, alluding to the measureless interior landscapes he is traversing and the cosmic connections he is making – except that he is wondering whether he has left his pen in the desk at Highlands.

Such natural theatrical genius, D.D. Rajendran marvels, as he waits by the open door for the guru to emerge, and as the small crowd gets ever more anxious and anticipatory.

Then, *here are my daughters*, comes to Swami, and he sticks a foot out of the car.

The crowd has been hushed by the delay. It murmurs and sways. DDR stands back and gazes at his creation, as Jodhi tugs Swami upright.

Swami feels the love of his daughters flow over him like warm fragrant water. Jodhi, Pushpa and Leela touch his feet respectfully, then cling on to him, trying not to weep but not succeeding very well, as they steer him across to Amma, who by now is very much at the back of the crowd. As for that crowd, the murmuring and swaying starts to develop into muttering and exclaiming and adaa-daa-daaing somewhat, and a fair portion of its individual members are gearing up to manoeuvre themselves into advantageous spots, from where they will be able to access the guru; but at the same time, there is something fiercely powerful about the family reunion, and as Swami limps over to his wife, people hold back.

Before she looks at him, she touches his feet. It is only in the act of rising up that their gazes meet. *Here is my wife.* They hold each other's gaze for a long while, and Amma says "Husband" without hearing herself do it.

"Swamiji," DDR is now saying, at his side, "Swamiji, many distinguished visitors are coming here to welcome you."

It is not that Swami has much interest in being rude or in asserting his own autonomy; it is more that what happens is what happens. He puts his hand on Kamala's shoulder as usual, and Jodhi takes hold of his hanging arm tightly, and they shuffle round and begin walking into the house.

"Swamiji..."

Amma, with her arms around Pushpa and Leela, walks close behind them, head bowed.

"Swamiji," says DDR, following up, "I am thinking you will like very much to be introduced to K.S. Ramachandran – he is the Junior Fisheries Minister from Chennai; the Chief Minister has sent him here to see you."

The family go through the open front door, trailed by D.D. Rajendran and some of his anxious associates.

"Shall I escort you to reception room for meeting the many prestigious admirers?" DDR tries, increasingly dismayed that this event is not panning out as he had intended. Poor old DDR, he doesn't understand yet that non-cooperation is a vital bit of kit in Swami's feckless, lucky arsenal. Nobody wants a doormat for a guru.

"Saar," Kamala says, "Appa needs a wash and a nap now, please show us a family room."

Swami and his women abandon the notables to their own devices, even the Junior Fisheries Minister, who has been sent here by the Chief Minister to suss out how much mileage there may be in visiting the guru during these early days of his fame.

* * *

Swami is alone with his wife and daughters in one of the rooms DDR has allocated them. He sits in an armchair, with Leela sitting on his lap. Amma and the other girls are at his feet, cross-legged on the floor.

"Pushpa did not get very finest marks in geography test," Amma is saying.

"It was trick question Appa, about Narmada dam."

"Appa, you are slightly little bit less cuddly," Leela says.

"Leela, don't tell Appa he used to be fat."

"I don't want to be in this big house, I want to go home, when will we go home, Amma?"

"What are you talking about, Kamala? How can we take your beloved Appa to our little house? Police are guarding it to make sure the devotees aren't stripping it bare!"

"But we can't stay here for ever, Amma."

"Yes yes, God will do everything," Amma points out, gesturing towards her husband in a vaguely complacent fashion; she could get used to staying here for ever.

"When are they bringing more tea?" Jodhi complains. "They said they would be bringing the tea."

"Did you ever see a room like this one?" Pushpa says, gazing around; it is far larger then the bungalow. The huge bed at one end is twice as big as Number 14/B's kitchen, and all four of its legs once belonged to a fierce wild elephant shot by the Maharaja of Mysore in 1907, after the animal had been rendered safe, drunk and incontinent with three gallons of toddy. Rugs, hand-woven for years on end by the nimble fingers of infant Afghanis, are scattered over the marble floor. There are antique chests and teak cupboards, idols carved from sandalwood and ivory, and at the end where the family is gathered is a group of western-style armchairs and settees, and a vast eastern-style recliner. French windows lead to a private terrace.

"Appa, you are not smiling much, but you are feeling happy," Jodhi says.

How should Swami respond? His speech is no better than before he died, and his inclination to employ it has become almost non-existent. After coming back from death, he doesn't care any more if he can't express himself. People seem to understand this, no one seems to expect him to say anything anyway – in fact, the less he says, the more they are in awe of him. He is content to exist in peacefulness, with his family all around him, talking their nonsense.

After a while the family decides to take a nap. The elephant-limbed bed would fit four of them, the recliner would fit three, each of the two settees could take two sisters at least... They go to sleep on the floor, all together on a rug, Pushpa hanging on to a corner of Jodhi's *chudidhar*, Kamala's fingers trembling as she dreams inexplicably about playing the piano on top of a skyscraper in New York, Amma snorting cacophonously while she dribbles onto DDR's $14,000 antique rug, and Leela burbling her oddities – "give me a blue dust and I'll go," she announces.

At some point Swami wakes up without waking up, feeling Leela's knees twitching against the backs of his thighs. His wife and daughters are all around him, in their dream world. On the other side of the room the white man is asleep in the vast bed. *Oh, there you are,* goes Swami, and there is a *Yes I'm here* from the sleeping white man.

10

Maybe there is some cosmic logic playing out in the way that Swami has ended up at D.D. Rajendran's house. Although the banyan tree in the garden is neither so vast nor so ancient nor so steeped in God as the one in Chennai, in the grounds of the Theosophical Society, near the bank of the Adyar river, yet it is certainly very large and very old and full of God. Many many years ago, when Mullaipuram was little more than a stronghold next to a rock, and had no burgeoning brash developments pressing out in all directions, no soft-drinks factories (quarter-owned by DDR) sapping the water table and ruining the farmers thereabouts, this banyan tree belonged to nobody and everybody and all the villages around. Untold thousands of home-made religious rituals have been undertaken in the presence of its spirits. Murtis of Mariamman and many other local deities – some of them forgotten now – used to be lodged in the crevices of its trunk and in crannies of its gnarls, placed in the whorls at its base. Long-dead mothers brought their babies here to ask for protection and prosperity; long-dead priests performed pujas for worshippers who brought their upturned coconut halves, flames flickering within on a wick stuck into a daub of clarified butter.

About ten years ago in Mullaipuram there was sporadic outrage and a badly organized protest when the compound of DDR's half-built house mysteriously outgrew the limits indicated in the building plans, to incorporate this sacred tree of everybody and nobody into its grounds; a couple of people ended up in hospital after a terse dialogue with some of DDR's least verbally gifted associates. One of them sustained a broken cheekbone that didn't get set properly, and even now he is still known as Banyan Balu. But maybe the appropriation of this natural temple into the gardens of DDR's house is in the best long-term interests of the tree and of all the spirits it shelters. Mullaipuram's ever-growing outskirts are not noted for their sensitive touch; they blindly envelop everything in their way, whether beautiful or ugly, covering it all with low-rise blocks of flats, new roads, warehouses and factories and ostentatious company headquarters and stinking shanty towns. And maybe, as has been noted, there is a deeper logic in these things, beyond our easy comprehension – because, by and large, any serious guru requires a damn good tree.

As soon as Swami sets eyes on it, just before sunrise the following morning during a solitary amble, when his daughters are sleeping and his wife is preparing to do her morning darshan in a puja room, he feels a terrific charge of recognition and acceptance. This tree, it's been waiting for a man like him. He threads himself through its natural pillars – the branches of the banyan tree grow up and out and round and then down, down into the earth, where they root, so that the whole structure is like nature's pillared temple. All manner of exotic ill-kept hounds from DDR's collection are following him, sniffing and trailing him but not harassing him. He circles the tree several times.

The nightwatchman on his patrols stands and watches in the dissipating gloom of the dawn, his hands in an unseen respectful *namaskaram*, as the guru finishes

his perambulations and sits down at last at the base of
the tree, half-obscured by the pillars of branches diving
into the earth. The story the nightwatchman will relate
later, to the gardeners, to his wife, to a delivery man,
to his six-month-old baby, to himself in his prayers, is
only slightly garbled and enhanced by the time it gets to
DDR's ears much later still; the guru glided round the
tree with a supernatural grace in a clockwise direction,
almost as if he were approaching the inner sanctum of
a temple, while all the dogs in the garden fell silent and
watched.

* * *

The balance of power in the marriage of Swami and
Amma has shifted. It's hardly surprising; marriage
guidance counsellors would be the first to concede that
when a husband has walked with God and accessed
the infinite pure essence that lies behind all experience
and causation, there may be a few changes afoot do-
mestically.

Which is not to say that Amma doesn't remain a very
determined, resourceful operator. For example, she is
still convinced that Jodhi's best interests lie in a union
with Mohan. Yes, she has set her heart on that boy,
despite the fact that the computationally gifted whizz-
kid is a social catastrophe, and despite the fact that Jodhi
will neither confirm nor deny that she harbours the
sweet feelings for another boy.

It is 5.45 a.m. While her daughters are sleeping, Amma
is in a puja room, improvising her darshan. Mariamman
is not present in this place, but Lord Murugan is here
– a metre tall, in cool grey stone, dressed in a luxurious
embroidered silk cloak, with a real bronze lance slotted
into his hand. She straightens his outfit and garlands
him with petals, not at all overawed that he is far more

resplendent in DDR's house than in her own. She recites the mantras she has recited every morning of her married life, holding a lighted candle and circling it before the god. At the end of her ritual devotion, she informs the god that she is going to make one last-ditch attempt to mastermind a successful outcome for Jodhi and Mohan. She suggests that Lord Murugan, whom she knows must be on intimate terms with her husband's godly essence, should help her to persuade her husband that Mohan is the boy for Jodhi – for no one will be able to prevent this marriage if Lord Murugan and her husband the guru provide their blessing... She bows to the god and with a last yearning glance at his handsome countenance she goes, rejuvenated, to wake up her daughters for breakfast. Despite the disappointment of D.D. Rajendran, who was hoping to eat with them so he could plan Swami's day, Amma has made it clear that her family will eat their idlis and chutneys by themselves.

In the room where they are served breakfast there is an old dining table surrounded by eight stately chairs – all fashioned out of a single slab of teak – that once belonged to a rich Chettiyar merchant. The table is set with all manner of valuable crockery and mysterious implements, such as the girls have never seen before, which has them umming and ahing dubiously. But Swami and his women sit on the floor with their plates of idlis and sambar, their dishes and pots of coconut chutney and coriander chutney and curds spread in the middle of them. The more exotic foodstuffs go untouched; Bobby, who amongst many eccentricities prefers highly spiced vegetables to meat, will be enjoying an unfettered luxury stuffing later on.

Two bemused servants are standing tense and upright nearby. Only Swami seems unfazed by their presence.

"Sister," Jodhi whispers to Pushpa, "coconut chutney."

One of the servants swoops down on the silver dish just as Pushpa is about to pick it up; he gets there first, and wordlessly sets it down by Jodhi and serves a well-judged daub of it next to her idli. He returns the pot to the centre of the spread, then goes back to his sentry duty. Jodhi opens her mouth, nearly says thanks, closes it again. Meanwhile the other servant has knelt down besides Swami to flick away a fragment of food that has the temerity to be resting on his knee.

"Ayyo-yo-yo," Amma breathes. On the one hand she feels gratified by these ministrations, they make her feel like a maharani; and on the other hand she feels a surge of wifely indignation, almost as if these stiff-backed fellows are impugning her. But most of all, she is longing to talk, and her daughters are longing to talk – they are all looking at each other like children admonished into silence during an event of great excitement – but how can anyone talk when there are two gloomy fellows watching your every chew and grunt?

"Kamala," Amma says, nodding towards the water jug, but it's no good – although Kamala goes for it with the speed of a striking cobra, the nearest servant is quicker, and within an instant he's refilling Amma's glass, calibrating the speed of the water's flow in a manner designed to impart maximum deference.

"Ayyo-yo-yo," Amma blows at last, exasperated, "that's enough, what are you doing, do you think my daughter doesn't know how to pour a glass of water?!"

"No Madam, sorry Madam," the poor man says, standing up.

"How can we eat our breakfast in peace if every time we blink there are two men jumping into the middle of our masala dosa?!"

"Sorry Madam, yes Madam."

"Amma, there isn't any masala dosa," Leela says.

"There is no masala dosa!" Amma complains.

"Sorry Madam."

"If there was, you would be jumping all over it!" Amma accuses the servants. She fans herself with her hand, half exhilarated at the sudden power that has been invested in her – normally she only gets to shout at her children, and at beggars in the street.

The daughters look at their mother aghast. Swami is unperturbed, he has his head down and is tucking into his breakfast with the single-minded application of a normal Tamil man.

"Well, we are wanting the family talk, so please be leaving us."

The servants make small respectful bows, and with a last uncertain glance at the breakfast vista they troop out of the room. As soon as the door closes the girls erupt into life:

"Amma you are embarrassing us, Amma!"

"I thought I was going to explode!"

"Every time I blinked the short one put another idli on my plate!"

"I thought they were going to take hold of my jaws and move them up and down, to save me from the hard labour of chewing the food!"

"This is the life of the rich people! Having the fellows like that to do everything!"

Swami vaguely gestures to the coriander chutney, and a daughter leaps into action and serves him a dollop.

Despite the novelty of Swami being amongst them once more, and despite the surprising new context of their family interactions, ordinary life must continue. After that breakfast of idle chat and affectionate squabbling and servant abuse, Pushpa and Leela must get ready for school. Meanwhile it is agreed that Kamala will go to Number 14/B with some of D.D. Rajendran's staff to collect some essential possessions. In another ten minutes, only Swami and Amma and Jodhi remain.

It is time for Amma and Lord Murugan to gang up on Swami and Jodhi.

"Weeks and weeks and weeks and weeks," Amma is saying, glaring at her eldest daughter indignantly, then turning back to her husband once more. She scratches an itch on her cheek aggressively, walks around Jodhi disapprovingly, all the while looking at Swami. "Weeks and weeks and weeks and weeks!" she emphasizes – it seems that four "weeks" is no where near enough, and even eight is barely adequate. Perhaps she should go for a round dozen.

It is not always easy to guess what Amma is going to say – in fact at times it's difficult to guess what she's already said, never mind what might be coming up next – but at this particular time, as the ninth, tenth, eleventh and twelfth "weeks" are violently dispatched into the atmosphere, it seems reasonable to assume that the problem exercising her anxieties is the lack of progress in the marriage arrangements for her eldest daughter. She has held back long enough. More than twelve hours have passed since her husband came back from Thendraloor, and the obsession of the previous weeks must be resolved. The mother of six daughters and no sons cannot squander time and perfect boys willy-nilly.

Swami is sitting in an armchair, looking straight at his wife as she rants and raves. He finds her inexpressibly beautiful this morning. Amma's brisk, plump movements and gestures and expressions are selected from a repertoire of scolding that has been generated from pure love and that has been refined by years of practice. She performs the routine with a genuine passion, and with the perfect trained instinct of a dancer. Adaa-daadaa, Swami's mind goes, as Amma charges up to him, wags her head and points a finger upwards with harsh philosophy, then wags that finger at Jodhi while still addressing Swami.

"...best boy!... Superhighway Endowment Scholarship!... incredible prospects!..." she raps.

No species of activity in Swami's brain lasts for any length of time these days, certainly not long enough to outlast one of Amma's rants. The empty blankness of his wisdom's nothingness is soon taking over again.

This expression of Swami's – the almost blank one that trains itself on an agitated talker like a bank of lights – has facilitated grief-wrecked parents to cease sobbing and cling to half an hour's soul-rest. It gives nothing and it takes nothing, and yet it is the face that has helped an alcoholic wife-beater to go home one evening and tell his children a bedtime story for the first time in three years. This is the face that has already inspired hundreds to get closer to their idea of God. This is the face that thousands glimpsed ecstatically at Mullaipuram Bus Station. And you won't find a more fervent advocate than Amma as to the spiritual powers of her husband – but Amma, being married to him, is more immune than most.

"...three lakhs of rupees annually!... very stubborn girl!... wilful ingratitude!..."

Swami hears what she says and doesn't hear what she says. It is as though he recognizes the general shape of her words and the weight of their meaning, without engaging with her real purpose.

"And now look what is happening!" Amma bewails. "This marriage is almost definitely over before it has almost definitely started! Parents of the boy are almost pulling out of all arrangements! Parents of the boy seem to know more about my daughter than I do! Parents of the boy are saying our Jodhi is having the sweet feelings for somebody else!" It's possible that the shocking nature of this notion requires some amplification. Fortunately amplification is one of Amma's primary talents: "A somebody else who is not the somebody he is supposed to be! A boy who is not Mohan! The wrong boy!" she rounds off. "And our daughter here, she is not explaining to me anything, she is not denying there is a boy who is not Mohan!"

While Swami is looking at his wife distantly, with a kind of abstract technical pleasure in the life animating her body and language – it courses through her like the timeless flow of the rivers that nourish Mother India's body and spirit – Jodhi is sitting cross-legged on the floor, her shoulders hunched, her head down, examining the patterns that her ten fingers make when interlocked together in a variety of pointless ways.

"Whatever Appa tells me to do, I will do," she says now – in a small pause that Amma has accidentally left vacant.

"Husband, tell your daughter – tell your daughter – tell your daughter to tell me if there is another boy she is having the sweet feelings for!"

Jodhi and Amma stare at Swami in a new and full-blown really long silence.

Swami is in love with his family. Now that he has broken free of the self-imposed shackles of misery, he could wallow in his family's life for whole seconds at a time, the beauty of their half-conscious doings, the richness of their interlacing lives. Look at the heaving bosom of his agitated wife, her pursed lips and her gleaming eyes, she is every mother; and as for his daughter, look at her, this solemn and dignified young woman, who submits, but who, in her own way, will not be cowed. All, finally, is in balance, the small things and the large things and the everything – even if none of it means anything much.

If he could think about anything for very long, Swami wouldn't bother to consider the notion that Jodhi has another boy – he would find it too ridiculous and unlikely. Nevertheless, she does. Swami doesn't know everything, you know – far better gurus than him have made much bigger mistakes than that. Jodhi is head over heels in love with another boy, she is besotted. But as far as Swami's intermittent attention to this topic is concerned, Jodhi has done nothing wrong except to be unimpressed by Mohan – an outbreak of thundering good sense for which anyone but Amma would feel the utmost sympathy.

"Husband, are you so busy with the gods that you don't care if your daughter has secret love interest when she is supposed to be engaged to Mohan?... Ayyo-yo-yo!" Amma erupts. "What am I doing to deserve it all, someone tell me! Daughter is a beauty, boy is a wonder, husband is a god, and still the marriage is not taking place!"

Beautiful, Swami thinks. But he has wafted in and out of this last fifteen minutes of existence like smoke blowing in and out of a room. He is about to shut down and roam around randomly in that mysterious place of the spirit where confronting problems with solutions is considered neither impressive nor effective, nor considered at all. Not that this will shut Amma up. At this moment in time, Swami could be visibly penetrating the starting point of the centre of the spiral of all knowledge – only death can stop Amma carrying on carrying on.

"Everything I have to do!" Amma complains bitterly. "Nobody is helping me! Parents of the boy are not believing Jodhi any more, they are not believing me any more – but they will believe the guru! He, at least, they believe! Daughter, you listen to me, I have been to the parents of the boy, I have told them how your Appa is definitely agreeing that their son is marrying you! Understand? Answer me Jodhi!"

"Yes Amma, I understand." Jodhi pulls her hands apart, wiggles her fingers, locks them together again.

"I have explained everything to them every which way, from upside down to flat on the face until I'm blue in it!" Amma declares; in terms of strict grammar, she is ceasing to make sense, and the semantics are becoming hazy too, but her general feeling seems to be coming through loud and clear.

"I *told* you Amma," Jodhi answers wearily, "I am doing what Appa is telling me to do."

"Appa is telling you to do what I am telling you to do," Amma replies.

Mother and daughter gaze at Swami, like claimants in a land dispute who are waiting on an arbiter's enigmatic ruling. He doesn't say anything. He rarely does.

11

It is ten days since the Guru Swamiji took up residence at Mullaipuram Mansions. If it's true that he once walked with God, then today he will walk with God again. He will also walk into a baying mob of two or three thousand people, and he will discover that he has only twenty-four hours in which to determine Jodhi's destiny. Even for a guru, it's a demanding schedule.

Despite the best efforts of Amma and D.D. Rajendran to manage Swami to their own advantage, a routine of his own organic and unconscious making has been developing, just as in Thendraloor. Everyone must bend to it finally – though Amma does tend to dash her head against it instead, out of habit – and when they do, they find it is for the best. With each passing day, DDR in particular realizes more and more that Swami seems to have a hotline to a higher order of strategic planning than he can comprehend; for although his efforts to steer Swami towards various desirable objectives are continually thwarted, yet he finds that the end result constantly surpasses his hopes. So they do move in mysterious ways, the gods; either that, or they don't exist. That is the only sensible thing that anyone can say about them.

It is long before dawn, and the girls are still sleeping.

"Tomato," Leela mumbles from within a very unusual dream. It is a dream in which tomatoes play their part.

Amma and Swami rise together. Amma helps Swami to perform his ablutions. She is not yet fully habituated to the luxurious nature of the bathroom – its hot and cold running water, emanating from configurations of spouts she has never seen before, into receptacles large and small whose purpose she is uncertain about. The only bidet in the whole district resides in this bathroom, and its function has exercised the imaginations of far more sophisticated guests than her. "Gold-plated tappings!" she murmurs, shaking her head. It's not gold really, but she likes to think it is.

After they have washed, she gets Swami dressed in a pure white ironed lungi and a pure white shirt, then heads off to the puja room to conduct her fastidious and emotionally charged interactions with Lord Murugan.

It has become understood that the guru should be alone and undisturbed at this hour. Swami limps down the hallways and chambers of the house, not noticing the servants and staff going about their business, who stop respectfully and grant him their silent *namaskarams*. A guard waiting at the front door lets him out silently, and the guru slips into the darkness of the pre-dawn day. The encampment of devotees situated outside the compound is yet to stir.

It is very cool at this time, a mere thirty degrees centigrade. Most of the dogs are waiting for him – they're sticklers for routine, dogs, given half a chance – but he ignores them as always. They walk companionably behind him and around him as he perambulates through the grounds for ten minutes, until he gets to the banyan tree.

Maybe there is something, after all, in this three-times-round-the-tree-anti-clockwise malarkey. These days, the base of the tree is regularly hosed down to disperse the urine from the dogs, so there is no longer any pressing practical need to approach the tree tentatively, at an

oblique angle to the stench. And yet Swami circles the
tree three times before he settles down, as the sun comes
up, threading himself between the branches that have
rooted into the earth. The dogs appreciate this. They like
to turn around three times too, before they settle down.

A certain cleft of the trunk at the base affords a
satisfying grip on Swami's bottom. He eases himself
into it, and exhales.

He has visions when he sits here. Not every morning,
and they aren't very good. Really, your lowest class of
fakir has better visions than these ones. Some of them
are so enormously long and dull as to be mysteriously
pointless. Yesterday, in this very spot, Swami had a vision
lasting a full ninety minutes in real time. It involved
living the entire experience of sitting on an unknown
doorstep of an unknown building and watching two
unknown men unload 10,000 cans of paint – of an
unknown hue – from the back of one huge lorry into
the back of another huge lorry. Swami experienced
every aspect of the visionary transaction, saw each bead
of sweat on the men's foreheads as it emerged and grew
and, at a certain point, became too big to maintain its
purchase on the skin, rushing down in abrupt defeat;
he noted the way in which the ridged base of each can
slotted into the grooved lid of the can below it. Each can
of paint was helpfully inscribed with the words *Nerolac
Paints* in the first truck, but with something unreadable
in the second truck. You see, the trucks were identical in
all respects – the same bright yellow metalwork hand-
painted with images of the gods and Sachin Tendulkar
and Tamil film stars, the same scratches and dents and
patches of dirt – except that they were mirror images of
each other.

That vision of Swami's yesterday – it was rubbish.

Today's is a bit better. Within minutes of sitting down,
after he has thought about thought, and then thought

about Jodhi, and then not thought about thought, nor thought about Jodhi, nor thought about anything, the emptiness settles – the emptiness he doesn't know he has. His blank gaze somehow hints that the world might be relevant in some small way – perhaps this is why strangers get such succour from it? His lungi is hitched up so that he can flop his knees out to the sides, his spine hugs the banyan bark, and the slightly pointy bit at the back of his head rests against that 1,000-year-old tree. An immense vulture comes flapping over the roof of D.D. Rajendran's tasteless residence and lands unceremoniously in front of Swami. Without hanging around or waiting for permission, it takes a couple of jumps forwards into Swami's lap, then incorporates itself into his matter. Once it is part of him, it starts flying around his mental landscape of unbroken mountains and noisy jungle and, for some reason, a vast bicycle parking lot. Swami watches it fly around inside his head. Sometimes it descends onto a dead body – a decomposing goat, for example, or maybe just an ugly trunkless leg of some unidentified monster – and tears away at it, gobbling it down greedily till there's nothing left but white bone. After a while it can't find any more rotting matter to dispose of. Swami watches the bird emanate from his stomach and lurch onto the grass. It is noticeably fatter than before, and has some trouble taking wing, but finally it lumbers into the air and crests – just – the rooftop of DDR's house.

Going on strictly spiritual criteria, that vision isn't so impressive either – but at least it means something, probably.

After returning to the house for breakfast with his family, Swami goes and sits in a reception room in the main part of the house. He does this every morning these days, so that various people can access his silent wisdom – old acquaintances, visiting notables. DDR schedules the appointments, and administrates hefty donations from the rich towards his aspirations for an ashram. Kamala does her best to look after her father and make sure he doesn't get too tired. But really, there's nothing very tiring about doing nothing at all. It just requires sufficient peace of mind to be completely uninterested in what people say, and in who they are, and in what they think of you. Most of them give up talking when they get no reply, and many of them fall into Swami's blankness with relief; they subside into a new state of consciousness, if only for an hour, one that they never quite forget even when going back to their compromised lives; one that changes some of them for the better.

"Swamiji," says the director of a private university near Coimbatore who accepts large bribes to matriculate very stupid boys, "what is honesty?" – he thinks that philosophy will help his low-down dirty doings. But Swami isn't very good at philosophy any more.

"Swamiji," says an expensively bejewelled woman whose distinguished husband removes the kidneys from the torsos of poor malnourished landless labourers and puts them in the torsos of rich overnourished foreigners, "Are there limits to matrimonial love?"

"Swamiji," says a gloomy youth sent here by his rich father for unspecified reasons, "why am I here?" – and that is definitely the best question so far.

Swami sits on the simple, low platform that DDR has cobbled up at one end of the reception room, thinking and not thinking, ranging his glance over the faces that come and go, come and go, seeing some of them and not others. Sambrani incense is smouldering away in two elaborate copper holders, one on each side of the room. Kamala sits at the edge of the room – very occasionally she steps in to arrange Swami's clothes, or to give him a glass of water. There is a small audience of other visitants waiting to see the guru. That is why most questions to the guru are couched so obliquely. Who wants to admit in public that he's fleecing disabled pensioners of their alms money – even in front of some other crook who is stealing and selling off the state-subsidized cooking oil of a dozen orphanages?

You're putting on weight, says the white man – he is abruptly present, and for the first time Swami realizes that the white man's mouth doesn't move when he talks, even now, when he's sitting next to the disconsolate youth in full bodily apparition.

There's no exercise here, Swami tells him. *Am I really a god?*

Take your pick.

I wasn't sure...

Everyone is, now and again. Few realize it when they're alive.

Is that what you realized when you died?

I don't know.

"Beautiful," says Swami, aloud, his eyelids flickering, his back hunching, his bad hand beginning to quiver.

"Swamiji," says the suspicious youth – his father once had sex with his wife and a prostitute on the same morning, and then in the afternoon cut a deal with a state politician that kept an innocent man in prison, so no wonder he thinks his son needs spiritual guidance – "Swamiji, you have gone all strange, please tell me what I am getting in my mid-term electrical engineering examinations."

"Shut up boy!" cries some voice offstage. "He is having the godly visitations!"

Kamala is trying to keep people back, but the hue and cry is building up among the enthralled spectators, people surge forwards, within seconds the whispers are rushing down the corridors of Mullaipuram Mansions, expanding into open chambers, crashing like breakers upon various assemblies of astonished VIPs and elated servants; people start crowding into the room, and there's nothing that Kamala can do about it. The Guru Swamiji is walking with the gods in front of everyone's very eyes.

His body slips into a slack and precarious posture, drooping over to one side. His eyelids have stopped flickering, but his eyes are listless and half-closed, and there is some dribble hanging off his lower lip; it swings gently to and fro several times before latching onto his shirt. There is quite a crowd in the reception room now, and a whole heap of adaa-daaing, and here comes D.D. Rajendran sweeping into the room in a state of imperious anxiety.

There is the Swami who is in some kind of catatonic trance – that particular Swami is being propped up by Kamala on the platform, quivering gently – and there is the Swami who is talking to the white man – this Swami, whether he exists in the spiritual world, or in Swami's deluded head, or perhaps both if they ever prove to be much the same thing, has six arms. The three on the right side are a little weak and withered.

Sometimes I know I have to tell everyone I'm not God.

Go ahead. It doesn't matter. They wouldn't listen.

I never do anything,

Excellent. The living are always doing things.

Why do I have to wait?

I don't know. Look, you've got six arms – you know what that means...

Swami looks down at his six arms, and moves his six hands around under his own gaze – turning up the palms of one or two, clenching a fist with another and then opening it again, wiggling the fingers of a couple more. *Oh my God!* he exclaims.

It's wise not to get overexcited when this kind of thing occurs, because it might mean nothing. A really choice spot of science might ruin it all for ever one day. But it's undeniably impressive when it seems to happen – even to Swami, who at this moment certainly appears to be a god, or as near as damn it, and a pretty substantial one too.

The white man starts to ascend smoothly, levitating through the ceiling, disappearing.

Are you coming back? Swami says with a note of regret, as he watches the ceiling suck up the white man's thighs, knees, shins, ankles, feet.

Swami keels over on his side in front of his rapt audience, who squeal and scream and yelp and hiss and whistle and shout and even pant with concern, and Kamala and DDR lay him out on the floor as some of DDR's staff start to clear the room. Swami has a really lovely sleep.

12

"Guru or no guru, walking with the gods or not, this cannot carry on any more!" Mr P is announcing at a small family gathering – they are supposed to be celebrating Anand's amazing admission into one of the few colleges within a hundred miles that hasn't rejected him several times before, or kicked him out already. The world-class expert in sleeping, with his penchant for writing unreadably bad poetry and contemplating the three dimensions of mundane objects for reasons that he can't or won't articulate, has been forced by his parents into studying for a Masters in Business Administration.

The ghastly apparition of Anand's brother Mohan is ruining this happy gathering. Mohan exudes the *joie de vivre* quotient of a depressive who has been charged with escorting a bleating kid through a compound of starving tigers, and the mild-mannered Mr P, whose bad tempers normally only get as far as exasperation before subsiding once more into affability, has had enough.

"We must have a resolution!" he declares. "It is becoming an insult!" he more or less thunders.

Maybe it's the authority vested in his uniform that is making him so vigorous at this moment, for he is testing out a new uniform, identical to his old one in all respects except that it is slightly bigger. It is slightly bigger because he is slightly bigger. He has been getting slightly bigger all his adult life. Mrs P is looking forward to polishing the buttons on that jacket. She likes her husband to have the second-shiniest buttons at Mullaipuram Station. She feels that only the Station Director should have shinier buttons.

"Look at the boy!" Mr P instructs everyone, pointing at his middle son. "He is complete nervous wreckage!"

Everyone's gaze follows the jabbing prompt of Mr P's dark hairy index finger, and fixes on the wreckage he is indicating. The cumulative weight of disbelieving pity in the gazes of those five people – Mr P and Mrs P and Anand and Devan and Mrs Devan – would inspire most people to snap out of it, or to muster enough altruism to quietly end their lives. But Mohan, his lower lip trembling above his unshaven chin, is unreachable in his misery. He is beyond doing anything so optimistic as killing himself. His shining eyes are haunted by the awful fear of losing Jodhi, and the space just behind them is tormented beyond endurance by the hopeless hope that he might still get her. What a mess. He has stopped eating, stopped studying, stopped building super-computers before breakfast. He has even stopped having difficulties below the belt. Nothing stirs down there any more, he is far too depressed for that.

"The mother is 100% certain that Jodhi wants to—"

"You women!" Mr P shouts at his wife. He doesn't shout much, Mr P, and overall he's not very good at it. "You women!" he tries again. He isn't sure what he wants to accuse women of – something to do with never making a decision about anything, or with making decisions too quickly – but he does want to accuse women of something or other, if only in a general fashion. "You drive me mad!" he shouts.

"Depression," Mrs Devan observes, indicating Mohan.

No one says anything for a while. They fume and chew their food and sip water and sigh.

"The mother says that Jodhi wants to do exactly what the guru decides," Mrs P tries again; she hasn't eaten anything in ten minutes, despite the array of edibles all around – it's an indication of how upset she is.

"If she's liking another boy," says Devan portentously, "then there is no point in this marriage, even if it's agreed on all sides. Find another girl." Devan is the most sensible person here, because he was born without an imagination. It's a rare gift, but one with which his wife is also blessed.

"Back-up plan," she says.

"No!" Mohan breathes. The tormented space behind his eyes is throbbing with pain. "I'm wanting that girl, only that one – I am in love with that girl!" he declares. "You know I want that girl! That is the girl I want! That girl!" He shakes his head in despair. "That," he says. "Girl," he adds.

Nobody responds to this. It is perturbing to hear Mohan say he is in love. The word should not be spoken like that, the idea should not be exposed in this raw and vulnerable way. Devan picks up a *vadai* and starts chewing. He is an incredibly noisy eater, one of the noisiest in Mullaipuram, a town where many of the menfolk take a fierce regional pride in the volume and speed at which they can eat. He chews so noisily that everyone can hear him, even above the noise of buses roaring past outside.

"What if the father—" Anand says.

"The guru," says Mrs P.

"Yes, the guru, what if he is saying no to this marriage?" There is a slightly hopeful air to his question.

"He walked with God yesterday morning," Devan says matter-of-factly, through food-flecked teeth.

"How do you know he walked with God?" Anand asks his elder brother irritably.

"Because a roomful of people saw him do it!" Devan replies, rather more irritably, through his chews.

"What, they saw God walking with him? How did they see him walk with God if they did not see God walk with him? And if they did see God, then they are the gurus too!"

"Idiot," Devan says. He has no time for people who question anything anyone says with the word "God" in it.

"Anand, please don't talk in this way," Mrs P says nervously. Her youngest son is always showing signs of not believing in God. He hangs back at religious ceremonies and festivals, he smiles in kind and enigmatic ways when elderly relatives quote from the *Vedas*, and he reads improbable books about philosophy whose titles Mrs P doesn't understand. It makes her nervous just to think about all the things her youngest son might not believe in. "The guru will not say no," Mrs P insists, "his wife is 100% certain that—"

"His wife is 100% full of the crazy nonsense-making!" Mr P points out.

"It doesn't matter what you say, husband, I am the mother, I can feel the connection – I know the Guru Swamiji will say yes to my son."

"Then he can say yes by tomorrow, because we are not waiting any longer than that!" Mr P says. "Guru or no guru, he has till tomorrow night to say this thing or that thing. That is my final word on this matter!"

Mohan looks down at the table, a spasm of instant nausea and imminent diarrhoea clutching at him.

"Husband, not tomorrow night, that is too little time."

"They've had months! In the mean time our boy is dying of a broken heart. And are we to endure this cretinous lover-boy for the rest of our lives? Better to find out by tomorrow night. This is my final word."

Mohan's head slumps into his arms – *Oh God*, he

implores, *let the guru say yes.* Anand plays with his chutneys in an abstracted fashion. Devan and his wife are nodding implacably. And as for Mrs P, she is already scurrying out of the room to go and see Amma without delay, and impress upon her that her husband has been unfortunately manly in a very deplorable way, and is imposing a final deadline on the pressing, complicated business of the marriage.

"Life," says Mrs Devan, still nodding; this is the nearest she gets to philosophy.

"More," says Devan, pointing at the snacks.

"Existence," says his wife, as she serves him.

* * *

Ever since the guru came home to Mullaipuram, thousands of ordinary people have flocked to Mullaipuram Mansions to be near him. They wait outside the compound day and night, neglecting their families, risking their jobs, getting ill, and engaging in many other strenuous proofs of their commitment to spiritual enlightenment. An encampment has established itself, and hawkers have already set up stalls selling votive offerings. During the daytime the throng's collective hum of excitement and frustration and living activity goes vibrating throughout the mansion and its grounds. Those exalted individuals inside the building can never quite get away from it; it throbs in the air, it informs all frequencies that the guru belongs to the people, that the people are angry with DDR, that they want their guru.

At first D.D. Rajendran had fought this alarming phenomenon, treating it as an unfortunate distraction from the main event, as an operational challenge requiring his powers of logic. Those powers of logic brought him to the view that the most appropriate response was to arrange for the police to break up the crowd with tear gas. When that strategy proved to be of only temporary success, he tried making all manner of threats to the common people hankering after their Swamiji; and when that didn't work, he issued numerous lavish promises about the "dedicated Guru Swamiji ashram of the future" that he is already planning, where tens of thousands of the guru's devotees will be able to access their hero. But it's no good – people want to be near the guru now, not in a year's time. They will tear down the compound wall brick by brick if Swami is withheld from them for much longer.

Today, that low throb of communal dissatisfaction is turning into something more threatening. A humming twang of mutiny is in the air. DDR is in despair as to how to solve this problem. He has asked the guru about it, several times over the past few days, but the guru merely looked at him in a calming manner.

At this moment, a baying mob outside the gate is hurling stones and refuse at an abusive man addressing them from within the compound through a distorted megaphone; this man – who is undoubtedly one of DDR's least fortunate associates at this moment in time – is cowering behind the rudimentary defensive emplacements that the bodies of two guards can afford. These two guards are DDR's most unfortunate employees in an absolute and objective sense.

It seems that all megaphones in India – whether manufactured at home or imported from abroad – take whatever sound is fed into them, distort it until it is incomprehensible, and then amplify it to a volume at which it can puncture the eardrums of most mammals. Nothing can be done about this. People are used to it, and they can't understand a word unless the megaphone is seriously defective. It is a kind of homage to how megaphones in India have always been.

"Mr Rajendran," the man is bellowing into his hissing

instrument, "Mr Rajendran is respectfully imploring you to go home, go home while the guru and he devise best possible arrangements for fair and future visitings!"

"*Herrriiinnnjjeee ferrrriiinnnnjjjeee merrriiinnnjjjeee!*" shrieks the megaphone, in various permutations.

Everyone understands perfectly, and by way of reply to this abject failure to give them their guru and his spiritual peace and wisdom, they renew their pelting of the poor speaker with their stones, and shout at him that he is a stupid bastard.

"*Kerrriiinnnjjjeeee meliiiinnnjjjeeee baliiinnnjjjeee!*" the megaphone man shouts back, unwisely – it is an action that he is in no position to execute – so that the missiles rain down twice as ferociously; the guards flinch and grunt as they take the impact, until one of them slumps to the ground with a moderate head wound.

It is into this unpromising scenario that Swami comes walking. Nobody notices him at first – hurling missiles at a man with a megaphone is an absorbing business, being both fun to undertake and yet harbouring an underlying seriousness of intent. The missiles are still raining down as he walks calmly past the injured man, straight up to the gate.

"Swamijjjiii!"

"Guruji Swamijjiiii!"

"The guru has come!"

The gates open, Swami walks through them, and in a series of muscled pulsing ripples, the crowds prostrate themselves in awe. Swami walks into the middle of the people, finds a five-foot-tall tatty goat-gnawed bush, sits down next to it, and doesn't speak. It is his very vulnerability that seems to keep him safe.

From now on Swami will come here every day, leaning on Kamala's shoulder, sharing his serenity with the god-hungry desperados of far and near. The hour of silence has come to Mullaipuram.

13

Swami is not very good at doing anything, or remembering anything, or deciding anything. In fact Swami is not very good at anything – that might be the best way of putting it. He doesn't mind this, or notice it – he's not very good at minding things either, or noticing them. And anyway, although doing has its place, being is more important – that's a little something he somehow understands since coming back from the other side. And how could anyone expect a man like Swami to do anything much? He barely engages in ordinary human consciousness for more than fifteen minutes in every hour, and those minutes are getting fewer every day; the rest of the time his mind is knocking about in accidental states of the most profound banality, while everyone around him and beyond him interprets the vacuum. And yet there are two persistent problems from the outside world that press against his minutes so relentlessly that they sometimes coincide with his more lucid human desires to do something about them... There is Jodhi's marriage, of course – Amma's obsessive interest in securing Mohan for her eldest daughter is still dominating family life. And there is the problem of whether to tell the world that he might not be part of the godhead – though during any lucid moments that he happens to stumble into he would be the first to admit that maybe he is not the best-qualified person to judge.

One day, after Swami has passed in and out of attentiveness during a morning session with VIP devotees who are fervently hoping that he's going to perambulate with a series of notable gods before their very eyes, this pressure about whether he is a god or not becomes keener. He finds that he is looking at D.D. Rajendran, Murugesan and Apu. The three of them are cross-legged before him, all wearing white clothes and expressions of sublime self-sacrifice. They have been waiting in front of him in silence for at least ten minutes, although Swami has only just noticed them. Today is the day that they are choosing to reveal to the guru ("He is already knowing anyway," Apu insists) that they understand the sacrifices he requires of them. Swami's comprehension of the details is pretty hazy, to be honest – he only catches a quarter of what is said, and only understands a quarter of what he catches – but even with just one sixteenth of the dialogue to go on, he has an awareness that these men are deluded.

"Swamiji," Murugesan is saying at one point, "some twenty-five years I have known Swami, but Swamiji I am not knowing at all, I did not even recognize Swamiji when Swamiji arrived. Only with Swamiji's incredible patience has everything become plain to me."

"Swamiji," Apu is saying at another point, weeping in soft ecstasy, "I know you know what I did! You have not told anyone! You have taught me what I must do! Let the Destroyer with the third eye in his forehead come, but I will do it! Thank you Swamiji!"

"Swamiji," DDR is saying at a further point, "my life was empty of meaning, and you have filled it. I see my destiny ahead, entwined with yours, serving you – but in the past I did not listen to you, and I abused you," he observes, in self-disgust.

What are they saying? Swami asks the white man, who appears to be lying on his side nearby, resting his head on his hand.

It doesn't matter, comes the reply.

There is a hazy patch in the middle of all this, during which who knows what DDR and Murugesan and Apu have been revealing, and then Swami finds himself looking at all three men on their knees in front of him, prostrated. Curiously disembodied observations come to him – *I didn't realize Murugesan's hair grew so far down the back of his neck*, and *I've seen this young man before, where was it?*

This is the main bit. The white man says. He is sitting in a chair now, watching with some interest.

But what are they doing?

Weren't you listening?

I don't know, wasn't I?

They think they killed me. You too.

Killed us?

One of them thinks he tortured me and forced me to jump from a window, another thinks he covered up the investigation into my death, the third one thinks he hushed everything up so his reputation wouldn't suffer.

It isn't true?

Yes yes, all true. It always is. And one of them threatened you when you were about to kill yourself – you had a heart attack instead. They did these deeds – but that's just the detail. I had to jump, it was arranged like that. It was all so that you could become what you are becoming.

What am I becoming?

You don't need to know. The part of you that cares about such things is dwindling. That is why you are becoming it.

Murugesan – whose moustache-twitching ended for good some weeks ago, when he submitted to the guru – is painfully reconstructing for Swami's benefit the process which has been taking place:

"...supernaturally masterminding all my... spiritual development... struggled with... conscience... overriding love and wisdom... only now... understanding... by refusing to lead me... bless with the chance to take responsibility... ready for..."

What is he saying?

Some nonsense.

Which one thinks he killed me?

They all look the same to me.

Yes that is the problem, Swami agrees. *The shapes of their thoughts, they're all the same. I can't tell them apart.*

It's because they're alive.

Am I alive?

Oh, the white man comments, as though responding to an unwelcome summons, and he's going – this time walking out of the room in an ordinary way as Swami looks on.

Can I come with you? Swami asks.

You are me, comes the answer – and then, more faintly, *only greater.*

"We are going to report ourselves, Swamiji," Apu is mumbling into the rug half hysterically. "I will lose my job and go to prison for some years – oh, how my child will suffer!" he adds, with a flash of pride. "Forgive me, Swamiji!"

Swami shakes his head with some vigour. "Don't do it," he wants to say. After all, why are these men opting for public disgrace when they could be doing something much more sensible instead, like getting away with it? But no sounds will come out of Swami's mouth. What to do? At this moment, as Kamala looks at him a little anxiously, hoping he will stop this session soon – he is too tired, too much has happened today – Swami receives an image of himself standing up strongly, casting his arms out wide, trumpeting like an elephant just to prove his vigour, and then bellowing,

"I am not a god!" If he could persuade these fools that he isn't a god, perhaps they wouldn't voluntarily choose to be so self-destructive.

But Swami cannot say "I am not a god".

For a full hour DDR, Murugesan and Apu are prostrated before the absent guru. They are watched by a small group of distinguished devotees as they spill their guts out in every particular as to how they executed all manner of sins and colluded in covering them up. They are elated. They finish each other's sentences, rephrase the worst aspects of their crimes, wallow in their guilt. They await the guru's response in much excitement.

"Appa is tired," Kamala says gently – suddenly there behind the guru, helping him up.

"But—"

"Yes but—"

"What—"

The deflated men and their bemused audience watch the guru walking out without a glance at them.

Idiots, Swami thinks.

* * *

It is the middle of the night in Mullaipuram. Murugesan stirs in his sleep, whimpers – he is dreaming that his moustache has started quivering again – and clobbers his wife with a hairy spare arm. D.D. Rajendran sits at a desk in an office, with a snoring Bobby, ogling a series of technical drawings in which Mullaipuram Mansions is extended, expanded, transformed into a vast ashram complex centred on the Guru Swamiji. In a much poorer part of town, in a one-and-a-half-room rented flat, Apu and his wife are sleeping on a bed mat with their child between them; all three of their faces are streaked with tears.

Swami has taken to getting up in the night and going

for solitary walks, attended by a company of dogs and, at a respectful distance, two nightwatchmen. He limps around the unkempt gardens. He feels more human at night than at any other time. Perhaps he is. Perhaps it is because darkness and unconsciousness nudges everyone else closer to the gods, easing people into their subconscious topographies where they can cavort without bodies and consequences.

Sometimes he walks along the wall until he reaches the gate, then sneaks a look at the outside world – he sees a growing shanty town of devotees, he sees locked-up stalls selling everything from milk to mobile phones, the hawkers stretched on the ground next to their stalls, and he sees clusters of men sitting around fires in the dark, talking and playing cards. Just once, he'd like to be a man who could sit with other men at one of those fires, talking and playing cards. But that will never happen again.

It hasn't been mentioned yet that sometimes Swami receives an overwhelming and convincing signal that he is going to die imminently – it could happen any moment, such as this one now, as he spies on the world he has left behind him. When those signals come in, he immediately waits to be dead – not in despair or in pleasure, but with acceptance. But so far the feeling has always passed, in a confusing and trivial fashion, as though the death that is going to take him but doesn't is on a par with a sneeze that nearly comes but won't. Death only matters if life matters too, but maybe life doesn't matter much to people at their highest levels of wisdom. Perhaps Swami doesn't die because he isn't wise enough yet. In any case, death doesn't take him, and as he limps away from the no-show sneeze of it, head down, he thinks *Poor Jodhi* – in a sudden surge of feeling. Hasn't Amma all but ruined her prospects by turning her into a laughing stock?

By the time he is standing on the verandah outside his

family's rooms, looking in through the window, he has largely forgotten the pity that has brought him here, but he stares at those recumbent forms anyway. It seems incredible to know that four of those lives would not be existing without his existence first. A vague image of happy times in a different era is still swimming about half-known in what's left of his old mind, memories of sitting on the little verandah of Number 14/B, reading some books – what were they, those books? What did they say? – while his daughters attended to him.

Yes, I will renounce all this guru nonsense, he tells himself, *go back to being the father of my girls. I don't need – there is no need – I don't...*

Bats are zipping in and out of the gloom around him, and his glance latches onto an indistinct form, follows it flitting around, loses it in less than a second – and thought is over for Swami for the next hour. He sits down on the verandah, nothing more than a detached observer of the landscape unfolding in the constructions of the brain in his head. The half-glimpsed bats make strange patterns in the air around him, and Swami loses any sense of selfhood or identity as these patterns inhabit his mind, for seeing things is really being here.

The nightwatchmen later report that the guru, after checking on his family, stayed on the verandah for an hour and delved into the blackness.

* * *

Given Jodhi's astonishing fortitude in contemplating the kind of betrothal that would inspire many women to make enquiries about government sterilization programmes, and taking into account her endurance in suffering so many private humiliations and public embarrassments not of her making, a dispassionate commentator might conclude that Swami and Amma's eldest daughter has something almost superhuman about her. Maybe it's in the genes? Her father seems to be no slouch in the spiritual-achievement stakes, and look at Granddaddy – although unheralded, his visions are ten times more impressive than the guru's. Granddaddy is so superhuman that sometime he plays his flute even while asleep. But no, Jodhi is not of this bent. With Mr P's manly deadline ticking down relentlessly, and with Amma insistent that the wedding will go ahead because Swami will endorse it, and with Swami failing to do anything to prevent it, Jodhi's fortitude is disintegrating. Though she has made a good stab at trying to accept her fate with equanimity, behind her calm façade she is suffering more than anyone involved in this matrimonial saga – except for Mohan, of course. Nobody is suffering more than Mohan. A few hours ago he inexplicably cut up most of his clothes into very small pieces – only a genius of unsurpassed lovelorn misery can suffer more than that.

Pushpa wakes up in the night from a strange sense that something is dislocated or wrong. Amma is snoring like a dam burst not far away, so that's okay; Leela is babbling about tyres, plinths and condensation, which seems largely normal; Appa is away on one of his night-time ambles, which is not unprecedented; Kamala is silent and unmoving, which is absolutely typical; and Jodhi – Pushpa props herself up on an elbow, what are those noises? – Jodhi is crying. Jodhi is not weeping inconsolably or keening in despair – that would not be her way. But she is softly crying, she is issuing low-volume whimpers, discreet but distressing catches of the throat. Pushpa watches and listens, wondering what to do. After a while she feels a hand on her waist, and looks over in the gloom to see that Kamala has woken up and is also looking at Jodhi. The two of them shuffle over to Jodhi, and whisper, and stroke her hair.

Some minutes later, the three of them are sitting together by the far wall of the room, huddled in the dark. "I must do my duty," Jodhi is saying in a tragic whisper, while Amma and Leela sleep on.

"He is a very handsome boy," Kamala says valiantly.

"His prospects are excellent," Pushpa confirms, uncomfortably, feeling that this is a very grown-up thing to say.

"A wife's duty is to love her husband and support him in all his endeavours," Jodhi instructs herself.

"You could do a lot worse than Mohan," Pushpa points out, still with half an eye on how grown-up she is.

"That is true," Jodhi says – but then again, she could do a lot better – and she breaks down again, snivelling and snorting gently.

"Hush Sister, hush, don't worry, everything will be all right, let us not wake Amma – imagine the commotion!" Kamala whispers, and she glances across at snoring Amma and babbling Leela – "Don't step in the wet cement," Leela is moaning.

"Don't cry, Sister – you'll get used to Mohan."

"I am in love with Anand!" Jodhi splutters.

As she covers her face in her hands from shame and hopelessness, Pushpa and Kamala stare into each other's chronic amazement through the gloom. Kamala glances across at Amma fearfully, but it's all right, Amma is still snoring like a hibernating bear.

"Come," Kamala hisses decisively, getting to her feet, pulling up her sisters after her, making for the safety of a locked bathroom and the kind of in-depth crisis conversation that can only be generated by three sisters, a disastrous would-be and a secret love interest.

"That's not a bucket!" Leela nearly declares; but she decides against it.

* * *

"...All these crazy emails I was getting from Mohan," Jodhi is explaining – the three of them are perched on some of DDR's most ostentatious bathroom fittings. "He is telling me you don't know what rubbish, he is completely crazy, and then one day Anand sent me an email too, and we started writing, every day..."

"Ayyo-yo-*yooooooo*..." Pushpa breathes.

"...and we are enjoying it like anything, getting on like a burning house, talking about everything under the sun..."

"...oh my God..." Kamala breathes, the latent lover in her getting uncomfortably excited; she wonders what it would be like to know a boy like that, to get on like a burning house, to talk about everything under the sun.

"...and all the time he, him – Mohan," Jodhi forces herself to say, "he is sending me these pledges about how he would do anything for me, he is making me the world-champion-beating anagrams of Graham Greene, and saying he will eat silicon chips if I ask him to, and—"

"Eat silicon chips?"

"Yes! Eat silicon chips! But how can I marry a boy who would eat silicon chips if I asked him to?"

Even that notable text, *How to Attract Women*, did not advocate the eating of silicon chips.

"He would eat silicon chips for you," Kamala repeats, with a slightly dreamy air; perhaps she would like to meet a man like that. Not every man is capable of such love. But she rouses herself and demands, indignantly, "What kind of a boy would do that?!"

"For all I know he's munching through a whole dish of them right now!" Jodhi sobs in despair, and for a few moments they all nearly giggle as they catch each other's eye – but Jodhi's situation is too desperate for that. "I only agreed to go to the cinema because I thought Anand would go, I just wanted to... just see him, look at him... and when he wasn't there I felt – you don't know how I felt – you can't know how bad it feels until you've felt how bad it is."

"I was there, it felt very bad," Pushpa points out.

"And then, while Amma is chasing around Mullai-puram worried that I'm wearing jeans and what-all, I am bumping into Anand one day outside the Bharat Petroleum garage – just passing by—"

"But how are you just passing by, in Thenpalani?"

"—just... passing... and... you see... when we met... it's difficult to explain..." Jodhi peters out.

"And what, Sister?"

"We are just seeing each other and knowing," Jodhi says simply, flushing.

"But – knowing what, Sister?"

"Yes Sister, what is the knowing?"

"Knowing. It is the knowing. Just – knowing. It is knowing the beautiful thing."

Kamala bursts into tears – perhaps she somehow senses that she will never know the beautiful thing.

"And then he is saying to me – things, and then... and now... We haven't seen each other since, we haven't spoken, didn't email. The situation is too very hopeless! How can I marry Mohan?" she pleads. "Even if Appa is the God, the God can't stop the Amma," and she bursts into tears once more, and this time she will not be consoled.

Though Jodhi's estimation of the power of the God in relation to the power of the Amma may or may not be accurate, yet she is completely unaware of the power of the Leela.

* * *

When Amma wakes up later in the near-darkness, on the end of a snore that could make any nearby tree shed all its leaves, she finds that she is alone. Never in her life has she been in this situation – not one sleeping moment of her existence has been passed in a room by herself. The glass doors to the verandah are wide open, and a slow hot breeze is oozing in.

"Husband – help – Daughters – thief – help!" she moans incoherently, lurching up into a sitting position, looking around her wildly. "Husband – Jodhi – murder!" she cries, her voice rising in pitch and panic.

Leela comes in from the verandah, saying, "Yes Amma, don't worry, everything is fine."

"Where is my family?!" Amma cries.

"Calm down Amma, everything is fine, they are just chatting."

"Chatting?" Amma asks incredulously. "It is the middle of the night! Where are they?"

"Bathroom," Leela admits.

"Bathroom?! Why are they chatting in the bathroom?" comes the disbelieving response.

At this point Swami comes limping in from the verandah. He carefully gets to his knees next to Amma, lies down on the rug with a grunt and a shiver, and as Amma and Leela watch – one in indignation, the other in admiration – he falls asleep in less than five seconds.

"What are you doing?" Amma cries abruptly, shaking him awake, "What is going on? I am waking up all alone and my family is having secret meetings all over the place about who knows what, and later you must be telling the boy's family that Jodhi will marry him, and all you are doing is being the guru and roaming around and sleeping!"

"Anand," says Swami's dislocated voice, in the gloom – and Leela slinks away, to lie down on the rug, hoping to put herself out of the way of Amma's suspicions. For Leela has tried to make up for all her gossip with some new, different, better, more accurate gossip.

Swami hasn't spoken for a long while. Amma processes the phenomenon like a bemused traveller testing a new foodstuff on the tongue.

"Anand," she repeats, "Anand... Anand..."

Swami is already falling asleep again.

"Anand?!" Amma exclaims – she shakes Swami again. "Husband, yes yes, thank God, you are making the decision at last! But it's Mohan you mean, isn't it!"

"Anand," says the voice, in the gloom.

"Husband, what are you talking about, the boy is called Mohan, Mohan is the boy – Anand is the brother who is no good at anything, he is the useless one, he is the one who won't be earning 300,000 rupees per year, you are confused! This is not what you are saying! Thank God you are making the decision. Mohan! Thank you husband, at last you are – you are..."

Swami is struggling to sit upright. Amma helps him, and then finds herself helping him to stand up. Once he's on his feet, Swami walks over to a table lamp on a table, and switches it on. Light floods the room. Swami limps over to his wife and looks deep into her eyes.

"Jodhi," he says. "Anand," he says. "Fifty-Seven," he says.

And even as he is getting back down on the rug to fall asleep – Swami no longer dreams when he sleeps, by the way – a stricken Amma is crying out for a copy of *The Sacred Couplets*.

Epilogue

In the future, not less than five years away but no more than ten, a family visit is coming to a close in the little bungalow of Number 14/B. Jodhi and Mohan are sitting on the floor with the children, six-year-old Rajah and five-year-old Geetha, playing snakes and ladders on a small cardboard grid from *The Big Bumper Box of 101 Board Games*, a recent purchase by Mohan. It is a cheap and underwhelming present, but it is all he can afford, and the children are young enough to like it. But at a sudden shout from outside, the children are on their feet and scampering out, scattering the pieces heedlessly, squealing "Me first, me, me!" as they rush into the backyard.

Mohan looks down at his hands as he listens to them laughing and shrieking:

"Does anybody want to buy my salt!
Does anybody want to buy my salt!"

"I am playing this game too when I am a child," he says, smiling awkwardly. He is gaunt, and strained, and shabby. The pocket on the breast of his shirt has come unstitched.

"Yes, and I was playing this game, and our parents, and our parents' parents."

"Yes, that is so," Mohan concurs.

"The children's children will play this game."

"Yes, and their children too."

This is among the best and longest conversations they have ever had. Maybe, one far-off day, when they are old, they will always talk so easily.

They lapse into their usual excruciating silence, and pretend to be absorbed in listening to the game going on beyond them, instead of being lost to melancholy.

"Amma," says Rajah running in, "Appa is letting Geetha have two goes in a row, but that is not fair!" He looks to be on the edge of tears.

"Uncle will let you have three goes in a row!" Jodhi claims, and as Rajah races back outside she smiles at Mohan, who is dutifully lumbering to his feet. Soon she is watching from the open kitchen door as her husband and her brother-in-law cavort around the small backyard carrying the children around like gunny sacks. Everyone is laughing, but only the children are happy.

Apart from taking advantage of Number 14/B – the Indian Police Service would like to have the bungalow back, but does not like to press its claim – Anand and Jodhi have stepped outside the all-encompassing world of the Guru Swamiji Ashram. All the other members of the family live on the complex. Kamala is Swami's devoted personal assistant – a mini sub-cult of Swami's followers almost venerate her, in a very minor way. Pushpa is engaged to the fellow whom D.D. Rajendran has appointed as Assistant Director of the Guru Swamiji Educational Outreach Program – instigating and arranging that match kept Amma happy for six months. Leela is a junior dance instructor at the Guru Swamiji Cultural and Traditional Activities Centre. Suhanya and Anitha live with Swami and Amma and Kamala in a simple, purpose-built bungalow at the edge of the ashram, from where they go to college each day. As for

Swami and Amma, they have hardly changed – except to become more and more like themselves – while DDR, President of the Guru Swamiji Ashram, has been steadily building up the infrastructure, scope and reach of the project. Swami doesn't do much these days – less than he ever did, as befits a man who is much better at being than doing. He has almost ceased to exist in any mode that an ordinary human being can comprehend. He hasn't spoken in three years now. The last time he did so he said a number, but there is a dispute as to which number it was, and to which sacred couplet it referred, and to what that sacred couplet might mean, and in what light the Guru Swamiji's citation of it should be interpreted. Some are still arguing about it – the debate can be followed in *The Silence and the Breaking of the Silence* (Guru Swamiji Press), which can be found in the Guru Swamiji Devotional Bookshop, amongst many other tracts and publications.

The core of Guru Swamiji's message is still centred beyond articulation in his deeply affecting hour of silence, a practice which benefits countless thousands from all over the world. Nobody knows how it works, only that it does. An impressive tiered amphitheatre now surrounds the ancient banyan tree where, each day, Kamala leads the guru – escorted by K.P. Murugesan, who heads up security, or his deputy S.P. Apumudali.

Jodhi and Anand have not been drawn into this parallel society. Anand is losing money hand over fist on the literary magazine he has founded. He secretly publishes his own poetry in the journal under a series of pen names – perhaps that's why no one is buying it? Jodhi is in charge of the production side of things. It is too much for her to handle; she is also in the middle of her doctorate, while holding down a full-time job as junior lecturer at the Madurai University-affiliated local college. In fact, though no one says so, to all intents and purposes Anand is Mullaipuram's first and only house husband. Jodhi would never admit to it, but Amma was 100% correct about several aspects of Anand's uselessness. His sleeping powers, without question, are unusually over-developed, and he does indeed spend far too much time contemplating mundane objects for reasons that no one can fathom. Yesterday he spent over an hour looking at a wooden spoon. As for his poetry, it has got steadily worse, and from a very low starting point.

Mohan no longer lives in nearby Thenpalani, and can bring himself to visit only once each year. He has not fulfilled the high expectations that were vested in him. Though a convincing recipient of the *Sri Aandiappan Swamigal Tamil Nadu Information Superhighway Endowment Scholarship*, and a worthy student at the South Indian Institute of Integrated Information Technology in Bangalore, he dropped out of his studies after losing his IT hunger. Unrequited love tends to do that to a man's interest in information technology. He lives in a tiny, dirty, sub-subletted room, on the seventh floor of a perilously built and very ugly block of flats, in a teeming neighbourhood of Chennai, some 200 miles away. He spends his days puffing on bidis, exhaling the smoke out of the window and onto the city, and repairing the second-hand computers of the lower middle classes.

After a while Anand and Mohan stop playing with the children in the backyard, and it is time for Mohan to go back to his parents' house in Thenpalani before catching the overnight train back to Chennai.

"I'll go and come back," he says, at the door.

"Yes please come back very soon," Anand says, "children always asking for Uncle."

"Very soon I am coming back," Mohan agrees.

After a few steps, he turns around to give an awkward wave to his brother's family. He sees Anand's hand resting on Rajah's shoulder, while Jodhi holds her daughter on her hip.

"Uncle!" says Geetha, and bursts into tears, as Mohan walks away, tall and stooped, past the crumbling wall that the British built.

Acknowledgements

Heartfelt thanks to Alessandro Gallenzi, Elisabetta Minervini, William Chamberlain, Christian Müller and Jonny Gallant at Alma Books for their talent and hard work; I am particularly indebted to Alessandro and Elisabetta for their long-standing support. I am deeply grateful to Dr Bharat Srinivasan in Chennai for providing feedback under severe time constraints – his input has improved the novel in many places. A.M. Rajah, R. Jayanthi and M.A. Sundar kindly supplied all kinds of useful information which has found its way into the book – thanks to all of them. My thanks are also due to Dr James Jobanputra for his feedback on medical issues. Finally, many thanks to my brother Paul, whose eye for grammar is ruthlessly beady, and from whom I have received much encouragement over many years. All the people mentioned here have improved the book; the flaws and errors that remain are a result of my own stubbornness in occasionally not taking their advice.